PPP

F
Sedley   Sedley, Kate

Nine men dancing

$ 27.00   8/0 3

DUE DATE

NINE MEN DANCING

NINE MEN DANCING

Kate Sedley

This first world edition published in Great Britain 2003 by
SEVERN HOUSE PUBLISHERS LTD of
9–15 High Street, Sutton, Surrey SM1 1DF.
This first world edition published in the USA 2003 by
SEVERN HOUSE PUBLISHERS INC of
595 Madison Avenue, New York, N.Y. 10022.

British Library Cataloguing in Publication Data

Sedley, Kate
    Nine men dancing. - (A Roger the Chapman mediaeval mystery)
    1.   Roger the Chapman (Fictitious character) - Fiction
    2.   Peddlers and peddling - Fiction
    3.   Missing persons - Investigation - England - Fiction
    4.   Great Britain - History - Edward IV, 1461-1483 - Fiction
    5.   Detective and mystery stories
    I.   Title
    823.9'14 [F]

ISBN 0-7278-5977-3

Typeset by Palimpsest Book Production Ltd.,
Polmont, Stirlingshire, Scotland.
Printed and bound in Great Britain by
MPG Books Ltd., Bodmin, Cornwall.

One

I suppose it's an integral part of the human condition that everyone, on some occasion or another, should experience feelings of guilt; and this applies particularly to men with wives and children who, like me, value their independence and need, from time to time, to escape from the ties of family life. (At least, I used to when I was younger. Now that I'm an old man, I have to submit, however unwillingly and ungraciously, to the petty tyrannies of my sons and daughter; especially the latter, who persists in regarding me, now that I'm in my seventies, as just another of her offspring. The idiot one!)

Certainly, after an autumn and early winter of intense domestic activity, I was more than ready, following the Christmas festivities of that year of 1478, to take my chapman's pack and be out on the open road again, with the solitude and silence that only a winter landscape can offer. Even before the church services had run their course, before the waits had finished singing carols from door to door, before the Boy Bishop had preached his sermon and doffed his mitre for another year, I was dreaming of sodden bracken squelching underfoot, of the naked trunks of birch trees seen tall and straight through a mesh of purple twigs, of frost-bitten grass and early morning, knee-high mists . . .

Fortunately for me, my wife, Adela, was the most understanding of women and rarely made over-exacting claims on my time and patience. By the middle of January, she knew that I was near the end of my tether. Of course, she could easily have pointed out that with three small children, one of them a baby of six months, to look after – not to mention the flea-bitten

1

mongrel who had attached himself to us and become the household pet – she, too, was at the limit of her endurance. But she didn't. The Virgin only knows why not! Adela wasn't a saint by any stretch of the imagination, but her love for me gave her a tolerance for my loutish, unutterably selfish behaviour that I didn't deserve and of which I took endless advantage.

Our two elder children, Nicolas and Elizabeth, were now four years old, with only a fortnight's difference in their ages. This apparent phenomenon is easily explained. Nick is Adela's son by her first husband, Owen Juett, while Bess is my daughter by my first wife, Lillis Walker. The baby, Adam, was born on the last day of June, a year after Adela and I were married. His half-brother and -sister, who were (and still are) devoted to one another, had not taken kindly to his appearance in their midst and had, for a time, deeply resented him. But they were by now more reconciled to his arrival, even condescending, on occasions, to entertain him. Nevertheless, it had not been an easy six months.

To make matters even more difficult, I had inherited a house; a gentleman's town house in Small Street, Bristol, where we lived. Prior to this, our accommodation had been a one-roomed cottage, rented from Saint James's Priory in Lewin's Mead, outside the city walls. How I came into possession of this house belongs to an earlier story, and I refuse to go into details again here. But what, at first, had seemed like the answer to prayer, turned out to be a double-edged sword. The resentment of many of our erstwhile friends to this outstanding piece of good fortune was palpable. That a mere, common, low-born chapman from the small Somerset town of Wells – who didn't even have the courtesy or common sense to be born a native Bristolian – should become the owner of a two-storey dwelling with a yard and a privy at the back, was more than most of them could stomach, and they choked on their own bile. They had long envied the fact that, trained for a life in Holy Orders, which I had rejected, I could read and write. Now, here I was, set up for a life of ease.

Well, that was their version of my future!

Like our former friends, our new neighbours in Small Street were equally resentful and waited eagerly to see what a pigsty we would make of the place. After all, our home now consisted of a hall, a parlour, a buttery, a kitchen and three bedrooms. It was impossible that we should have enough sticks of furniture to equip the house in any sort of comfort. What no one knew but ourselves was that after the last favour I had done for the Duke of Gloucester – or the last commission I had carried out for His Grace, as Timothy Plummer would have preferred to phrase it – Prince Richard had given me two gold pieces for my pains. This had been more than enough to furnish the house, if not luxuriously, at least adequately, and yet again, my detractors were frustrated in their desire to see me fall flat on my face. What they failed to realize was that, in the future, I should have to work twice as hard at my peddling in order to keep us in the style to which we had all too easily, and in very short order, grown accustomed.

This was the situation, then, after the twelve days of Christmas, 1478, when I began, once again, to feel the well-remembered itch to be free of domestic ties and encumbrances and to take to the road with my pack and cudgel.

'Go!' said Adela. 'Get out from under my feet before you drive me mad with your grumblings and your bouts of ill-temper.'

'I don't like leaving you. Not in the present circumstances,' I cavilled, while not admitting to her accusation of bad behaviour.

She laughed, as well she might, knowing me quite as well as, if not better than, I knew myself.

'I'm perfectly capable of dealing with any unpleasantness that might arise,' she argued.

This was true. Adela treated everyone, however awkward, with an unfailing courtesy that disarmed them and made them ashamed of their boorishness. It was also true that as far as the children were concerned, she was better at controlling them than I was. Whereas I shouted and bribed, veering between heavy-handed tyranny and abject sycophancy, she spoke

3

quietly, but firmly, and if she uttered a threat, it was not an idle one.

'Besides,' she added, 'Margaret' – Margaret Walker, my quondam mother-in-law and Adela's cousin – 'has promised to shut up her cottage in Redcliffe and stay with us while you're away.'

No doubt, I thought sulkily, the whole thing had been arranged between them, behind my back and before I was even aware of what I wanted myself. My wife saw the look on my face and laughed again. She put her arms around my neck, pressing close to me with an affection that I couldn't, and wasn't meant, to mistake.

'You can have until the beginning of March,' she told me. 'I shall expect you home well before Saint Patrick's Day. And I mean that, Roger. I don't want you turning up three weeks later, hoping that I'll accept some lame excuse for your tardiness, because I shan't.'

'What would you do?' I grinned, returning her embrace with lascivious interest.

But just at that moment, our two elder children burst in and, in spite of having the hall, the kitchen and their two bed-chambers as alternative playgrounds, announced that the parlour was the one place in the house where they intended to be for the rest of the morning.

Nothing had changed.

Three days later, I was on the road, heading north towards Gloucester, a full pack strapped to my back, a good thick cudgel (my 'Plymouth Cloak') grasped in my right hand and a small, nondescript dog trundling happily at my heels. (I had been forced to take Hercules with me because Margaret Walker had recently acquired an equally small, equally aggressive, black and white dog who had been abandoned by his owner, and whose presence in his new house deeply offended Hercules.) And now, in this last week of February, the pair of us were on the road home, in excellent time to reach Bristol well before the Feast of Saint Patrick on the 17th of March.

*   *   *

Nine Men Dancing

On my northward journey, I had taken my time getting to Gloucester by visiting even the smallest, out-of-the-way hamlets, tucked snug as mice in their nests beneath the rising folds of the Cotswold hills. From Gloucester, where I did good business and made a pilgrimage to the tomb of the murdered Edward II, I struck south-east, through the little slate-roofed villages and prosperous sheep farms, to the market town of Cirencester, the ancient Corinium Dobunnorum of the Romans, where, yet again, I had no difficulty in selling my wares. By now, February was well advanced and it was time to turn my footsteps south-westward if I was to be home by the middle of March.

I had chosen, conveniently, to forget Adela's instruction of 'well *before* Saint Patrick's Day', but an unexpected twinge of conscience led me to attempt a short cut, leaving the well-worn track between Cirencester and Tetbury and taking to a path recommended by a local forester. As this led through a densely wooded area, I should have known better, but the man's eager assurances that, this way, I should reach Tetbury before I knew where I was proved irresistible. Unfortunately, it also proved prophetic in the sense that, before very long, I *didn't* know where I was, and was totally lost. To make matters worse, it had begun to rain, cold, slanting spears that stung my face and made Hercules whimper with indignation and stare up at me accusingly as he trotted by my side.

'All right,' I muttered as he yelped pathetically, 'I know I'm a fool. You're hungry, I'm hungry. We're both wet, chilled to the marrow and dog-tired – if you'll pardon the expression – but there's nothing I can do about it. We can only keep on along this path and hope that it leads us somewhere . . . Christ Jesus! What was that?'

Something hanging from the branch of an oak had brushed my face. I swung round, cudgel at the ready, while Hercules growled and bared his teeth. Happily, there was still sufficient daylight filtering between the overhanging canopy of trees for me to see what it was that had struck my cheek. A corn dolly, with a nail driven through its heart swung from a twig, while a bunch of mistletoe had been placed at the foot of the oak. I shivered, but made no attempt to touch either. Hercules shrank against my legs. I could feel him trembling.

I looked higher up the tree. Long strips of cloth, sodden and darkened by the rain, were tied to some of the other branches. This was an old Celtic custom and indicated the presence, somewhere in the vicinity, of a well or spring, once sacred to the local god of the place (something I had learned from my first wife, Lillis, who was of both Cornish and Welsh descent). And yet I had neither heard nor seen any sign of water for quite some while.

'Let's get out of here,' I muttered to Hercules, picking him up and tucking him under my left arm. He was still shaking and I soothed him as best I could, glad of the warmth of his little body close to mine.

Suddenly, the crowding trees seemed to draw back and we were in a clearing. In spite of the fact that the light was bad, I could see that there were strangely shaped humps and bumps amongst the general scrub and undergrowth. A closer look at one of them convinced me that there was stonework beneath the encroaching ivy and layers of moss. Young saplings, thrusting heavenwards, had dislodged one or two of the stones, which lay scattered around on the grass. Further investigation suggested that a house of some size had once stood on the site, and its broken stumps of walls accounted for the hummocky landscape.

I put Hercules down and he at once began his own inspection, eagerly sniffing everything in sight and leading me on until the path we had been following suddenly reappeared, snaking ahead of us to vanish into another belt of trees. And it was at this point that I stubbed the toe of my right boot against something lying hidden in the undergrowth and measured my length on the ground. For a moment, I was winded and half stunned; then, cursing roundly and fending off the dog's well-meant attentions, I picked myself up and turned to find out what had felled me.

I knew from my aching ribs that I had fallen across something hard. Tearing aside the long stems of winter-bleached grasses, I soon revealed a large, round wooden cover with a handle. This, when raised – not without a good deal of swearing and exertion on my part, and excited barking on that of Hercules – revealed the dark, rank-smelling depths of an old well, which had once, presumably, provided water for the ruined house. The canopy of the well, the winch and bucket had long since disappeared, but the shaft remained; although, as far as I could make out in the poor remnants of daylight, there was no water in it (I threw a stone down, but heard no splash). A narrow iron ladder, about a foot in width, was attached to the wall of the shaft, disappearing into the murky gloom like the descent into Hades.

I stood up, rubbing ineffectually at the damp and muddy knees of my second-best pair of hose, thankful that at least I hadn't ripped them. Then I dragged the lid of the well back into place, making sure that it fitted snugly around the ring of stones bordering, and standing slightly proud of, the shaft's rim, just as I had found it.

I shifted my almost empty pack, which had slipped sideways, to a more comfortable position on my back, and looked down thoughtfully at my discovery. I wondered who had made the lid and fitted it. Such care for the well-being of human and animal life (perhaps not necessarily in that order) argued a settlement, a village or a hamlet, somewhere not too far distant. If that were so, then Hercules and I might hope for food and a place to sleep for the night. Greatly cheered by this reflection, and praying that I was right, I urged a willing Hercules onward.

We followed the path into the trees and, almost at once, found ourselves on a gentle slope, descending almost imperceptibly into an as yet invisible hollow. The rain had ceased and a thin, watery ray of light slanted through the leafless branches overhead. There was the sudden glint of sun on water – and so it was that I saw, even before I heard, the little rill, purling over its stony bed, that had suddenly appeared and was accompanying us downhill. Where its source lay, I had no idea, but it encouraged me to believe that my reasoning was correct, and that we were within reach of warmth and shelter.

The trees ended abruptly and Hercules and I were once again in open country, on an incline whose lush grassland, in spring and summer, would be white with sheep – those four-legged moneybags that made Gloucestershire farmers the envy of all Europe. But for the present, after the lambing season, most of the ewes were still indoors, in barns and folds and hovels, and only a few dotted the horizon. And even as I watched, a man came out of the farmhouse, just visible away to my right, striding purposefully towards them, crook in hand, ready to pen them up for the night. He waved to someone further down the slope; someone beyond my range of vision in the rapidly advancing dusk.

It was indeed growing dark, and my obvious course of action would have been to make for the farmhouse, had I not at that very instant noticed the fugitive twinkle of lights in the hollow below me. I strode out with renewed vigour, whistling tunelessly and encouraging Hercules to hurry along with promises of a bowl of scraps eaten by a warm fireside.

The distance between us and a night's shelter was, however, greater than I had estimated. We passed the farmhouse and its attendant barns and outhouses, now nothing but black, papery shadows set against a stormy evening sky, and, some little way further on, a much smaller homestead, again only a dark shape on the horizon. It was perhaps another quarter of a mile before Hercules and I found ourselves crossing the wooden footbridge over a broader stream, fed by the rill that had been our companion for the past half-hour.

Beyond the bridge, lay one of those little Cotswold hamlets of slate and stone, lying like a wisp of grey smoke between the surrounding hills. As far as I could see at first glance through the increasing gloom, this one consisted of half a dozen cottages, a tiny church thatched with rough grass and bracken, a mill and – a sight to gladden my heart – an alehouse.

This last was unmistakable. The door stood open, showing an oblong of smoky red light across which flitted a procession of figures. Raised voices could be heard inside, laughing, complaining, shouting, arguing or drunkenly singing snatches of a bawdy song to the accompaniment of a reedy pipe and the scrape of a badly tuned fiddle. A pole with a bunch of leaves tied to its top – its 'bush' – indicated that food was available. My empty stomach was already rumbling.

I gathered up Hercules and pushed my way inside, my head knocking against the door's lintel. The general hubbub faltered and slowly died as all eyes gradually swivelled in my direction. Not for the first time in my life I cursed the great height that never allowed me to enter any room unobtrusively. I brazened it out and gave a mock bow.

'Roger Chapman,' I announced. 'A poor pedlar who has lost his way. Hungry, thirsty and more than somewhat tired.'

By now, my eyes were growing used to the smoky atmosphere, and I could see by the guttering candlelight that there were probably a dozen or so people in the alehouse, most of them seated at the central table. The fiddler and piper stood near the hearth at the far end of the room, while a few others were sprawled on stools ranged against the walls. I remembered the corn dolly with the nail driven through its heart, and shivered inwardly. But I kept up a brave front.

A young woman of some sixteen or seventeen summers pushed between the customers, ignoring with practised ease the jocular, even ribald, comments of the men as she brushed against them. Onc man caught her around the waist and kissed her cheek, but she fended him off without giving offence, smiling at his boldness and generally implying that she was not displeased.

'Come in, chapman,' she invited. She eyed me up and down. 'You look a starving wreck, I must say' – everyone laughed – 'but I daresay you need a good deal of feeding. Come and sit by the fire. Josh Rawbone! Get up off your backside and let the pedlar have your stool.' She added, 'I'm Rosamund Bush. My father's the landlord of this place.'

'William Bush, at your service,' said a harassed voice just behind her, and a lean, dark man in a leather apron gently put

Kate Sedley

her to one side. It was obvious at a glance that his daughter must get her fair, curvaceous good looks from the distaff side of the family. 'What can I do for you, sir?'

'A bed and supper for me, and a bowl of scraps for my dog, if you please.'

'Call that thing a dog?' queried some wit from out of the smoky depths, and there was another roar of laughter.

Hercules, always swift to sense an insult, bared his evilly pointed teeth and growled. His spirit was instantly applauded, as, with a cry of 'Oh! What a dearling!' Rosamund Bush seized him from my arms and crushed him against her ample bosom. Hercules rolled an alarmed eye in my direction.

'It's all right, boy,' I assured him, thinking him an ungrateful little cur. I don't suppose there was a man in the room, including myself, who didn't envy him.

'I can give you supper, you and your dog, but the Roman Sandal isn't a hostelry,' William Bush explained apologetically. 'There's no call for accommodation in these isolated parts. And upstairs, there's no room for more than my goodwife and daughter and me.'

'I can sleep on the floor by the fire,' I said. 'I've slept in many worse places in my life.'

The landlord looked as though he would demur, but Rosamund – at that moment equally as fair in my view as Henry II's Rosa Mundi – pleaded, 'Let him stay, Father. What harm can he do? He's lost, and it's going to be a stormy night. The wind's rising. I can hear it.'

There was a general nodding of heads; but the final decision was taken out of Master Bush's hands by the appearance of his wife, who arrived in the ale-room, presumably from the upper storey and by way of the outside staircase I had noticed as I entered. She was a pretty, plump woman and, as I had guessed, an older version of her daughter. Her eyes were the same soft blue, and doubtless the hair, decorously concealed beneath a linen cap, was the same pale straw colour as the younger woman's.

She had evidently overheard a part of the conversation, and was able to fill in the rest for herself.

10

'Let the man stay, William,' she said briskly. 'He's welcome to sleep by the fire if he wants to. We can lend him a blanket to wrap himself in. Goodness me!' she went on in a scolding tone. 'It's not often we get a visitor in Lower Brockhurst at this dead time of year. And a Chapman at that! The women won't thank you for letting him go until they've inspected the contents of his pack. Go and sit down by the fire, Master, and Rosie here will give you some soup from the pot.' Her gaze homed in on the same young man who had been picked on by her daughter, but her voice, when she addressed him, held a vindictive note. 'Shift yourself, Jocelyn Rawbone, and let Master Chapman have your seat!'

As I rescued Hercules from Rosamund Bush's fond embrace, the youth – I judged him to be about twelve, maybe thirteen years of age – rose sulkily from his stool, slouched past his fellow drinkers, past me, managing to knock into me as he did so, and vanished into the darkness outside.

'Good riddance to bad rubbish,' Rosamund said, with a hostility that now rivalled her mother's.

To my surprise, the seemingly mild-mannered landlord nodded in agreement.

'Like uncle, like nephew,' he muttered, adding, almost under his breath, 'Like the whole damned Rawbone family.'

I doubt if anyone other than his wife and daughter and myself heard what he said, as the noise had increased, louder even than when I came in. But the expression of anger on his face was apparent to anyone looking in his direction, and I saw one or two people glance significantly at each other, while several more dug one another knowingly in the ribs. A local feud, doubtless, and none of my business. I recollected Adela's parting injunction to me, to keep my nose out of strangers' affairs. But, of course, I was agog with curiosity. Nosiness was my chief failing as my mother, both my wives and former mother-in-law had always made plain.

I was determined, however, to amend my ways. I would be home before the Feast of Saint Patrick and prove to Adela what a good husband I was. I made my way to the vacated stool by the fire and stretched my feet to the blaze. Hercules lay down beside me with a sigh of contentment, while Rosamund Bush appeared with a bowl into which she ladled a rich-smelling stew from the pot suspended over the flames.

'When you've finished,' she smiled, handing me the bowl and a spoon, 'fill it again for your dog. Now, he does look as though he could do with some flesh on his scrawny little frame.'

Two

F or the next quarter of an hour I was too busy filling my stomach to join in any of the conversations going on around me. I persuaded the fair Rosamund to bring a separate bowl for Hercules, so we could eat together; but although our mouths were stopped, our eyes and ears were not. The piper and fiddler had paused in their labours for refreshment, so I was easily able to overhear an animated discussion being carried on behind me, by three or four men seated at the long table, at the end nearest to the fire. The topic being hotly debated was the varying merits of different manures.

'I don't reck'n much to pig dung. Does more harm than good. My old father—'

'Horse dung, forked in with a nice bit o' straw, you can't beat that fer corn. Stands to reason. Horses eat corn. So their droppings must be good fer it.'

'Nah! Cow dung's better. Or root veg'tables ploughed back into soil. What I say is—'

'My old father,' insisted the first voice, forcing its way back into the argument, 'reckoned human manure's as good as pig's any day. Better, in fact. He maintained—'

'God's teeth!' exclaimed the recommender of root vegetables. 'Human shit stinks. It's bad enough cleaning out the privy without havin' to spread it on the crops.'

'It's all right if it's mixed with wood ash,' protested a fourth man. 'I don't see nothing wrong with it. Although, myself, I use sheep dung. Plenty o' that in these parts.'

The babel of talk increased until one voice, louder and more

13

insistent than the rest, suddenly demanded, ' 'Ere! What d'you think this young fool's been doing?'

I eased round on my stool so that the group were at last within my range of vision. There were indeed four men, skin like leather, cropped hair, dressed in rough, serviceable countrymen's clothing, and a young lad, whose cherubic, normally ruddy face beneath a shock of unkempt brown hair, was now as scarlet as a rose in summer.

The speaker continued, 'Only putting the Rawbones' sheep in the same pasture as Mistress Lilywhite's geese.'

'*What?*' His listeners were united in horror and condemnation.

'Don't you know, you stupid young fool, that geese droppings is death to sheep?'

'Ar! Gets in their innards and kills 'em, it does. D'you mean to say you don' know that, Billy Tyrrell, and you born and bred in these parts?'

'Boy's a bloody idiot! Ned Rawbone and old Nathaniel'll have his guts fer tripe if he ain't more careful.'

'It was only once and it were an accident,' the boy pleaded, close to tears. 'The flock were over by the stream and Mistress Lilywhite's geese had somehow wandered in. 'Tweren't on purpose.'

'Well, you'd best be carefuller than that,' said the first man, 'or Ned Rawbone'll be looking fer another shepherd lad.'

There was a general murmur of agreement from his companions, while Billy Tyrrell looked both defiant and ashamed. 'Weren't my fault,' he kept muttering.

The two musicians now started up again, a jolly jig of a tune that soon had all the customers stamping their feet, and it was no longer possible to eavesdrop. I finished my third bowl of stew and decided that enough was enough. Even Hercules had only eaten half of his second helping and was now stretched out in front of the hearth, exhausted after his long, wet tramp through inhospitable woodlands. I wondered idly who the Rawbones were, remembering that the lad who had been forced to give up his stool to me had been of the same name. A local family, obviously, and one, I guessed, of some importance. But a family that had its enemies: William Bush and his womenfolk did not seem to like them. Or, maybe it was just the young man, Josh or Jocelyn, however he was known, who had incurred their ill-will.

The thought had barely taken shape in my mind, when a man stormed furiously through the open doorway and, ignoring everyone else, walked up to William Bush, seizing him roughly by the throat.

'What do you mean,' he snarled, 'by turning my nephew out of this piddling alehouse? He's as much right to drink here as anyone else in this village.' He gave the landlord a shake. 'Well, answer me!'

There were murmurs of protest from the assembled company, but the young man, toughly built and somewhere around my own age of twenty-six, I reckoned, was in an ugly mood. For the moment, at least, there was a general reluctance to go to Master Bush's assistance on everybody's part, except one. Rosamund Bush flung herself on her father's assailant from behind, scratching viciously at his neck and face, and spitting like a cat.

'Leave him alone, you great bully! You beast! You treacherous bastard!' The ladylike mask had slipped to reveal a virago underneath.

But her onslaught had the desired effect. The young man was forced to release his prey in order to protect himself from her nails and teeth (the fair Rosamund was not above biting as well as clawing) and eventually managed to get hold of her wrists. This time, however, there were plenty of would-be rescuers, all seeking an excuse to wrest that seductive body from his un-chivalrous grasp. Those too slow or too far away to be of any practical use, contented themselves with a volley of insults.

'Let her go, Tom Rawbone! You're a bloody bully, like she says!'

'You got no right coming in here, abusing people, not after what you done to this family, you fucker!'

'Murderer, more like! Ask 'im what 'e did with Eris Lilywhite. What d'you do with 'er after you killed 'er, Tom, eh?'

'Yeah! What d'you do with her body? Answer us that!'

The young man released Rosamund into the arms of her champions and turned furiously on his accusers.

'I did *not* murder Eris Lilywhite!' he roared. 'How many times do I have to tell you? I don't know what happened to her any more than the rest of you! Maybe she isn't even dead! Can't you get that fact into those turnips you call your heads? Perhaps she's still alive, living in Gloucester or some other place.' He dabbed ineffectually at the bleeding scratch marks on his face, then rounded once more on William Bush. 'I warn you, landlord, don't throw out any other member of my family, or you'll be hearing from me again. And next time, I won't be alone. Ned and Josh and Christopher will all be with me. Yes, and my father, too.'

'How is Nathaniel?' the landlord enquired mildly, working, presumably, on the principle that a soft answer turns away wrath. 'He hasn't been too well of late, I hear.'

The tactic was not a success.

'Mind your own business!' Tom Rawbone shouted; and, having made the point, he departed as precipitately as he had entered.

There was a collective sigh of relief. The musicians retuned their instruments (not that this made the slightest difference to their tooting and scraping) and started playing again; conversations resumed where they had been broken off; William Bush submitted to his shaken wife's embraces, before strolling off to broach another cask of ale as though nothing at all had happened; while Rosamund Bush freed herself from her admirers' clutches and came to sit beside me, pulling up another stool to the fire.

'So, Master Chapman,' she smiled, a little breathlessly and smoothing back a strand of corn-coloured hair that had come loose from one of her plaits, 'what's been happening out there, in the big, wide world?'

'Nothing much, Mistress,' I said, returning her smile with interest, and accepting her implicit ruling that the recent incident was not open to general discussion. 'Things have been quieter in the country this past year than I can remember for quite some time. The Duke of Gloucester has retired to his

Yorkshire estates, and, from what I can understand, won't be shifting from them unless forced to do so by a royal summons from his brother, the King. His other brother, of course, is dead and buried—'

'Oh, I know *that!*' Rosamund interrupted scornfully. 'Tewkesbury Abbey, that's where the Duke of Clarence is buried. Though how he died is more than anyone seems to know.' She pouted prettily. 'Is that all you have to tell me? It's not very exciting news.'

'Thank God,' I answered, adding in reply to her raised eyebrows, 'Exciting news usually means trouble. More fighting. More Tudor plots . . . Ah, I nearly forgot. I met a friar in Cirencester who'd come from London. The Queen's given birth to yet another baby girl.'

The blue eyes sparkled. 'Why didn't you tell me that first? Men never seem to know what really interests a woman.' She tilted her head provocatively. 'Do you have a wife?'

'I do. And three children.'

'Mmm . . . I guess you keep Mistress Chapman happy then. You look the passionate kind.' It was just as well that the fire was hot or she would have seen me begin to blush. She went on musingly, 'I was betrothed once.'

'To a local lad?' It was not my business, but some response seemed to be required of me.

She wrinkled her nose in distaste. (It was a mistake: that member was not quite so small and dainty as she so obviously thought it was.)

'Believe it or not,' she said, 'to that ill-mannered oaf who was in here just now.'

'Tom Rawbone?' I asked in astonishment, my interest suddenly aroused.

'Yes, him. How do you know what he's called?'

'I heard someone name him. I'm not surprised you ended the betrothal. A very bad-tempered and belligerent young man by the looks of him.'

'Oh, I didn't end the betrothal,' was the surprising answer. 'He did. He decided he wanted to marry Eris Lilywhite instead.'

17

I frowned. 'The girl someone accused him of murdering?'

'Yes. Oh, don't take any notice of that. Whatever else he might be, Tom's not a killer. He wouldn't harm a fly.'

'That's not the impression he gave me,' I retorted. Women's reasoning frequently left me floundering (and still does). 'He struck me as extremely dangerous.'

'Only when he's angry.' Her logic reminded me forcibly of Adela's. 'And I used to take care not to make him angry. It's different now, of course.'

'Of course.' I should have liked to pursue the subject further, but my companion had suddenly tired of it. (Either that, or she decided she had confided too much to a stranger.) She turned a little away from me and began to tap her feet in time to the music. So, instead, I asked, 'What's this village called? I didn't quite catch its name.'

'Lower Brockhurst.' She looked round again, relieved that I had voluntarily changed the subject.

Brock Hurst: the old Saxon words meaning Badger Wood. 'Why "Lower"?' I asked. 'Where's Upper Brockhurst? I haven't seen another hamlet or settlement for miles past.'

Rosamund laughed, showing small, even teeth like a child's. 'You won't,' she said. 'It's nothing now but a ruin, all overgrown. The trees have taken it back for their own.'

For some reason, her words sent a shiver down my spine. Hercules, curled up at my feet, stirred in his sleep and whimpered. Our Saxon forebears worshipped and sacrificed to the gods of the trees long before Saint Augustine brought the Christian faith to these shores, and deep within all of us still lurk some of the old pagan beliefs and superstitions.

The music had stopped again, and one of the men seated behind me – he who had been so earnest an advocate of human manure – had turned the tables by listening in on my conversation with Rosamund.

'That's right,' he confirmed, putting a very dirty and extremely smelly hand on my shoulder. 'Upper Brock'urst disappeared some year back.'

' "Some year back!" ' repeated a scathing female voice from

my other side. 'Well over a hundred years back, you silly old fool! Take no notice of anything these idiots tell you, chapman. The entire population of Upper Brockhurst was wiped out in the Black Death, and the place has fallen into ruin.'

I glanced round and saw a tall, gaunt woman, with a thin, lined face, standing beside my stool. She was respectably dressed in a dark woollen cloak that had fallen open to reveal a matron's linen apron, worn over – as far as I could see in the fire- and candlelight – an unpatched and undarned skirt of another dark material. Her voice had that harsh burr and flat intonation peculiar to the West Country and Cornwall, and which, amongst other things, denotes our almost total lack of Danish ancestry. She also spoke with a clipped precision that indicated urban origins. I suspected her to have grown up in a town or city; Gloucester or Cirencester perhaps.

I got to my feet, offering her my stool, but she declined, pressing me down again.

'I prefer to stand, thank you, young man.' She was, I guessed, nearer sixty than fifty, and a wisp of hair peeping out from her linen coif was iron grey.

'Upper Brockhurst,' I mused. 'Would that be the place in the woods, some mile or so uphill from here? Fragments of stone walls buried in the undergrowth? Oh, and a well that's been very commendably covered over.'

My companion shook her head. 'That's not the village,' she said, 'which is a bit further to the east. No, what you've obviously stumbled across is the remains of the Hall. Its owners, two brothers and the last of their line, also died of the plague. As for the well . . .' She broke off, shrugging. 'There's a strange story attached to that. But you'd better ask one of these yokels about it. I've only lived here for the past six years, since my son, who misguidedly married a local girl, died. So I'm still regarded as a stranger, thank God!' She added proudly, 'I was born and brought up in Gloucester.'

She had raised her voice slightly as she finished speaking, and there was a general guffaw at her last words from those near enough to hear them.

'That ain't nothin' to boast about,' jeered one of the men behind me. 'City dwellers is ignorant bastards by my reck'ning.' There was a chorus of agreement.

'You should think yerself lucky, Theresa Lilywhite,' someone else chipped in, 'that yer son married a good country girl like Maud Haycombe, who brought him a decent dowry and his own smallholding when 'er father died. Your Gilbert wouldn't have done so well in Gloucester, digging wells.'

'He was a good weller,' my informant snapped. 'Gilbert knew his trade inside out, and made a sufficient living to support me and himself.'

'He came down 'ere looking fer work, though, didn't he?' scoffed yet another of the little group seated behind me. 'Not enough work in Gloucester, was there? And once Maud Haycombe set 'er cap at 'im, he didn't hesitate. Knew a good proposition when it presented itself.'

The woman addressed as Theresa Lilywhite snorted derisively, but made no further remark except to say, 'I'm away home.' she pulled her cloak about her and disappeared into the night beyond the open door.

I swivelled round on my stool, and as the fair Rosamund was now delighting the company by adding her voice to the musicians' fiddling and piping, I wormed my way into my neighbours' conversation. Well, to be truthful, I was more impolite than that. I simply cut across what they were saying and asked, 'That woman! What's her relationship to the girl somebody claimed was murdered?'

'She was 'er grandmother,' answered the shepherd lad, Billy Tyrrell. 'Ain't that right, Rob?'

The man to whom he had appealed, nodded.

'Tha's right. She's a widow woman from Gloucester. Come down here some year back, to live with Maud and her daughter after Gilbert Lilywhite died. Don' think Mistress Lilywhite asked 'er. Just come fer the funeral and stayed.'

'True enough,' another of the men corroborated. 'Reckon she was the one who was lonely, fer all she said she was keeping Maud and young Eris comp'ny. Reckon they didn't want 'er

20

there, but couldn't get rid of 'er. Now, of course, there's just the two of them.'

'Was this Eris Lilywhite murdered?' I asked, my thumbs beginning to prick with curiosity.

'Maybe. Maybe not.' This was the man who had recommended horse dung mixed with straw. 'But there's this much certain. She disappeared on the night of the great storm six months ago, and hasn't been seen nor heard of since.'

There was a nodding of heads and a pulling down of mouths.

'You all believe she was murdered,' I suggested.

'We-ell, given the circumstances, yes,' the man called Rob admitted (he was the one who had advocated cow manure).

'And what were the circumstances?' I pressed them.

But just at that moment, the singing and the music stopped yet again, and Rosamund returned to join me at the fire. A brief silence ensued before my new-found friends suddenly began a vigorous discussion of the next day's weather. Young Mistress Bush laid a dimpled hand on my arm.

'How long do you intend to stay in Brockhurst, Master Chapman?'

'Call me Roger,' I invited. She gave me what she plainly thought was a seductive look from under her long, fair lashes, but which, unfortunately, only made me want to laugh. Carefully controlling this impulse, I continued, 'I had intended going on my way tomorrow. But I daresay I could spare another morning, if you think the goodies of the village would be keen to buy any of the things left in my pack. Sadly, most of what I started out with has already been sold.'

She pouted. 'Oh . . . Couldn't you stay longer than that? At least until the day after tomorrow? I want you to be one of my players.'

'Your players? I'm sorry, I don't understand.'

The hand slid from my arm, coming to rest lightly and seemingly accidentally on my right thigh. Again, she gave me that upward, slanting glance.

'Lambert Miller, over there, has challenged me to a game of Nine Men's Morris.' And she indicated a handsome, florid man of some thirty summers, seated directly beneath a wall torch whose smoking light showed up his impressive physique to the best advantage. I was not fooled for a moment by his apparently white head of hair. It was obvious that his calling was the same as his name. His broad shoulders also bore a faint dusting of flour.

Of course, I knew the game Nine Men's Morris. Played on a board with little wooden balls as counters, it was, and still is, called Morrells (or sometimes Merrills, depending whereabouts you come from). But in my young days, there was another version of it, in which the 'board' was drawn on a beaten earth floor, or, in summer, out of doors on any grassless piece of ground, and in which the counters were real people. The twenty-four holes on the board, into which the wooden morrells are slotted, were, in the larger game, indicated by markers. The 'counters', nine for each of the two players involved, wore distinguishing scarves or sashes (just as morrells are painted in two different colours).

For anyone who has never played the game, the object is for each protagonist to try to place three morrells, or human counters, in a straight line, either horizontally or diagonally, while preventing the other player from doing the same. Every time a player achieves this, he can remove one of his opponent's pieces from the board. The winner is the person who first manages to capture seven of his adversary's nine counters. When the game is played with people, the resulting moves are reminiscent of a morris dance, hence its name.

'And when is this game?' I asked.

'Tomorrow night, here in the Roman Sandal, after supper.' Rosamund gave me yet another winning smile. 'The tables will be pushed back against the wall and the board positions drawn on the floor. Everyone's promised to come. Everyone I've invited, that is.'

I assumed that the Rawbone family, however many of them there were, had been excluded from this invitation; but with nine human counters apiece to find for herself and Lambert Miller, I guessed that most of the other villagers had been pressed into attending. Rosamund even seemed to be in need of my services.

I hesitated for a second or two, knowing that I really should be on my way in the morning if I were to abide strictly by the terms of my promise to Adela. But I can't truthfully say that there was ever a moment's real doubt in my mind that I would stay. The mention of the word murder, and the whiff of mystery that surrounded the disappearance of this girl, Eris Lilywhite, had already cast their magic spell. I had to find out more.

But, having agreed to remain in Brockhurst for another day at least, and to act as one of her 'counters' in the following evening's game, the next question I put to the fair Rosamund had nothing to do with the puzzle that was uppermost in my thoughts.

'Why is this alehouse called the Roman Sandal?' I enquired.

Someone must once have told her that she looked pretty when she pouted, because Rosamund did it again, pulling down the corners of her rosebud mouth in an exaggerated moue of protestation at my lack of continuing interest in her and her affairs. But I soon realized that she was neither as flighty nor as empty-headed as she would have people think her, and after a word or two of explanation, she even warmed to her theme.

'It wasn't called so originally. It was just known as "the alehouse". Well, in a village this size, that's what you'd expect. There's not another inn for miles around. However, some time ago –' she paused and her lovely eyes glinted wickedly as they encouraged me to join in the joke – '*some year back*, as my parents and everyone else in these parts would say, Father found an ancient Roman sandal under a loose flagstone in the cellar. It was falling apart, of course. The leather straps were crumbling and the buckles had turned green, but you could see what it was. Father Anselm – he's the priest at Saint Walburga's church – says the Romans were all over this part of the country in centuries gone by. Cirencester was one of their most important towns.'

I nodded. 'Corinium Dobunnorum.' She stared at me doubtfully. 'The Latin name for Cirencester,' I explained. 'They called Gloucester Glevum.'

'Oh.' I could see her storing the information away in her

memory for future use. The fair Rosa Mundi was most certainly more intelligent than she liked to be thought. She repeated her habit of cocking her pretty head to one side. (Something else someone had told her was an endearing trait?) 'You know a lot for a chapman.'

It was an accusation I was used to, having encountered it regularly for the past seven or eight years of my life.

'I was educated by the monks at Glastonbury. My mother intended me for the monastic life. But it wasn't what I wanted, so when she died before I'd taken my vows, I quit – with my abbot's blessing, I might add. I fancied the freedom of the open road, being my own master, sleeping under the stars in summer and in warm haylofts in winter, no responsibilities, going to sleep and getting up when I chose—'

She interrupted me with a laugh. 'So now you're married with three children!'

I sighed. 'Life eventually catches up with us all. Fortunately, I have a very understanding and long-suffering wife. She allows me to escape now and then.'

'I wouldn't let you escape if you were mine,' Rosamund said fiercely. 'I wouldn't willingly let any man I'd set my heart on escape me. And if he did, I'd make him pay!' The delicate mouth thinned to a hard, unlovely line, the blue eyes took on the harsh glint of sapphires.

'And how did you make Tom Rawbone pay?'

She was plainly taken aback by my question. She had forgotten telling me of her betrothal to him. She gave a nervous laugh, which she managed to turn into an unconvincing giggle as she dug me in the ribs.

'You mustn't take what I say so seriously. You saw for yourself that I've done nothing to harm him.'

She was right: the young man was whole and fit and well. But what about the girl he had jilted her for? What about the missing Eris Lilywhite? What had happened to her?

Three

T he musicians had started up for a third time, but my ears were now so attuned to their playing that I failed to notice. It was first brought to my attention when Lambert Miller rose from his seat and came across to Rosamund, trying to look modest and unconcerned about the effect his large, handsome face, and even larger, well-muscled frame was having on the women in the ale-room. And failing dismally.

'Mistress Rose,' he said, bowing fulsomely over her hand, which he clasped possessively in one of his own great paws, 'I know I speak for everyone present when I beg you to honour us with another song.'

His big, bland smile intimated he had no doubts that she would oblige him. So she did, but it was obvious to me, if not to him, that she was doing so only to please herself. As she rose to her feet, she said tartly, 'I've asked you before, Lambert, please don't call me Rose.'

The great oaf looked bewildered. 'But it's your name,' he protested.

'My name is Rosamund,' she explained impatiently. 'No one wants to be called Rose Bush, Lambert. It sounds ridiculous!'

'Oh . . . Oh, yes! I see.' He gave an over-hearty laugh. 'You are a wit, Rose – er – Rosamund.'

She gave him an enigmatic glance, but allowed him to lead her forward to stand beside the fiddler, then tapped his cheek affectionately – which caused Lambert's chest to swell to even more manly proportions than it aspired to already. But I couldn't help wondering what deep game young Mistress Bush was playing. I could have sworn that she despised her rugged

25

admirer, but she plainly had no intention of alienating such a catch. And who could blame her? She must have been humiliated in front of the whole village by Tom Rawbone's rejection of her in favour of the missing Eris Lilywhite. She would have been less than human had she not wanted to demonstrate to him, and to everyone else, that she was desired by probably the handsomest and most sought after man for miles around.

The group behind me, wisely ignoring the music, had progressed from the rival merits of manures to reach a general agreement on the superiority of Stockholm tar over the old-fashioned remedy of broom water for the removal of ticks from sheep. But when the one called Rob noticed me looking at them, he interrupted the conversation.

'You wanted to know about the well at Brockhurst Hall, chapman.'

'I was impressed by the excellent lid on it,' I said, 'and by the fact that it hadn't been left as an open snare for children and animals.'

'Ah,' one of the other men explained, 'some year back, a young chap from the village climbed down the shaft, slipped and broke his leg—'

'And 'is arm,' put in somebody else.

'Ay, and his arm. Weren't found fer nigh on two days. After that, village elders they instructed John Carpenter to make a cover fer the dratted thing. A good solid 'un, they said. Which he did, as you've seen fer yerself.'

'Wouldn't it have been easier just to fill the well in?' I suggested. 'I imagine it's been dried up for a good long time.'

'Ar, reck'n you're right,' the one called Rob agreed. Then, suddenly losing interest, they all reverted to the far more exciting subject of sheep.

A hand fell on my shoulder. Swivelling round on my stool, I saw Theresa Lilywhite, who must have returned to the alehouse without my noticing. She bent down to speak in my ear as most of the customers had now joined in the rollicking refrain of a highly improper song, which I had first heard sung by the sailors along the Bristol Backs. No doubt this was a cleaner version, in deference to the ladies present. I very much hoped so.

'I've spoken to my daughter-in-law,' she said, 'and if you don't fancy sleeping on the floor here, we can offer you accommodation for the night. Or for as long as you want to stay in Lower Brockhurst. There's only the two of us since Eris disappeared. You can have her bed.'

'There's the dog, as well,' I said, pointing to Hercules, snoring happily at my feet.

She nodded. 'You're welcome to bring him. Just keep him out of the way of our dogs, that's all. They'll think he's a rat. But they're tied up outside at nights, anyway.'

It was a more inviting prospect than sleeping on the straw-covered flagstones of the ale-room, particularly if I intended remaining in Brockhurst for longer than a single night. Besides which, I should be right at the heart of a mystery that was beginning to intrigue me. Surely I was bound to learn more about the missing girl from her mother and grandmother than from anyone else.

'Thank you. I accept,' I said. 'Do you want me to come with you at once?'

'If you would. We keep early hours. What else is there for two women on their own to do on long winter nights besides sleep?'

I hoped that on this particular evening I might tempt her and her daughter-in-law into conversation, but I didn't say so. I simply begged a few moments' grace to explain matters to William Bush and say goodbye.

The landlord, although patently relieved to be rid of me, nevertheless deplored my choice of alternative lodging. The Lilywhites obviously ranked alongside the Rawbones as people who had inflicted unhappiness on his daughter, and were not to be easily forgiven. They had spawned the siren who had stolen the affections of Rosamund's betrothed.

'Watch yourself then, chapman,' William advised, failing in his half-hearted attempt to persuade me to stay.

I had a suspicion that his daughter might try harder if she knew of my intention to leave, so, while she was still flirting with Lambert Miller, I gathered up my pack, my cudgel and an indignant Hercules and followed Theresa Lilywhite outside.

It was quite dark now, the storm clouds no longer great bastions in the sky, but torn to witches' hair by a rising wind. It was the dead time of year, cold and tempestuous, as late February so often is just before the earth begins to stir and put forth new shoots. The dank smell of sodden grassland teased my nostrils, and a few thin trees waved arthritic branches overhead as we crossed the wooden footbridge and left the village behind us. My cloak whipped around my legs, and Hercules cowered in the shelter of my arm, growling his disapproval.

'What's the stream called?' I asked Theresa Lilywhite as we started climbing the slope towards the homestead, halfway between the village and the farm that I had noted earlier in the evening.

She laughed, the sound streeling away like a banshee's cry on the cold night air.

'Nothing. It's just known as "the stream". It's probably got a name somewhere along its length, but not in Lower Brockhurst.' She raised her voice against the increasing violence of the wind. 'But the rill that flows down from the ridge, that's known as the Draco. Don't ask me why.'

'Maybe from *drakon*, the Greek word for a serpent. Or from the Latin for a dragon.' I remembered the snake-like meanderings of the little brook, although, as we trudged diagonally uphill across the sheep-bitten grass, it was lost to view in the darkness.

'What sort of pedlar are you?' panted my companion, as she pushed open a gate in a picket fence and led the way into a small enclosure.

Our entrance was greeted by the furious barking of two great hounds, each tethered by a long chain to a stake driven into the ground; while, somewhere on the far side of the one-storey building that stood in the middle of the compound, geese began to cackle loud enough to have awakened the whole of ancient Rome. Theresa Lilywhite yelled at the dogs, who, recognizing the voice of authority, slunk back to their posts and lay down. The geese cackled on.

'Sorry,' she apologized, 'but there's nothing I can do about those hideous birds. We'll just have to wait for them to settle.'

'The Romans found them better sentinels than dogs,' I pointed out, and once again, she laughed.

'I'll have your story out of you before we go to sleep tonight,' she promised. 'So be warned. I have a long nose.'

'So have I,' I admitted cheerfully.

She gave me a curious glance and ushered me inside the cottage, but said nothing more for the present.

The long, narrow room in which I found myself served as living room and sleeping quarters all in one, a heavy curtain of unbleached linen dividing the latter from the former. I had been in many such places during my travels and had lived in smaller. Beneath a hole in the roof was a central hearth on which logs were burning, gnarled and hoary and covered with grey-green lichen. They blazed fitfully, spitting out showers of sparks and bearded with fringes of woodash that trembled into feathery, fan-shaped patterns. Near enough to benefit from their warmth, but not sufficiently close to be scorched by their heat, sat a woman, staring into the flames. She had been spinning, judging by the wheel and basket of wool beside her, but had now abandoned this occupation. She looked up as we entered.

'Maud,' Theresa Lilywhite said, 'here's the chapman I told you about. He's happy to accept our offer of a bed, rather than spend an uncomfortable night on the alehouse floor. Chapman, this is my daughter-in-law.'

I gave a slight bow. 'Pleased to make your acquaintance, Mistress.'

Maud Lilywhite, who I judged to be somewhere in her late thirties, rose from her stool, a slight woman in a dress of drab homespun, whose tired, careworn features still showed traces of the beauty she must have passed on to her daughter. (In a place the size of Lower Brockhurst, it would have taken a girl of exceptional looks to eclipse the pink-and-white prettiness of Rosamund Bush.) Her dark, liquid brown eyes retained something of the lustre that must once have set pulses racing, and which, long ago, had ensnared a young man from the big city of Gloucester.

'Have you had food, Master Chapman?' she asked.

'Hercules and I ate more than well at the alehouse, I thank you, Mistress.' I set my shivering animal down on the floor, where he immediately made himself at home, stretching out luxuriously in front of the fire.

'Then you'll take some mulled ale,' the older woman suggested, coming forward and indicating the small iron pot that hung from a tripod over the flames.

I agreed very willingly; and while Theresa Lilywhite drew up two more stools to the fire, showed me where to put my pack and cudgel and hung my wet cloak on a nail behind the door, Maud Lilywhite fetched beakers from a shelf above the wall-oven and poured out three generous measures of the warm, sweet, cinnamon-flavoured drink.

'Your own brew, Mistress?' I asked, when I had slaked my thirst.

The younger woman shook her head. 'My mother-in-law's.'

There was a certain reservation in her tone that made me suspect she did not really like Theresa. I recalled the conversation in the Roman Sandal – '. . . Just come fer the funeral and stayed' . . . 'Reckon they didn't want 'er there, but couldn't get rid of 'er . . .' – and decided that my guess was probably correct.

'Have you come far?' Maud enquired politely, just as Theresa demanded more robustly, 'Well, and what's your story, then, chapman? A pedlar who knows Greek and Latin isn't an everyday occurrence, you must admit.'

'A little Latin and less Greek,' I amended, laughing. 'All right. I'll tell you my history in exchange for some local gossip. What do you say?'

I saw Maud Lilywhite shift uneasily on her stool, but the older woman cried, 'Done! It'll be a pleasanter way to spend a stormy winter's evening than staring at these four walls, or watching my daughter-in-law's interminable spinning.'

So, for the next hour or so, I told them my story and a few of my adventures, adding, as a bonus for their hospitality, various insights into the life of the royal family – some a little exaggerated, I have to confess – and was rewarded by their undivided attention and awestruck silence. But I could see that whereas the younger woman was most impressed by the people I had met, the dukes and princes I had talked to, Theresa Lilywhite was far more interested in the mysteries I had solved. I could guess the way her mind was working, so did nothing to minimize my successes. In fact, quite the opposite: I was positively boastful. And if, on occasions, I saw in my mind's eye Adela's face with its mocking expression, I managed to ignore it.

When, at last, I had finished speaking, both women drew a long, deep, satisfied breath.

'Well, that tale's worth your bed and board for at least a week, chapman,' Theresa finally remarked. 'Don't you agree, Maud?'

Her daughter-in-law nodded. 'And you really have met the King and His Grace of Gloucester and that poor gentleman, the late Duke of Clarence?' she asked wonderingly.

'I have. And I swear to you, in the name of my mother and the Virgin, that all that I've told you is true.' My mother could take responsibility for the bits that were almost, but not quite, true. Our Lady could sponsor the rest.

'So,' Theresa Lilywhite said, getting up to pour three more cups of ale and then settling down again on her stool, 'what do you want to ask us?' The younger woman made a little movement of protest, but was rebuked by her mother-in-law. 'Fair's fair, Maud. He's kept his part of the bargain, and handsomely, too. Now we must keep ours. We're waiting, chapman.'

I could tell by the guarded look on both their faces that they were expecting me to ask about Eris, but I nosed my way into their confidence gently.

'When we were talking earlier this evening,' I said, turning to Theresa, 'I mentioned the well I'd stumbled across, and you said it must have been the well at Brockhurst Hall. You also said there was a strange story attached to it and recommended

Kate Sedley

that I ask one of the villagers to tell me about it. Only, for one reason and another, I never got around to doing so. Perhaps you'd be kind enough to enlighten me now.'

'Go on, Maud!' The older woman looked across at the younger. 'You're a local girl, born and bred in Lower Brockhurst. You know all the stories concerning these parts. Tell the chapman what he wants to know. I've already told him that the population of Upper Brockhurst and the Hall were wiped out in the Black Death. Those turnip-heads in the alehouse would have had him think that it all happened "some year back"!' The contempt in her voice was almost tangible.

Maud Lilywhite flushed resentfully, but attempted no defence of her fellow villagers. Perhaps, over the years, she had grown tired of doing so. Or perhaps she felt as much contempt for her mother-in-law as an outsider as Theresa felt for people she regarded as ignorant country yokels. Instead, she turned towards me.

'Very well, then.' She gave a faint smile and I smiled back encouragingly. 'You know, of course, Master Chapman, that some communities were wiped out completely during the great plague of the last century, while others, only half a mile or so distant, survived intact. And that, it seems, is what happened here. Every single inhabitant of Upper Brockhurst died – nobody escaped – while in our village only three people were struck down, and even they recovered.'

She paused to take a sip of ale before continuing. 'Brockhurst Hall stood a little apart from the village of Upper Brockhurst and, as far as I can gather, occupied most of the ridge that overlooks this valley. According to my grandmother, who had been told the facts by *her* grandmother, the Hall had been in the possession of a family called Martin for as long as anyone could remember. It's said that the first Martin, who built the place, came to this country with William the Conqueror—'

'William the Bastard,' Theresa Lilywhite corrected her with quiet venom.

Maud repeated, 'William the Bastard,' with a look of scarcely veiled derision. For my benefit, she explained, 'My mother-in-law's family are of Saxon descent, or so they say—'

32

'There's no "say" about it,' Theresa interrupted angrily. 'My great-great-great-grandfather's great-great-great-great-grandfather was horsekeeper to Earl Godwin himself, at Berkeley.'

My brain was too tired to work out whether this was a feasible claim or not, and in any case, Maud had resumed her story.

'As I was telling you, chapman, whatever the truth about the first Martin, it's certain the family had lived at the Hall for a very long time. But by the middle of the last century, only two brothers, Tobias and Humphrey, remained. Both men were bachelors and seemed likely to stay that way. Even before the plague claimed their lives, it seemed that they would be the last of their line.

'Like many elderly, unmarried people they grew more and more reclusive as the years went by, so much so that they went less and less beyond the confines of the Hall. But there was a problem. The chief water supply for the area was the Draco, that little stream that flows downhill to join with the larger one at the bottom. It ran straight through Upper Brockhurst's main street, where it was deepest and widest. There was, of course, a well in the Hall's stableyard, but whoever sank it originally hadn't dug down far enough, and, in summer, the water level became extremely low. This had never worried earlier generations of Martins, who simply fetched extra supplies from the Draco, like the rest of their neighbours.'

'But that didn't suit Humphrey and Tobias?' I suggested, leaning down to pat Hercules, who had suddenly woken up with a snort and an urgent desire to hunt for fleas.

Maud shook her head. 'No. It seems that as well as becoming recluses, the brothers had also grown miserly in their old age. They'd turned off their last servant some years before, and looked after themselves. But they had to have water, and if, in times of drought, they weren't prepared to walk into the village and fill buckets from the Draco, then they had to have their own well deepened. My grandmother – or, rather, her grandmother – couldn't remember the details, but it seems that a couple of wellers, a father and son from Tetbury way, were persuaded to come to Brockhurst Hall and carry out the necessary work. This they duly did, but –' and here Maud lowered her voice impressively, indicating that she was approaching the climax of her story – 'two days after they'd finished, and said goodbye to the friends they'd made during their stay in the village, they were found murdered in woodland about a mile or so from the Hall. The backs of their heads had been battered in with two great tree branches that were left beside the bodies, covered in blood. But before the hue and cry could be raised, or a message sent to the Sheriff's Officers at Gloucester, the first case of plague arrived in Upper Brockhurst. Maybe the wellers had brought it, who knows? But within weeks, the entire population, including Humphrey and Tobias Martin, was wiped out. And in the meantime, of course, no one from outside the village would go anywhere near them. Lower Brockhurst sealed itself off from the outside world – nobody was allowed in or out of the village for more than three months – and consequently everyone survived.'

'So,' I said, straightening up on my stool as Hercules settled down to sleep again, 'no one has ever discovered why the two wellers were murdered, or by whom. But couldn't it simply have been footpads? Or outlaws? After all, the Martins must have paid them for their work before they left the Hall. They would have had money on them.'

Maud Lilywhite added another log to the fire, stretching her feet towards the flames.

'But according to my great-great-grandmother,' she said quietly, 'neither man had been robbed. Their money was still in the pouches attached to their belts. So it couldn't possibly have been footpads or outlaws.'

'An intriguing story, eh, chapman?' Theresa asked, offering me yet another cup of ale, which I declined, feeling I had already consumed enough for one evening. 'And one to which we shall, I'm afraid, never know the answer.'

'After well over a hundred years, I'm sure that's only too true,' I agreed regretfully, and she laughed.

'You don't like unsolved mysteries, I can tell.'

'No, I don't.'

I saw her glance narrowly at her daughter-in-law before saying forcefully, 'Well then, here's one recent enough for you to be able to unravel. Perhaps you can discover what's happened to my granddaughter, Eris, who went missing over six months ago on the night of the great storm.'

'Mother-in-law, leave it! Please!'

'Nonsense!' was the robust answer to this heartfelt appeal. 'Someone's got to find out what's become of the girl. If she's been murdered —' Theresa's voice cracked a little on the word — 'or if she has simply run away. Although, knowing your daughter, Maud, I hardly think that's likely. She was too much your child in that respect. She knew a good catch when she hooked one. She wasn't going to throw old Nathaniel Rawbone back into the sea. Not with the fortune he has salted away.'

'*Nathaniel* Rawbone?' I asked. 'Excuse me, but you must understand that I've already heard something of the story—'

'From Rosamund Bush, I'll be bound!' the older woman exclaimed. 'That one's going to play the part of the Wronged Woman for the rest of her life. What has she told you?'

'That she and *Tom* Rawbone — a member of the same family, I take it — were betrothed, but that he jilted her in favour of your granddaughter. It came out quite naturally in conversation. She didn't go out of her way to tell me.' I found myself springing to the Fair Rosamund's defence.

Theresa Lilywhite snorted disbelievingly, but made no comment.

'It's quite true,' her daughter-in-law put in, evidently deciding that, as I knew so much, I might as well know the rest. 'A year ago this month, Eris went to work at Dragonswick Farm — that's the building you can see higher up the hill — for the Rawbone family. They needed extra help in the house, there being seven of them in all, and their housekeeper, Elvina Merryman having recently been sick.' She added, looking defiantly at Theresa, 'It wasn't Eris's fault if Tom Rawbone fell in love with her and out of love with Rosamund Bush.'

'Maybe not,' Theresa retorted grimly, 'But having stolen

another woman's betrothed, Eris should have been content with having done sufficient mischief. She should never have permitted the attentions of a man old enough to be her grandfather, and also the father of the man she had promised to marry. But, of course, she was never in love with Tom. He was just a way of worming herself into the Rawbone family.' Theresa sniffed disparagingly. 'She'd not long turned sixteen, and as crafty as the serpent in Eden. Well, I'll tell you this, chapman! She didn't get her mercenary, philandering ways from *my* side of the family. I wasn't born a Lilywhite, but my husband's folk were as honest and God-fearing as any you'll find in England. There wasn't a woman in Gloucester who would have turned down an offer of marriage from my Gilbert.'

I said hurriedly, not wishing to be drawn into any quarrel between mother- and daughter-in-law, 'Are you telling me that Eris – that your granddaughter – jilted Tom Rawbone in her turn, and for the young man's father?'

It was Maud who answered, refusing to rise to Theresa's bait. 'Yes, I'm afraid so. No one knew how long the pair of them had been secretly carrying on a courtship. Nathaniel, for all he's nearly sixty, still has an eye for the women. We all know that. He's been a womanizer all his life. But no one expected him to look at a girl of Eris's youth. Nor did anyone know that Tom Rawbone was courting her as well, and secretly plotting to break his betrothal to Rosamund Bush. How in the Virgin's Name,' Maud finished on an anguished note, 'Eris managed to keep everything a secret in this village, whose very walls have ears, I shall never understand. Even I had no inkling of what was going on.'

'What Eris wanted, Eris was going to get, come Hell or high water,' her grandmother declared uncompromisingly. Theresa lowered her voice almost to a whisper and her face was suddenly grey with fear. 'Sometimes, I think Eris might have been a witch.'

Four

Maud was on her feet immediately, shaking with anger or maybe fright, perhaps both. I couldn't decide. But in the end, anger got the upper hand.

'You're a fool, mother-in-law, to say such a thing about your own granddaughter, and in front of a stranger, too! You could do untold harm. Not just to Eris but to us.'

Theresa had already realized the error of her ways and was looking at me, pleadingly.

'I didn't mean it, chapman. It was thoughtless of me. We all say stupid things when we lose our tempers.'

'No one will hear it repeated by me,' I promised and attempted a feeble joke. 'Of course, I can't answer for Hercules.'

They both smiled wanly, but were in some measure reassured.

'I knew you were a trustworthy young fellow the moment I saw you,' Theresa told me.

I laughed. 'Not so young any more. Last October, I was twenty-six. I've been married twice and have three children, two of my own and a stepson. So . . . Tell me about the night Eris disappeared. I've gathered it was stormy.'

Theresa glanced across at her daughter-in-law. 'You'll have to tell him. I wasn't here. Perhaps if I had been, things might have turned out differently. But I'd gone home to Gloucester the week before in answer to a summons from my sister, who was sick. When I returned here a month later, it was to find that Eris had vanished and the whole village was buzzing with gossip about her and the Rawbones.' She glared at Maud. 'No one had

37

seen fit to send to Gloucester and advise me what had happened.'

Maud Lilywhite sighed wearily, as one who had grown accustomed to the accusation.

'I've told you this many times, Theresa, but I'll say it again. There seemed no point in worrying you. All that could be done to find Eris had been done. Ned Rawbone and other men from the village had spent days searching the woods and surrounding countryside. Some of them had been to Tetbury and Cirencester and as far afield as Dursley. Ned Rawbone had even climbed down the Brothers' Well – that's what we call it in these parts, Master Chapman – but found nothing. There was no trace of Eris, either alive . . . or dead.' On the last word, her breath caught in her throat but she forced herself to remain calm.

I repeated my earlier question. 'What happened on the night your daughter vanished, Mistress Lilywhite?'

She seemed reluctant to answer, but with some prompting from myself and a scolding from Theresa, she eventually told me what I wanted to know.

'I wasn't present, of course, either at the Roman Sandal or at Dragonswick Farm on the evening of September the first, which was Nathaniel Rawbone's fifty-ninth birthday.'

I interrupted. 'The Rawbones seem a large family. Seven in number, I think you said. Will you name them for me?'

'Oh, I'll do that,' Theresa said, glad of an excuse to put herself forward again. 'Nathaniel, he's the head of the household. Fifty-nine now, as Maud just informed you, and a widower these many years, ever since Tom was born – or so I've been told – when Nathaniel and his wife were both well past thirty. The older son, Edward, must have been about fifteen at the time. Over forty, now, and the old man's right hand. Runs everything at Dragonswick Farm, does Ned Rawbone. His father'd be lost without him. Not that Nathaniel would ever admit as much. Ned and his wife, Petronelle, their twin sons Christopher and Jocelyn – fourteen, fifteen, are they? – Tom, of course, who isn't married, and Jacquetta Rawbone, Nathaniel's elder spinster sister, all live under the one roof. There's also Elvina Merryman – *Dame* Elvina, as she likes to be called – their housekeeper.' Theresa gave a dry laugh. 'Housekeeper, my foot! She's been the old man's mistress these many years, as everyone in Lower Brockhurst will tell you. So you needn't scowl at me like that, Maud.'

I thanked the older woman for her contribution – like many outsiders she was more willing to talk about her adopted community than were the locals – and turned back to the younger.

'So on the first of September, Nathaniel Rawbone's birthday, I suppose everyone would have been present at the farm for such an important occasion. And your daughter was helping out because the housekeeper, Dame Merryman, had been ill?'

'Oh, that was a year ago,' Maud corrected me. 'By the time of Nathaniel's birthday, Elvina was perfectly recovered. It was the old man who was sick by then. Not seriously, but he'd had one of those rheums that always seem worse in summer, with a persistent cough that took him a while to shake off. I went up to see him during the day to pay my respects, and I remember he was sitting huddled over the fire, one of his sister's old shawls wrapped round his shoulders. He was angry because he hates illness, in himself and everyone else. He's always been such a virile, forceful man.'

'A bully!' Theresa cut in. 'But a handsome one. Always been a devil with the women, I understand.' She added with a half-smile, 'He frightens a lot of people, but he's all right if you know how to handle him.'

The inference was obvious, but I didn't pursue it. Instead, I enquired of Maud, 'The birthday celebration hadn't been cancelled, then?'

'Certainly not, but it had been confined to members of the household: the family, Dame Elvina and . . . Eris.' Maud took a deep breath. 'You must realize, chapman, that what I'm telling you now is, of course, only hearsay on my part. I stayed at home that evening because of the weather. The wind had been rising all afternoon, blowing up for an autumn gale, the clouds marching in across the hills and heavy rain threatening. Mid-evening, just as dusk fell, the heavens opened. I'd brought the dogs inside, as much for company as anything. But if I'd gone to the alehouse, as I'd intended to do earlier in the day, I'd have witnessed the terrible scene when Tom Rawbone announced that he was breaking off his betrothal to Rosamund Bush in order to marry my daughter.' Maud's hand stole up to her mouth. 'It seems he just came out with it, in front of everyone. It was such a humiliation for the poor girl, it's no wonder she became hysterical and attacked him with a knife.'

'I thought Rob Pomphrey said that that was William,' Theresa objected. 'Or was it *Winifred* Bush? She's every bit as volatile as Rosamund.'

Maud made a little dismissive movement with her hands, as though brushing away some irritation.

'Well, whoever attacked Tom Rawbone, there was a terrible to-do, but for the truth of the matter, you'd have to ask the people who were present.'

'Go on,' I urged her.

'Well . . . Tom stormed out of the alehouse and went home, where everyone was waiting for him. Nathaniel was none too pleased, according to Elvina, at having been kept waiting, and was just about to go for his son, tooth and nail, when Tom cut him short by announcing that he had something to say, and proceeded to tell them all that he was no longer betrothed to Rosamund Bush, but was going to marry Eris instead.'

'And?' I asked eagerly as Maud Lilywhite paused, suddenly disinclined to go on.

'And then,' Theresa put in, as her daughter-in-law still remained dumb, 'Elvina tells us that the old man laughed. Nothing of the kind, he says; *he's* going to marry Eris, who's promised to be his wife only that very day. *Well!*' Theresa spread her hands wide in a gesture that was half despair and half something that might have been admiration. 'You can imagine the consequent uproar. No one approved of the match, but Tom Rawbone was beside himself with rage. It was the biter bit with a vengeance. Of course, at first, he refused to believe it.

Thought it was a bad joke of the old man's. But when Eris confirmed that she was indeed going to marry Nathaniel, it seems Tom went wild. Tried to choke the life out of his father, and after Ned had dragged him off, he turned on Eris and attempted to throttle her instead. Everyone was shouting and yelling at once. Then, Tom flung out of the house, cursing Nathaniel and my granddaughter in equal measure, Ned went out after his brother, but couldn't find him and came back. Petronelle and Jacquetta rounded on Eris, calling her all the names they could lay their tongues to, while the old man swore at everybody and told them that if they didn't approve of his choice of bride, they could all leave his house on the instant.'

Theresa paused to draw breath, and Maud took her chance to say repressively, 'I've no doubt that Elvina Merryman did her share of abusing Eris, as well as the other two women. I'm sure she always hoped that Nathaniel, if he ever wed again, would marry her. She's never scrupled to belittle Eris to my face, whenever we've met during the past six months.' She buried her face in her hands and began to sob, rocking herself to and fro.

'Pull yourself together, Maud,' her mother-in-law advised sternly. 'There's nothing to be gained by making a spectacle of yourself in front of a stranger. Crying won't bring Eris back or help us to find her.' She looked at me. 'Would you be willing, chapman, to see what you can do in this matter?'

I hesitated. I had promised Adela to be home before the Feast of Saint Patrick, but February was not yet out. A day or two's delay would surely do no harm. I could make a few enquiries.

'Master Chapman has better things to do with his time, Theresa,' Maud said, raising her tear-stained face and wiping her nose on the sleeve of her gown. She gave me a tremulous smile. 'We've no wish to detain you.'

'Well, if you don't want to know what's become of Eris, then I do,' the older woman retorted fiercely. 'Chapman, what do you say? Will you see what you can make of this business?'

'If it doesn't take too long,' I agreed cautiously. 'I must be in

Bristol by the middle of March . . . You haven't yet told me how it was that your granddaughter disappeared. What did she do when the Rawbones turned on her?'

'It seems she said she was going home and ran out into the storm. Nathaniel was going after her, but Ned told him not to be a fool; he'd go. It was half an hour or more before he reappeared, soaked to the skin, to say he hadn't found her.'

'Did he call here?'

Maud nodded. 'Yes. He warned me what had happened. I was shocked, as you can imagine. I had no idea of what must have been going on, right under my nose, for the past weeks, or perhaps months, between Eris and Tom Rawbone – let alone her and Nathaniel. He stayed with me a while, but . . . but Eris hadn't returned by the time he left.'

'You must have been worried.'

'Yes. But we both thought she'd turn up eventually. You know how it is when you're young and distressed. You don't notice things like bad weather.'

Theresa snorted. 'That wasn't bad weather,' she scoffed. 'That was one of the worst storms of the autumn. In Gloucester, it took the thatch off several houses and blew over George Thomas's hen coops.'

I leaned forward, my hands dangling between my knees. Hercules got up and licked them, just to reassure himself that I was still there, then settled down again with a sigh of contentment.

'But Eris didn't come home?' I asked softly.

Once more, Maud covered her face with her hands. But her mother-in-law, who plainly had no patience with such displays of emotion, said sharply, 'No, she didn't. And she hasn't been seen since. She *might* have run away, but I don't think that's likely. Eris was a strong-minded girl. If she'd made up her mind to become mistress of Dragonswick Farm, that's what she'd have done. She may have been a bit upset at the time, but she'd have gone back next day and faced down the lot of them, especially with Nathaniel to back her.'

'You believe she was murdered?'

'Of course I do! Tom Rawbone had already tried to strangle her once that evening. And he was out there somewhere, in the dark. He probably saw her leave the house. He was probably lying in wait for her.'

'Mother-in-law! You must not say such things!' Maud cried despairingly. 'There's no proof against Tom! If he killed her, what did he do with the body? Why has no one been able to find it? Where has he hidden it?'

'I don't know,' Theresa said shortly, then added defiantly, 'But I'm convinced he murdered her, all the same.'

I asked Maud, 'When Eris didn't come home, what did you do?'

She shivered. 'Around midnight, when the storm had eased a little, I went up to Dragonswick Farm and roused the household. Ned . . . Ned dressed and came out with me. He made another search, around the pastures and up into the woods, but there was still no sign of her. He said he'd have another look as soon as it was daylight, which he did, although the weather had worsened again by then. He opened up Brothers' Well and climbed down the ladder, right to the bottom, but it was empty, except for a foot or two of water. A couple of other men from the village were with him. They didn't do more than peer in, but they confirmed that Ned was telling the truth; that there was nothing there. So, if Eris *was* murdered . . .' Maud broke off, shrugging.

'Her body wasn't concealed in the well,' I finished for her.

'More's the pity,' remarked Theresa, getting up and starting to damp down the fire before we went to bed for the night. 'If it had been, we could have been sure that Eris was dead. There was no way she could have fallen in accidentally, because of that great lid . . . So, Master Chapman, I ask you once more, will you help us find out what really happened to my granddaughter?'

'I'll do my best,' I agreed. 'But I can't promise anything, and my time, as I told you, is limited.'

Theresa seemed content with that, but I suspected Maud would prefer me to leave matters as they stood. I didn't blame

43

her. She had no doubt come to terms with her daughter's disappearance and would rather not know the truth. While this remained hidden, she could persuade herself that Eris was still alive somewhere, perhaps even happy and contented. It was better to travel hopefully than to arrive.

But she didn't know me, nor that terrible curiosity the good God had given me in order to use me as His instrument in bringing felons to justice. I used to resent deeply the Almighty's deplorable habit of pushing me in the way of unresolved crimes and mysteries, but I had learned, gradually, the futility of either arguing with, or trying to ignore, Him. He always won, so nowadays I just got on with it. Of course, He had me by the short hairs, anyway, because He knew I enjoyed solving puzzles.

The two women dragged a narrow pallet bed from behind the linen curtain and positioned it close to the dying fire. Maud fetched a pillow and blankets from a wooden chest and piled them on the mattress, took me outside to show me the privy and the pump in the courtyard, then vanished with her mother-in-law into the farther recesses of the room.

Their preparations for the night were made in almost complete silence, with only an odd murmur here and there, and I wondered if they were always as quiet when they were on their own. I suspected that they were. The antagonism between the two couldn't be mistaken.

I went to bed in both shirt and breeches, in case of any unforeseen accident during the hours of darkness that might throw me into my hostesses' company (as Adela said, there was no point in making a laughing-stock of myself unnecessarily). But I lay awake for a while, listening to Hercules snuffling and snoring, and watching the shadows, made by the last flare-up of the fire, tremble and curtsey across the walls. My mind was full of all that I'd been told that evening, but, for the moment, the facts were like bits of flotsam bobbing around on the incoming tide of sleep. Suddenly, however, I found myself sitting bolt upright, asking myself a question that seemed, on the face of it, utterly absurd, but which had popped into my head as sharp and as clear as the chime of a bell.

What did the disappearance, last September, of Eris Lily-white have to do with the murder of two men over a hundred and thirty years ago?

The answer, of course, in the sane light of morning, was nothing. How could it? The idea was preposterous. And yet, the question continued to vex me.

I was awakened by Maud Lilywhite, in a chaste house-robe of the same unbleached linen as the curtain, shaking my shoulder and telling me that there was hot water in the pot over the newly made-up fire if I wished to shave. I thanked her, and she then retired to dress, reappearing once more by the time I had visited the privy and held my head under the pump. The jet of water was icy but not freezing, waking me up sufficiently to chase Hercules indoors before he could wander off to inspect the geese and trade a few insults with them. Theresa had also emerged from behind the curtain and was busy coiling two long, grey plaits of hair around her head, preparatory to putting on her cap.

'Did you sleep well, chapman?' she asked.

'I did, thank you. I hope I didn't snore too loudly and disturb your rest.'

'I snore myself. Or so Maud complains. I hope you'll be coming to church with us this morning.' She saw my look of enquiry and smiled. 'It's the twenty-fifth of February. Saint Walburga's Day. Saint Walburga is the patron saint of our church in Lower Brockhurst.'

Of course! I recollected that Rosamund Bush had mentioned the fact the previous evening, but I hadn't taken much notice at the time. Saint Walburga, like Saint Dunstan and Saint Alphège (or Aelfeah to give him his proper name), had been a West Saxon, Wessex born and bred. The daughter of an Ealdorman of Devon, she had been educated at a nunnery in Dorset, and had eventually embraced the religious life herself. Later, she and her brother, Winebald, had answered Saint Boniface's call to go to Germany and convert its heathen tribes. She was so successful, and became so beloved, that when she died, on the twenty-fifth of February in the year of Our Lord 779, her fame had spread throughout the whole of Europe. But there was a curious postscript to the story of Saint Walburga. On the first day of May following her death, it was decided to transfer her body to a more prominent tomb at Eichstatt, but the eve of May Day was a great pagan feast, when witches and wizards were said to ride the skies on their broomsticks and hold their revels. By some odd twist of fate, Walburga became associated with this pagan feast, which is still known by a corruption of her name, Walpurgis Night.

I thought of the corn dolly and the bunch of mistletoe laid at the foot of the oak in the woods above, and again experienced a little shiver of unease, as though someone had walked over my grave. I told myself not to be so foolish: as long as I had God's protection, the forces of darkness could not hurt me.

After a breakfast of oatmeal and fried bacon collops, and after the dogs and geese had been fed, I walked with the two women down across the gently sloping pasture to the village, leaving Hercules to guard my pack and enjoy yet another snooze, curled up beside the Lilywhites' fire. The weather had improved somewhat from the stormy conditions of the previous night. Through a watery break in the clouds could be glimpsed a shaft of iridescent light and the broken stump of a rainbow that seamen call a wind-dog. But rain still hung in the air. The outlines of the hills on the opposite side of the valley were smudged and misty, as though they had been flattened by a giant hand. A flight of crows circled above the distant trees, cawing and beating the air with black, sweeping strokes of their wings, and to our left, the Draco glistened with a faint silver radiance as it purled its way down from the ridge above.

As we crossed the footbridge over the nameless stream and cleared the surrounding belt of trees, I could see that Lower Brockhurst was a slightly larger hamlet than I had at first imagined in the fading daylight of yesterday evening. There were ten cottages, not half a dozen, and besides the church, the mill and the alehouse, there was also a forge, albeit a modest one.

Together with Maud and Theresa Lilywhite, I joined the flow of people entering the little thatched church, where the priest – Anselm I remembered Rosamund had called him – was waiting to greet his flock in a rusty black gown that had seen better days. The interior was gloomy and musty smelling: there were a couple of side altars, one supporting an image of the Virgin, but the other I was unable to see very clearly. Saint Walburga must usually have graced the central altar, but she had been removed ready to be carried in procession around the church. Lamps and candles burned in various wall niches, and in spite of its small size, there was a general atmosphere of peace and prosperity that characterized most of the Cotswold churches I had visited during the past few weeks.

Someone pushed past me wearing an amber-coloured cloak and hood, her nose held high in the air. Rosamund Bush was pointedly ignoring me as she swept forward to stand at the front of the congregation, in what I assumed was her accustomed place, closely followed by her parents. William gave me an apologetic smile as he went by, obviously embarrassed by his daughter's behaviour. He paused to whisper, 'Take no notice of her, Master Chapman. She's annoyed that you've chosen to stay with the Lilywhites. She'll get over it, never fear.'

I liked him, so I forbore to say that his daughter's airs and graces made no difference to me. I was not in the market for female approval: I was a happily married man. I smiled to myself as I noticed Lambert Miller edging his way forward through the crowd – for three dozen people were a crowd in that tiny church – to stand beside Rosamund.

There was a stir behind me and a murmuring amongst the congregation as though somebody important had come in. Turning my head, I saw that it was not one person, but seven or eight, and realized without Theresa Lilywhite hissing the name in my ear that this must be the Rawbone family. The rest of the people parted like the Red Sea before Moses to allow them to take their place at the front.

The leader had to be Nathaniel, tall, well set-up and with a spring in his step that might have belonged to a much younger man. But the abundant reddish-brown hair was iron grey at the temples and threaded with silver all over the leonine head that sat so proudly on his broad, sturdy shoulders. The handsome, weather-beaten face was seamed with the deeply carved lines of fifty-nine winters and summers, and his intensely blue eyes looked out on the rest of mankind with a certain contempt. This was a proud man, a confident man, a man who needed no convincing of his merit and worth. In this particular little pond, he was, in his own estimation, a very big fish. How others viewed him, remained to be seen.

Immediately behind him walked a man who could only be his son. Slightly shorter and stockier, Ned Rawbone nevertheless had the same shock of reddish-brown hair, the same very blue eyes, the same handsome, weathered face as his father. He did not display quite the same ease and self-confidence, but that was only natural in someone who must always have been overshadowed by his father.

Clinging to her husband's arm was Petronelle Rawbone, a thin, nervous woman, who was probably younger than Ned, but could have been older. Sharp-featured, with a sallow complexion and eyes of a nondescript colour that might have been grey or a very pale shade of blue, I doubted that she had ever been more than passably good-looking, and guessed that her marriage with the heir of Dragonswick Farm had been for commercial, rather than romantic, reasons. Her twin sons, however, had inherited the Rawbone looks and colouring. I discovered later that they had just passed their fourteenth birthday and were as arrogant as their grandfather, encouraged by a mother who thought them as perfect as they thought themselves.

The second and much younger of Nathaniel's two sons, Tom, I had already encountered. Suffice it to say that he was a Rawbone to his fingertips, although his hair was a little less red and his eyes fractionally less blue than his sibling. But he was handsomer than both his brother and father. I could see why Rosamund Bush had set her cap at him.

Bringing up this little procession, but only because she

walked slowly and used a stick, was Jacquetta Rawbone, Nathaniel's elder sister. Her expression was every bit as proud as her brother's, and she stared haughtily down the long, straight nose that was such a prominent feature of all her family. With her upright carriage, she followed the others to the front of the church and imperiously waved away the stool that the priest had hurried to offer her.

'I'll stand, man, like everyone else.'

Father Anselm beamed around at his flock. Now that the Rawbones were present, the service could begin.

Five

I'm afraid I paid scant attention to the service, moving through the ritual like a sleepwalker, with my mind on earthly instead of spiritual things. I have only the vaguest recollection of the shabby and faded statue of the saint being processed around the church. And even Father Anselm's short address on Walburga's life made no impression on me; I knew the story too well. I did realize that he had made no mention of the saint's later, and undeserved, association with witchcraft, but other than that, the Mass had ended before I was hardly aware that it had begun.

I had spent much of the time thinking about Eris Lilywhite's disappearance. Even from the little I had heard of her, I agreed with her grandmother: Eris did not sound to me like the sort of girl to vanish tamely just because life had grown too difficult, especially as the difficulties had been of her own making. She had obviously aimed to become a member of the wealthiest family in the district. Having snared the younger son, and having persuaded him to break his promise to marry Rosamund Bush, Eris had not scrupled to throw him over when a bigger prize was offered. The discovery that Nathaniel Rawbone had been smitten by her charms, and was also intent on proposing marriage, must have seemed like an opportunity that a girl as ambitious as she was could not possibly refuse. And she must have been prepared for Tom's reaction once he learned the truth, as well as for opposition from the rest of the family, all of whom could only have seen the union as a threat to them and theirs.

The first and most important consideration for the Rawbones had to have been that Eris was a young and nubile woman of childbearing age, while Nathaniel, at fifty-nine, was not yet too old to father children (one of the many unfair advantages that Nature has given men over women, who lose their fertility so much earlier in life). Any son born to the couple would not, of course, displace Ned as his father's heir, but offspring of either sex would mean more mouths to feed, bodies to clothe, dowries to find, both before and after Nathaniel's death.

Ned must already have suffered one such blow when Tom was born so many years after himself. He was therefore unlikely to take kindly to a second. And then there were his sons, almost on the brink of manhood, and whichever of them was the elder twin stood in direct line to inherit Dragonswick Farm in his turn. The more dependants to be provided for, the less for him and his heirs. Petronelle, too, would be alive to this danger to her sons' patrimony, and only the most unnatural of mothers is indifferent to her children's interests.

And what of Nathaniel's sister? She could well have had a good deal to fear from a young woman suddenly put in authority over the household, the darling of a besotted elderly husband, ready to pander to her every whim. Eris could have made Jacquetta's life a misery if, as seemed more than possible, the two women had no liking for one another.

Finally, there was the housekeeper, Dame Elvina, who, if Theresa Lilywhite was to be believed, had been Nathaniel's mistress for many years and who, again according to Theresa, was one day hoping to marry him herself. Eris had been a girl brought in to help her in the house. To have that girl suddenly elevated so far above her, to have to take orders from her instead of the other way about, surely any woman would have found such a situation intolerable.

So it seemed to me that a girl as calculating as Eris Lilywhite appeared to have been must have guessed in advance that her marriage to Nathaniel Rawbone would provoke opposition not just from his family, but from almost everyone. Why, therefore, if she were ready for this eventuality, would she have run away? No; it was far more likely that someone had murdered her, removing her once and for all from the scene. But who? (Not that there was a dearth of candidates, but then, that was part of the trouble.) And when? And what had happened to her body?

Yet another question distracting my attention from the Mass had been how to worm my way into Dragonswick Farm. But on this score, I need not have worried. As the Rawbone family followed Nathaniel out of church, Dame Jacquetta stopped in front of the Lilywhites and, raising her stick, poked me in the chest.

'Are you this chapman I've been hearing about?' she asked in a clear, ringing voice that possessed none of the feebleness of age, and which resounded throughout the tiny building, causing curious faces to turn our way. I muttered that I was and she poked me again. 'Come up to the farm after dinner with your pack. There are certain things I'm short of that you might have. Buttons, laces, pins. Can you oblige?'

I mentally reviewed my depleted store of goods, then nodded. I still had some buttons, I was sure of that, and would have lied outright just to get my foot in the door of the Rawbones' farmhouse.

'Stop loitering and come along, Jacquetta!' her brother ordered irritably from the church doorway. 'What are you doing back there?'

'Don't forget! As soon as you can after dinner,' the old lady instructed, poking me for a third time.

I rubbed my sore chest and began to move with the rest of the congregation, filing out into the cold winter air, where the inhabitants of Lower Brockhurst, like people everywhere, paused for a gossip before making their way home to dinner. Excusing myself to Maud and Theresa, I edged towards Rosamund Bush, where she stood, a little apart from her parents, who were deep in conversation with another couple of their own age. I reached her just ahead of Lambert Miller.

'Mistress Rosamund,' I said, giving her my best smile, which elicited no response, 'are you still wanting me to play in your team this evening? If you've made other arrangements I shall quite understand.'

'No, I haven't made other arrangements,' she answered

crossly. 'I'm still expecting you. If that's all right on your part,' she added on a more conciliatory note.

'Of course.' I tried another smile and was rewarded by a slight tilt at the corners of her mouth. And when Lambert would have interrupted the conversation, laying a possessive hand on her arm, the Fair Rosamund decided it was time to teach him a lesson. Her smile deepened until it was positively glowing.

'You were very naughty to run away like that last night, without even saying goodbye,' she pouted.

I took hold of one of her little hands and kissed it. 'It was very wrong of me,' I whispered, 'but Mistress Lilywhite wanted to leave at once and I was afraid to keep her waiting. She terrifies me.'

Rosamund giggled. 'Don't be silly,' she said, nipping my fingers and ignoring the expression of outrage on her would-be swain's face. 'Theresa's harmless enough. Besides, a great fellow like you isn't afraid of anyone, let alone a woman.'

'I wouldn't be too sure of that,' I grinned, releasing her hand. 'I'm a married man. Master Miller!' I went on, as if I had only just noticed him. 'As a member of Mistress Rosamund's side, I hope to have the pleasure of seeing you again this evening. You are her challenger, I believe, in this game of Nine Men's Morris?'

He glowered at me. 'I am. But if you have other things to do, pedlar, I'm sure I can find her another player.'

'Nonsense, Lambert! Master Chapman has agreed to be my man and I'm holding him to his promise.' Rosamund swept me a curtsey as William and Winifred Bush signalled that they were now ready to depart. 'I shall see you tonight then – Roger!' She peeped at me coyly from beneath her lashes before turning to follow her parents. But she remembered to kiss her fingertips to Lambert. She had no intention of antagonizing him too much.

I returned to the Lilywhites, who were waiting patiently for me, and offered the older lady my arm. Theresa accepted it gratefully, finding the climb back up to their homestead more arduous than the descent to the village. The weather had improved still further while we had been in church and a thin, watery sunlight now warmed the whole of the pasture. Only the surrounding woodland stood as though carved from thunder-clouds, black and menacing.

The dogs and geese set up their inevitable cacophony as we entered the enclosure, the former yet again being silenced by a word from Theresa. Not so Hercules, who came bounding towards me as soon as the door into the house was opened, barking like a fiend out of Hell and ignoring all my efforts to hush him. He had evidently become worried at being left so long on his own and was showing his disapproval in no uncertain manner. Eventually, however, I managed to convince him that I had not totally abandoned him, and was able to turn my attention to a matter that was troubling my conscience. This was prompted by the savoury smell of the rabbit and herb broth that was bubbling in a pot over the fire.

'Mistress Lilywhite,' I said, addressing Maud, 'if I am to stay here for any length of time, I must pay you for my food and lodging. I can well afford to.'

Both Maud and her mother-in-law were at first reluctant to agree. Quite apart from the hospitality that people living in remote places are expected to extend to strangers, I had also promised to do them a favour by trying to discover what had become of Eris. But after a little persuasion, we agreed on a sum for my and Hercules's continued bed and board.

'The dog and I have healthy appetites,' I warned them.

Theresa said she was happy to hear it: she liked a hearty eater, be it man or beast. But Maud's smile was perfunctory, and she continued to convey the impression that she would prefer me not to meddle.

'So!' said Theresa as we sat round the table to eat our broth. 'You have been invited to Dragonswick Farm after dinner, chapman. It will give you the chance to make some enquiries. You'll probably find Jacquetta Rawbone eager enough to talk. She didn't care for my granddaughter at the best of times, and hasn't had a good word to say for Eris since the night of her disappearance – the night she discovered that Nathaniel was planning to marry the girl.'

Theresa glanced at her daughter-in-law for confirmation of

her words, but Maud refused to comment. Her face was still closed, its expression almost surly. She did not want me to prove that Eris was dead.

It was getting on towards midday by the time I finally finished my dinner – I had disgraced myself by having three helpings of broth – and was able to rebuckle my belt over my woefully distended stomach. At home, Adela would have curbed my appetite by warning me of the perils of overeating – 'You're developing a paunch, Roger! You'll get fat and look old before your time!' – but without her watchful eye upon me, I had behaved like a little boy let loose in a cook shop. I knew I ought to have felt thoroughly ashamed of myself. Unfortunately, I didn't.

I walked up the hill, Hercules trotting at my heels, both of us a little somnolent in spite of the cold. I paused some distance from the Rawbone holding in order to survey it, ignoring the dog's impatient bark (he wanted to go rabbiting). The farmhouse was a substantial two-storey building of grey Cotswold stone, slate-roofed, much bigger than it appeared from further down the slope. A number of sheep were grazing the winter pasture, and I saw that each animal's fleece was marked with a red saltire cross, evidently the mark of the Rawbone family, and giving strangers notice that the sheep belonged to them. (I later learned that the pigment used was red raddle, the same as is employed for murals in our churches.) I recognized the shepherd boy who was keeping a watchful eye on the flock, his stick in his hand, his dog circling round him, as Billy Tyrrell, the lad who had been in the alehouse the previous evening. I called to him and he came to greet me, glad of anything to relieve his boredom.

'Hello, chapman! What are you doing here?'

'Dame Jacquetta wants to buy some of my goods. Where shall I find her?'

'Follow me,' he said importantly, and, instructing his dog to keep watch over the sheep, and requesting me to keep Hercules under control, he led the way towards the farm.

At the back of the house I could see the sheds where they

rolled the fleeces and weighed the wool after the summer shearing. The pigsty and cow-byre were both much smaller, suggesting to me that these animals were kept solely for domestic purposes. Sheep, and sheep alone, were the Rawbones' source of wealth, as they were of most farmers in the Cotswolds. Billy Tyrrell led me to the rear of the house, where he opened a door, then bade me a cheery goodbye before returning to his charges.

The fierce, strong-smelling heat of the kitchen almost overpowered me as I entered. The stone floor beneath my feet sweated with damp and the lime-washed walls, darkened by age and smoke, were here and there encrusted with lichen. There was one small window with its shutters half closed and, peering through the dreary half-light, I could just make out the bins of corn and meal, and the pendulous shapes of hams and other joints of meat hanging heavily from the ceiling. When my eyes had grown accustomed to the gloom, I could see that there was a young girl busily making pastry at a central table.

Without glancing up from her work, she demanded, 'And what do you want?'

'Mistress Rawbone asked me to call,' I answered mildly. 'I'm a chapman.' I indicated the pack on my back. 'She's in need of buttons.'

The girl did look up at that, her thin, plain face sharpening with interest. But all she said was, 'Which Mistress Rawbone? The older or the younger? Jacquetta or Petronelle?'

'The older. Dame Jacquetta.'

'Right. Come with me.' She wiped her floury hands down the sides of her skirt, but hesitated before leading the way to the inner door. She nodded at Hercules, tucked under my arm. 'You'd better leave that thing here. I'll look after him for you. She ain't keen on strange animals.'

Much as I resented Hercules being called a thing, I took the girl's advice and put him on the floor near the kitchen fire with instructions to stay there until I returned. He gave me a malevolent stare, but he was getting used to my disappearances and settled down, head on paws, with nothing more than a disgruntled sigh. I nodded to my guide and followed her through the door into the passageway beyond where there were still more doors, presumably opening into still room and larder, buttery and pantry. One was half-open and as I passed, I caught the glitter of polished surfaces and a glimpse of milk jugs and great, curving bowls for the making of cream. The Rawbones lived well, off the fat of the land.

The passage ran at right angles to another, but the kitchen maid stepped straight across this second one and knocked on a door immediately opposite the opening to the first. While she was waiting for an answer, I took a swift glance around. To my left, a flight of stairs rose steeply upwards to the second floor; to my right, the second passage, shorter than the one behind me, was faintly illuminated by a window of oiled parchment at the further end. There was sufficient light, however, to show me where one of the flagstones had been raised by means of a large iron ring, and as I watched, a plump woman came panting up from the cellar, holding in her arms two very dusty leather bottles which she set down on the floor before heaving herself up after them.

'That's the last time I'm doing that,' she announced breathlessly to no one in particular. 'If he wants wine in future, he'll just have to wait until one of the men can go down to fetch it.' She saw me and her eyebrows shot up. 'Who are you? Ruth! Who is this stranger?'

Before I could reply, Ruth had knocked on the door for a second time and a voice had called, 'Come in.' My guide pushed it wide and said, 'The chapman, Mistress,' jerking her head to indicate that I should enter and flattening herself against the door jamb. I smiled my thanks and went in.

I was in the main hall of the house, a room that the family used for eating, judging by the long oaken table in the centre and by the benches shoved back against the walls on either side. Three large bronze candlesticks, supporting three fat candles, stood in the middle of the board – they had already been lit because of the overcast morning. A fire blazed in the vast fireplace set in one wall, an armchair drawn up beside it. There were a couple of wooden chests, whose flat tops meant that they could be used as extra seats as well as for storage, and some scarlet cushions scattered on the broad ledge of a window that, by my reckoning, looked out over the approach to the farmhouse. I was unable to verify this as the shutters were half closed, diminishing the daylight still further. Finally, there was a second door in the wall to the left of me which I guessed led into a smaller, snugger parlour.

Jacquetta Rawbone heaved herself out of the chair, seized her stick, which had been resting against one of its arms, and limped towards me.

'You're late,' she snapped. 'I was expecting you half an hour ago at least. I suppose those Lilywhite women detained you with their chatter.'

'No,' I said, unstrapping my pack and beginning to spread the contents over the table. 'In fact, I find the younger Mistress Lilywhite rather quiet.'

Jacquetta snorted, but didn't contradict me. 'Not so her mother-in-law, though, I'll be bound. As nosy as they're made, that creature. A trouble-maker!' She started to examine my store of buttons, picking them up and putting them down again with her elegant, bony fingers.

'I wouldn't know about that,' I answered. 'I haven't known her long enough to form an opinion.'

My companion shot me a shrewd look from her deep-set eyes.

'Do you seriously mean to tell me that you've spent a whole evening and morning in Theresa's company and not heard all about the unhappy connection between our two families? Don't bother denying it. I'm not that gullible, chapman.'

'I wasn't going to deny it,' I retorted, directing her attention to a set of very pretty ivory buttons that I had bought from a ship moored at the Gloucester wharves, whose captain and crew had just returned from a long voyage to the east. 'And a very interesting story I found it. To be honest, I was going to mention it if you hadn't done so first. I'd be interested to know your version of events.'

Jacquetta pushed the buttons to one side, signifying that she would buy them, and turned to the pile of laces, testing their strength by jerking them hard between her hands and carefully inspecting their metal tags.

'Those boys, the twins,' she grumbled, 'they're always breaking their laces, with the result that their breeches are either falling down round their ankles or their shirts are riding halfway up their backs. And their mother does nothing about it.' The old lady spat into the rushes that covered the stone-flagged floor. 'Well, if Petronelle doesn't mind them going about the countryside looking like a couple of scarecrows, I do! I'll take all the laces you've got left. And two dozen pins. That's all then. What do I owe you?' And she loosened the strings of a velvet purse attached to her girdle.

When we had completed our transaction, she watched me stow away the rest of my unsold goods in my pack, then said abruptly, 'Stay awhile if you wish.' She motioned me towards the fire and waved a hand at the benches ranged against the wall on each side of the fireplace. 'I'm lonely, young man. My sight isn't as good as it was and I can't read as well as I used to. My brother and nephew, Ned, have gone down to the village to get some flour from the mill, Petronelle's upstairs somewhere and I don't ask what my younger nephew and the twins get up to all day. That's their business, and I'm content to leave it that way.'

I sat down on the end of one of the benches nearest the fire, while Jacquetta again settled herself in the armchair. I was amazed at how easy it had been to get my hostess to talk to me: I hadn't counted on the midwinter boredom of people, especially women, in remote villages who, until I came along, perhaps hadn't seen a stranger since the previous autumn. I looked expectantly at Jacquetta.

She laughed and wagged a witch-like finger. 'Oh, you're getting nothing from me, my lad, until I hear something of what's been going on in the world. Is it true the Queen's been brought to bed of another child?'

'So I've heard. At the beginning of this month. Another daughter. But don't ask me what they're going to call her. We have an Elizabeth, a Mary, a Cicely and an Anne already. They'll soon be running out of names.'

My companion laughed self-consciously. 'I was baptized Joan,' she said, 'but it was too ordinary a name for me. When I was nineteen, I rechristened myself after the present Queen's mother. She that was Jacquetta of Luxembourg and became Duchess of Bedford when she married one of the fifth Henry's brothers. Later on, after Bedford's death, she married his squire, Richard Woodville. What a scandal that caused, but she didn't care. That must have been a real love match, judging by the number of children she bore him.'

We chatted for a while longer about this and that; of Clarence's execution, a year ago now, and of the strange rumours that had surrounded it; of the odd fact that the Bishop of Bath and Wells, Robert Stillington, had been imprisoned about the same time, but later pardoned; of the rift it had caused between the King and his one remaining brother, Richard of Gloucester; of the Duke's retirement to his Yorkshire estates with his wife and son; and of his reported hatred for the Queen and all her kindred, holding them responsible, as he did, for the condemnation and death of George of Clarence.

'Well, there's one good thing,' Jacquetta concluded, leaning back in her chair and extending her feet to the fire, 'the King and Queen have those two dear boys. The succession is assured for the House of York. That's something to be thankful for.' (How ironic that sounds now, looking back on events from my old age and knowing what actually happened.) 'So, chapman, what do you want to know from me? And why?'

I shrugged. 'I'm just naturally nosy,' I said, unwilling to go into details of my past as I had done with the Lilywhites. 'The disappearance of this girl, Eris, sounds like an intriguing mystery to me. What do *you* think happened to her?'

'She ran away!' Jacquetta exclaimed scornfully. 'She suddenly realized what she'd done; that every man's hand was going to be against her. And every woman's, too. Especially the women's. She'd made too many enemies with her devious, underhand dealings. She got frightened and went.'

'On a stormy night of rain and wind?' I cavilled. 'And without going home first to tell her mother what she planned to do and at least to find a cloak? Forgive me, Mistress Rawbone, but it makes no sense.'

'It makes no sense to betroth yourself to one man and secretly plot to marry his father,' Jacquetta spat. 'I think it suddenly came home to her what havoc she was causing, not just for us, here at Dragonswick, but for Rosamund Bush and her family as well. Perhaps – and here I give her the benefit of the doubt – a shred of decency stirred in Eris Lilywhite and she decided to leave before she did more harm. Besides, she had a cloak, a good thick one. She was wearing it when she arrived here earlier in the day.'

I leaned foward. 'Dame Jacquetta,' I said gently, 'you don't truly believe, do you, that Eris left Brockhurst of her own accord? People like her don't have a conscience.'

The old woman eyed me sharply. 'What are you suggesting?' she demanded. 'That someone killed her?'

'It seems more probable, you must agree.'

I could see by the expression on her face that she did agree, but was reluctant to admit it.

'That family,' she snorted, 'the Haycombes, they've always been trouble. Maud Lilywhite,' she explained, noting my puzzled frown, 'was a Haycombe before she married that young man from Gloucester. Her father, Ralph Haycombe – she inherited that smallholding from him – was a wild lad in his youth. No girl was safe from his attentions, as I know only too well. Like father, like daughter,' she added spitefully. 'And like granddaughter, if it comes to that.'

The passage door opened and the woman I had seen coming up from the cellar entered the hall just in time to overhear Jacquetta's last remarks. She laughed nastily.

'I seem to have heard,' she taunted, 'that *you* were rather sweet on Ralph Haycombe, my dear. If my mother was to be believed, at one time you were even hoping to marry him. Unfortunately for you, he preferred her, but she was already spoken for by my father.'

61

Six

J acquetta turned her head and raked the newcomer with her
deep-set eyes, but otherwise seemed unperturbed by the
remark.

'Ah! Elvina! I didn't notice you there. But then, you do creep
about so, listening at keyholes.'

The housekeeper grinned, acknowledging a hit, and the
features of both women relaxed. I guessed that theirs was an
old, longstanding rivalry, no doubt damaging enough in its
heyday, but now a form of ritual gone through by two people
who, although not exactly bosom friends, were still allies
against intruders who threatened their peace.

'Talking about Eris Lilywhite, were you?' Elvina Merryman
asked and gave a chuckle. 'Soon found a way to get under your
skin, didn't she, my dear?' She looked at me. 'Discovered that
Jacquetta's baptismal name is really Joan and ever after called
her by it. It was Dame Joan this and Dame Joan that until I
thought poor Jacquetta was going to have an apoplexy. Made
the Master laugh, though.'

'That's true,' the older woman agreed without rancour.
'Made Nathaniel laugh almost as much as the way she imitated
you behind your back; your walk, the way you speak. He used
to call her a baggage, and encouraged her to disobey your
orders.' Jacquetta frowned suddenly. 'We were both slow there,
Elvina. We should have foreseen what was coming.'

'I never imagined your brother could be such a stupid old
fool,' was the vicious response. 'Nor did you. Don't blame
yourself or me, my dear. The girl was a bigger slut than either of
us thought her.' The housekeeper took a deep breath. 'Well, it's

62

all water under the bridge now. I'll leave you to your gossip with the pedlar here.' She winked. 'You always did have an eye for a handsome man. I just came to tell you that I've been down to the cellar and brought up the wine Nathaniel wants for supper. But I'm not doing it in future. Forty-five is too old to go prancing up and down those steps, I can tell you.'

'Oh, stop complaining, woman!' Jacquetta chided her. 'I can give you eighteen years and my left leg's practically useless, but you don't hear me whining all the time, now do you?'

Elvina Merryman snorted derisively. 'Don't come the old soldier with me, Jacquetta. We've known one another too long for that. Practically useless, indeed! I've seen you hopping along fast enough when you thought no one was looking. That stick and limp are just to make yourself interesting. There isn't much goes on in this house that you don't know about, and you don't get your information by sitting around all day.'

For a moment it seemed as if my hostess might set about the housekeeper with her cane. She half-raised herself from her chair, gripping its handle in a determined hold, but then fell back again, a wry smile twisting her thin lips.

'Oh, mind your own business, Elvina, and leave me to mine.'

The armed truce had been re-established between them and they again saluted one another with a nod and a grin. When the passage door had closed behind the housekeeper, Jacquetta settled herself in her chair and asked, 'Right! Where do you want me to begin?'

'I'm hoping,' I said, 'that you're going to tell me what happened on the night that Eris Lilywhite disappeared.'

She laughed. 'Oh, you are, are you? Has Maud Lilywhite put you up to asking these questions?'

'No.' True enough: it was Theresa. 'I've told you, I'm naturally curious. I can't keep my nose out of other people's affairs. If my mother were still alive, she'd tell you I was born like it.'

'Well, if it's simply nosiness, I've no objection to telling you what you want to know,' Jacquetta conceded. 'Elvina's right. If I have a weakness, it's for good-looking young men. And we don't get many of those wandering into this part of the world, especially in winter. So! Where shall I start?'

'It was your brother's birthday, I believe. At least, according to the elder Mistress Lilywhite.'

My companion nodded. 'The first of September. Nathaniel was fifty-nine. Everyone had been summoned for the feast. Most of Lower Brockhurst was expected to attend. But then, a few days before, Nat developed a nasty rheum that descended to his chest. So the general feasting was cancelled. Eris Lilywhite and Ruth Hodges from the kitchen were sent down to the village to tell everyone not to come. But the family were still expected to be present, that went without saying. My brother's nothing if not patriarchal. He likes to keep us all under his thumb, especially his sons. The farm and its land are not entailed, you see . . . Ah! I can see by your face that that's shocked you.'

It had, indeed. Such a circumstance had not occurred to me. It put an entirely new complexion on Nathaniel's proposed marriage to Eris Lilywhite. A child of theirs could have inherited outright under the terms of any new will that Nathaniel decided to make. I became more certain than ever that Eris had been murdered.

Jacquetta went on, 'Tom's always been a bit of a rebel. Edward – Ned – my elder nephew, is fifteen years older than his brother and has always been Nathaniel's right-hand man, ever since he was old enough to help around the farm. He married to please his father. Petronelle's a local girl who brought a decent dowry with her. A good, hard-working lass – well, woman now: she's thirty-eight and more – who's presented the old man with two strapping grandsons. She wouldn't have been Ned's choice I'm sure, left to himself, but Nathaniel insisted and, as ever, my nephew did as he was bidden. So Tom, you see, has always presumed that Ned will inherit Dragonswick and has never seen the need to toe the line in quite the same way that his brother does.

'Mind you, that isn't to say that Tom doesn't respect his father nor want to please him. He knew that Nathaniel would be delighted when he got himself betrothed to Rosamund Bush. William Bush is known to be plump in the pocket and Rosamund's his only child. We were all delighted, if it comes to that. Rosamund's a very pretty, pleasant and friendly girl. She'd have been an asset to this family in more ways than one . . . I'm assuming that much of this story is already familiar to you, chapman. It should be if you've been in Lower Brockhurst for nearly twenty-four hours.'

I laughed. 'All villages are the same, Mistress; hotbeds of gossip. But you're right. I didn't arrive until late yesterday afternoon, and it seems as if I'm already acquainted with everyone's business.'

Jacquetta leaned forward and gripped my left knee, then let her long, bony fingers splay into what was a surprisingly sensuous caress. Perhaps she felt the sudden tension of my body, because after a moment she gave a dry chuckle and withdrew her hand. 'Where was I?' she asked.

'Your nephew Tom's betrothal to Rosamund Bush.'

'Mmmm.' She sucked her teeth, thought for a few seconds, then spat into the fire, making the flames leap and sizzle. 'Time to move on to Eris Lilywhite. She'd come to help out in the house a few months earlier, because Elvina was poorly and Ruth Hodges . . . well, you've seen her. A sickly child, always ailing. Not like Eris, who was as strong and healthy as a young horse.' I noted that Jacquetta spoke in the past tense, but I didn't comment. 'And beautiful, I'll grant her that. I don't think I've ever seen a lovelier girl. She had her mother's eyes; those great, dark, liquid brown eyes that Maud inherited from *her* mother. And hair, an abundance of it, russet, the colour of leaves in autumn. Skin like milk. Dear, sweet heaven! I should have recognized her as trouble from the moment she set foot across the threshold. I'd seen her around the village, of course, ever since she was a child, but she was one of those girls who blossom suddenly and late. At fourteen, she was a whey-faced, skinny little thing with red hair, and not much better at fifteen. I'd lost sight of her throughout the winter – I don't go out much during the bad weather – and she came to us in late February, last year, a month after her sixteenth birthday.' Jacquetta took a deep breath. 'I hardly knew her. She'd filled out . . . Curves everywhere! She was like a flower that had suddenly unfurled its petals overnight.'

She paused, and, although I could guess the answer, I asked, 'Prettier than Rosamund Bush?'

'Can you compare a star with the sun? One twinkles, the other dazzles. However, it didn't take me long to discern that the girl had a hard edge to her. A brittleness, a sharpness that was ugly. And having discovered as much, I shall blame myself to my dying day that I failed to guess what might happen. Not, as Elvina said, that I could ever have anticipated that my brother would be smitten but, Tom, yes, I should have expected that. With hindsight, I recall the way his eyes used to follow her every time she entered and left the room. I remember him arguing with Ned one day when Ned complained that Eris was slow in bringing him his ale, saying she was overworked and that his brother was being too rough on her. Worse than that, I recollect one time seeing him catch her round the waist and kiss her cheek.' Jacquetta beat with her fists on the arms of her chair. 'What a fool I was! What a purblind fool! But I thought it just a bit of fun. I thought Tom safely in love with Rosamund Bush. I didn't think him capable of looking seriously at another woman.'

'And your brother? You suspected nothing there?'

'Nothing,' was the fervent answer. 'Eris was just sixteen, Nathaniel old enough to be her grandfather. If he favoured her – and, looking back, I think perhaps he did – I considered it no more than the soft spot an elderly man might have for a young and beautiful girl. If he ever thought of marrying again, which I doubted, I expected it to be with Elvina . . . I expect Theresa Lilywhite has told you the gossip concerning her.'

I nodded, realizing that we had wandered yet again from the subject of Eris's disappearance. 'Master Rawbone's birthday . . . ?' I suggested tentatively.

'Ah, yes! Nathaniel's feast day. It had been quiet in general, except for the weather, which started clouding over in the afternoon and by evening had developed into a full-blown storm. Maud Lilywhite called in the morning, just after dinner, but she didn't stay long. I don't know why she came: she's never much liked any of us except Ned. But then, he's friends with everyone because he never lets on what he's really thinking. In the afternoon, the meal was laid out on the table here, and by the time Elvina had turned the hourglass for the start of the fourth hour, we were all present, dressed in our Sunday clothes (even Ned, who had penned the sheep early and sent Billy Tyrrell off home). All, that is, except Tom. Well, time went on. Five o'clock, six o'clock, seven o'clock came and went and still he didn't appear. We ate our meal without him, Nathaniel growing more and more furious with every passing minute. The storm by now was raging and we were beginning to get worried, wondering if Tom had had an accident and was lying helpless somewhere in the wind and the rain. Ned eventually said he was going to look for him, and my brother told him to call on Maud Lilywhite at the same time to say that Eris – she'd stayed on to wait at table – wouldn't be going home that night. The weather was too bad. She could share a bed with Elvina. But just at that very moment, the door, the one over there –' Jacquetta indicated the door on the opposite side of the room that opened on to the front yard – 'burst open and Tom was literally blown into the room.

'He was soaked to the skin, but other than that seemed perfectly sound in mind and limb and in tearing spirits. My first thought, and probably that of the others, was that he'd been drinking and had got into a fight. He was very flushed and had a cut under one eye as well as several scratch marks on his cheeks. Nathaniel heaved himself out of his chair, absolutely livid with temper, but before he could utter a word, Tom crossed the room, seized Eris Lilywhite about the waist and spun her round, shouting, "I've done it! I've done it! I've told old man Bush and his fat, frumpy daughter that I'm going to marry you, not her." And he kissed her in front of everyone. Then he turned to Nathaniel and said, "I don't care what you say, Father, Eris has promised to be my wife and I intend to wed her whatever measures you may take to try to prevent me." '

'What happened then?' I asked, as my companion broke off, staring into the fire, obviously reliving the moment in her mind. 'Dame Jacquetta?' I leaned forward and gently touched her arm.

'What?' She jumped and turned a blank face towards me. Then understanding flowed back and she apologized.

'I'm sorry, lad. I was lost in my own thoughts . . . What happened, you want to know. Well, I'll tell you. My brother started to laugh, that's what happened. Nathaniel sat down in his chair again and laughed until the tears ran down his cheeks. "You minx! You baggage!" he kept on saying to Eris. Then he grabbed her away from Tom and pulled her down on his knee. "You're not going to marry her, my boy," he said. "*I* am!" One of the twins, I remember, started to laugh, a loud, embarrassed sort of laugh, and the rest of us smiled feebly thinking it was either a very poor joke, or Nathaniel's way of ridiculing Tom. We were all feeling shocked and someone, Petronelle I think, shouted, "You can't do that, Thomas!" Though why she thought he would attend to anything she said, I've no idea. And, of course, he didn't even hear her. He was staring at his father, absolutely transfixed.'

'So when did you realize that your brother was serious?' I asked.

'Almost immediately. Nathaniel stopped laughing and just stared at us all until he had reduced us to silence. Then he said quite quietly, "You're wrong if you think I'm funning. Eris promised to be my wife only this morning." He kissed her cheek. "Tell them, my girl. Go on, don't be scared. I won't let them hurt you." *Scared!*' Jacquetta's lips very nearly disappeared and she breathed heavily. 'That hussy wasn't scared! She just smiled serenely at us and said, "It's true. I'm going to marry the Master. I'm sorry, Tom, but I didn't think you'd be going down to the Roman Sandal today or I'd have told you earlier. You'd better try to make your peace with Rosamund."''

Jacquetta rubbed a hand wearily across her forehead before continuing. 'As you can imagine, Tom went wild. He caught hold of her wrists and pulled her off his father's lap, then put both hands round Nathaniel's throat and tried to strangle him. If Ned and the boys hadn't managed to drag him away, it would have been a hanging matter. Tom would have killed him, I'm sure of that. But Ned and the twins had no sooner released him than he turned on Eris and tried to throttle her instead. Ned had to haul him off again, by which time Tom had begun to come to his senses. He tore himself free and flung himself away towards the outside door, cursing both his father and Eris. It was shocking to hear, but I don't know that any of us blamed him. "May your soul rot in Hell this very night!" I remember him shouting at Eris, and then he rushed out into the storm.

'Petronelle started shouting at Eris, too. "Go home!" she kept screaming. "You slut! You scheming little whore! Go home and tell your mother! We'll see what Maud has to say about it!" Ned told her to be quiet. He was still attending to Nathaniel, who was very white and shaken, but beginning to come round; enough at any rate to tell us that if we didn't like his choice of bride, we could all leave his house on the instant.'

'And you . . . and Mistress Merryman . . .' I suggested hesitantly, 'did you say anything?'

Jacquetta looked a little sheepish. 'Probably,' she admitted at length. 'Although exactly what, I can't remember. Petronelle was still yelling at Eris to go home. I went over to calm her down because I thought her in danger of having hysterics. I could understand why, of course. She could see that if my brother and Eris Lilywhite had a child, a son especially, Nathaniel was going to play God with Ned's and the twins' inheritance. Ned wouldn't be able to call his soul his own: he'd be under constant threat of being cut out of his father's will unless he obeyed every order to the letter.'

'Had he never faced this threat from Tom?' I queried.

My companion shook her head. 'No. Tom has never been his father's favourite. In many ways he's too like Nathaniel for them to get along without bickering. The same traits in each irritate the other. Besides,' she added viciously, 'any idiot could see that Eris was going to be able to twist my brother round her little finger. The stupid old fool was besotted. And she'd take good care that any children of hers were given priority.'

'Your nephew, Ned, went out after his brother, I believe.'

'Not immediately, and not for long. He came back in about ten minutes, saying there was no sign of Tom and it was too dark and too stormy to go looking for him. I'd managed to quieten Petronelle down in the meantime, but as soon as she saw Ned she started up again and suddenly flung herself at Eris, clawing, kicking . . . That was when Eris left. She grabbed her cloak from the peg, announced she was going home and burst out sobbing. No tears, though, that I could see: it was all a fake for my brother's benefit if you want my opinion. Then she ran out. Nathaniel was all for going after her, but Ned said his father was in no fit condition: he'd go. He was absent a lot longer the second time. When he did return, he said he'd called on Maud Lilywhite to tell her what had happened. Poor soul! She was as shocked as he was, and he'd waited a while with her, both of them hoping that Eris would appear. When she didn't, he came on home. Of course, we all thought she'd turn up eventually. Although where we thought she was or what she was doing on a night like that, I now find it hard to imagine. But at the time, none of us was thinking properly. Nathaniel began shouting at Ned to go and look again, upbraiding him for not doing enough to find Eris, but suddenly Ned had had enough. He looked ghastly, absolutely exhausted, and so did Petronelle. "Fuck you, Father!" he said. "I'm going to bed!" And he seized Petronelle's arm and pushed her out of the hall ahead of him and upstairs to their bedchamber. I heard him slam the door.'

There was another pause, so lengthy that I thought Jacquetta must have finished her tale, but she suddenly stirred and went on, 'That was when Nathaniel said *he* was going out to search for Eris. Elvina and I told him not to be a silly old fool – he had a cough bad enough to see him six feet under – but he wouldn't listen. He put on his cloak and took a lantern. The twins tried to stop him, but he cursed them and pushed them away, so they went with him. Needless to say, they lost one another in the dark. The lantern got blown out in the gale, and they came straggling back one at a time; Nathaniel after about half an hour, then Christopher and lastly Jocelyn. Josh said he'd even been down to the village, but didn't do more than look up and down the main street. It wasn't a fit night for a cat to be out in, let alone go knocking on doors. Besides, as you can guess, neither of the boys was that anxious to find Eris. If she never came back, it would be too soon for them. They're not stupid: they knew very well what their grandfather's marriage to her could mean, for Ned and for themselves.'

I stretched my legs and eased my shoulders, aware that I had been sitting in a hunched position, leaning forward on my knees, for far too long. My companion's appreciative glance made me ask hurriedly, 'When Eris failed to turn up, Maud Lilywhite says she came up here and roused the household. Your nephew, the elder one, got up and dressed and went with her for another search of the pasture and woods.'

'That's true. Poor Ned! But at least he'd had a few hours' sleep when Maud came hammering on the door, and the storm had abated a little by then. We all got out of bed and went down to see what the matter was. Except Tom, of course. He hadn't come home. Goodness knows where he spent the night; he's never told us. I think Nathaniel hoped that it was Eris knocking: if I'm honest, I'm sure the rest of us were hoping that it wasn't. Well, we had our wish. Although Ned went out with Maud again that night and searched, and again with other men from the village all the next day and the day after that – in truth, for the best part of a week – we never set eyes on Eris Lilywhite again. She'd run away and thank God for it, say I! Oh, it didn't end there, naturally. Nathaniel had people looking for her as far afield as Gloucester and Dursley, but her whereabouts were never discovered. So, there you are, chapman. I've kept my side of our bargain. That's the story of Eris Lilywhite and the night she vanished. She was ashamed of herself and ran away.'

'You don't believe that,' I said.

She challenged me with a look. 'Don't I? What do I believe, then, my know-it-all friend? You tell me.'

'All right! I will.' I leaned forward again, holding those deep-set eyes with my own, daring her to drop her gaze. 'You think Tom killed her. He was the only one out there in the dark when Eris said she was going home and ran out into the storm. He'd already attacked her once and he must still have been in a

71

murderous rage. He'd been made to look the most goddam fool, not just in front of his family, but, as soon as the news became general knowledge, in front of the whole village, as well. How Rosamund Bush and her parents were going to sneer at him! He'd be the laughing stock of Lower Brockhurst and beyond. It would be too good a story for the villagers to keep to themselves. Everywhere they went, they'd be repeating it. A young man robbed of his sweetheart by his father, who's twice his age . . . Oh, yes. I feel sure you think your younger nephew killed her. It's the obvious thing to think. He was still loitering near the farmhouse when Eris left. The temptation to finish what he had been prevented from doing inside was too great. That's certainly what they believe happened in Lower Brockhurst, judging by what I saw and heard yesterday evening.' And I described the scene in the Roman Sandal when I had first clapped eyes on Tom Rawbone.

'I wouldn't give a groat for anything that rabble down there think!' Jacquetta declared scornfully. But her eyes had shifted away from mine and refused to look back. 'And if Tom did kill her,' she added triumphantly, 'where has he concealed her body? Because it's never been found, as you must know.'

'I didn't say that *I* believed your nephew murdered Eris Lilywhite,' I corrected her. 'I said you did. And in spite of the mystery as to where the body is hidden, you still do.'

'Nonsense!' she answered stoutly, then glanced at me curiously. 'Why don't you think Tom killed her?'

'I'm not saying he did or he didn't. I'm keeping an open mind. But in my experience, things are often not as simple as they seem. On the face of it, allowing for possibility and probability, for motive and the opportunity to commit the crime, your nephew, Tom, appears the most likely person to have done it. But apart from your brother, everyone in this house would have liked to see her dead.'

'Not liked,' Jacquetta protested. 'But . . . Very well! I agree that, except for Nathaniel, we're all glad that she's gone. And I think even my brother is beginning to realize that he might have had a lucky escape. Life is quieter without her.'

'The old well in the woods – the one belonging to Upper Brockhurst Manor – was searched, so Mistress Lilywhite informed me.'

'The Brothers' Well? Yes, that's so.' And Jacquetta confirmed Maud's story. Ned had climbed right down into the well the following morning, using the iron ladder and watched by a group of men from the village, including Father Anselm. The others didn't bother going down after him, because they could see by peering over the rim that there was nothing there. A foot or two of brackish water, but that was all. 'The well dried up,' Jacquetta explained, 'when, some years after the great plague the villagers of Lower Brockhurst diverted the course of the Draco to flow directly downhill in order to augment their own supply of water, that stream at the bottom of the pasture. I've always understood that before the plague, the Draco meandered in a curve through the main street of Upper Brockhurst. But sometime in the latter half of the last century, men from the lower village cut a new straight channel, so that the Draco flowed faster and more efficiently into the stream below, thus giving a better head of water for the mill race.'

I asked, 'Do you know anything about the murder of two men that took place in the woods around Upper Brockhurst, just before the outbreak of the plague?'

My companion laughed. 'My word, you have learned a lot about this place in less than twenty-four hours, chapman. I congratulate you. And I thought I was nosy! But in this case, I'm going to disappoint you. All I know is probably what you've been told already. Two wellers from Tetbury, who'd dug a well for the Martin brothers, the owners of Brockhurst Hall, were found battered to death in woodland not far away. But the story goes that they hadn't been robbed. If true, it would seem to have been a motiveless killing. But before anything could be discovered concerning the murders, the plague arrived in Upper Brockhurst and, within weeks, everyone, including the Martins, was dead. But that was all a hundred and something years ago. It has nothing to do with Eris Lilywhite. Has it?'

73

Seven

J acquetta was looking puzzled, as well she might by this sudden change of direction in my questioning. She asked again, 'What has this to do with the disappearance of Eris Lilywhite?' but got no further before a woman I recognized as Petronelle Rawbone entered the room.

'Ned and Nathaniel have returned,' she said. 'Tom and the boys are with them.'

The words were hardly out of her mouth, when the front door was flung wide on screeching hinges and the Rawbone men surged into the hall on a great tide of energy, all talking at once. A strong smell of ale hung in the air, and it was no surprise to learn that they had all met up with one another in the Roman Sandal. (Presumably, as far as William Bush was concerned, business was business and resentment on his daughter's behalf did not extend to turning away so much custom.) They were all heatedly debating the truth, or otherwise, of a rumour concerning a murrain of cattle in neighbouring Wales, and the possibility of it spreading across the Severn into Gloucestershire. Jacquetta and Petronelle were inevitably drawn into the conversation, firing off worried questions at their menfolk until Nathaniel roared for quiet.

'You're behaving like a lot of hysterical women, the pack of you!' he shouted. 'It ain't likely a disease'll cross water, but if it does, we'll deal with it when it happens. And you can be sure that I'm not killing off my sheep for anybody.'

No one was taking any notice of me, so I decided it was time to be on my way. I picked up my pack and tiptoed out into the passage, closing the hall door softly behind me. As I crossed the flagstones to enter the other passage opposite, I glanced to my left. The trapdoor of the cellar was still standing upright, and, with a few strides, I was beside it, crouched on my haunches, staring into the void. A narrow stone staircase disappeared into what would have been pitch darkness had the housekeeper not forgotten to douse the wall cresset she had lit earlier. On a sudden impulse, I dropped my pack and, after a quick look around to make sure that no one was watching, descended the well-worn treads.

As cellars go, it was not large; long and low-ceilinged, but very narrow. I soon realized that this was because the farmhouse had been built into the side of a hill and its foundations in the front were lower than those at the back. The ground floor had been levelled, leaving this oddly shaped space beneath it; a space that had been utilized as an undercroft, except that, in this case, there was no access to it from the outside. Logs and smaller pieces of firewood were stacked against the outer wall; some leather bottles, containing, I supposed, more wine, were ranged against the inner; while anything that seemed to be in need of a stitch or a nail by way of repair, had been bundled down there out of sight (and presumably out of mind), a fact that said little for the housewifery and economy of either Petronelle or Jacquetta or Elvina Merryman.

But however much this fact would have been deplored by my wife and former mother-in-law, Margaret Walker, it was not what interested me. I paced the length of the cellar, my eyes fixed on the ground, searching for traces of any disturbance to the beaten-earth floor that might indicate a recently dug grave. But there was too much clutter for me to arrive at any firm conclusion; and I was suddenly aware of voices overhead calling for the housekeeper to bring ale. Hurriedly, I retraced my steps and clambered up out of the cellar just in time to see Elvina disappearing into the hall, demanding irritably, 'What's all the noise about? What do you want? Can't one of you come to find me in a decent, civilized fashion, instead of bawling yourselves hoarse like this?'

I grabbed my pack, stole down the corridor, turned into the other at right angles to it, then headed for a door halfway along and entered the kitchen. Ruth Hodges was still there, putting a pie into a wall-oven and cursing as she burned her fingers, while Hercules, who had been lying resignedly by the hearth, came hurtling towards me, jumping up and barking loudly. I hushed him, found my cudgel and cloak, said my farewells and made my escape from the house before Jacquetta realized my absence, and decided she wanted me back to answer a few of *her* questions.

The afternoon was now some way advanced and the weather had worsened. The distant trees were tossing and billowing, and above them, huge clouds rode like galleons in the storm-tossed sky. Below me, I could see the Lilywhite holding and a woman I thought was Theresa crossing the back yard, battling against the wind, to feed the geese. Below that again, in the valley, the village lay snugly tucked behind its belt of trees, its inhabitants no doubt busy about their work, but eagerly anticipating the evening's entertainment and the game of Nine Men's Morris to be played at the alehouse. I must remember that I was expected, or I should once again be in Rosamund Bush's black books.

But there were some hours yet to nightfall, so I considered what to do in the meantime. Hercules was capering around me, telling me as plainly as he could that he needed exercise, and the evil way in which he was eyeing up the placidly grazing sheep made me anxious to comply with his wishes. So I took the liberty of stowing my pack inside the Rawbones' cowshed and strode off uphill, across the pasture, to the woods foaming along its crest.

I decided to follow the course of the Draco, and after walking for about half an hour – slow going over rough, thickly wooded terrain, even though the land had levelled out somewhat – I came to the dried-up watercourse, mentioned by Dame Jacquetta, where the stream had once diverted through Upper Brockhurst. Now it flowed downhill in a more or less straight line from somewhere ahead of me, swollen by the recent rains until it had almost breached its banks. The original channel, still vaguely discernible, had filled, over the years, with a mixture of earth and a mulch of dead leaves until it had become very nearly a part of the woodland floor, supporting an ever-increasing growth of scrub and young trees. Whistling to Hercules, I set out to follow its path as best I could.

After walking for another quarter of an hour, I was unsurprised to find myself moving in a gentle curve, in a landscape reminiscent of the previous day, when I had penetrated the remains of Upper Brockhurst Hall. Here and there, I could plainly see the jagged teeth of ruined buildings pushing between the encroaching foliage, giving me notice that men had once lived here, where now only badgers and other woodland creatures were in occupation. In a long-gone village street, that had echoed to the sound of people laughing, talking, singing, there was now nothing but a dry, rustling noise, so faint that it made me starkly aware of the dead weight of silence all around me.

Hercules, tail erect, nose quivering, was searching for any rabbit foolish enough to leave its comfortable burrow for the cold and wet of a miserable, late February day. He had just found a promising hole and was snuffling at it in eager anticipation, when he suddenly stopped and raised his head, ears pricked, his little body tense and troubled.

I stood stock still. 'What is it, boy?' I hissed, whispering although I had heard nothing. Then a twig cracked somewhere, as if it had been snapped underfoot, and Hercules let out a whine. Unbidden, a vivid picture, clear and fully-formed, sprang into my mind of two men walking through these self-same woods, pleased with a job well done, the prompt payment they had received for their work jingling in the purses hung from their belts. They were going home after – how long? A month? Six weeks? More? I had no idea of the time needed to sink a well. But whatever length of time it had taken, the wellers, father and son, must have made friends in Upper Brockhurst during the period of their stay. And if the Martin brothers had really been as parsimonious as Maud Lilywhite had described them, they were unlikely to have offered the two men bed and board of an acceptable quality. So the wellers had probably lodged with the villagers, who would have welcomed strangers from the larger community of Tetbury in their midst.

(Both the Brockhursts, Upper and Lower, were off the beaten track and news of the outside world would therefore have been slow to reach them.) What proved to be the last weeks of the unsuspecting villagers' lives were no doubt enhanced by the pair's presence.

And so father and son had finally set out for home, looking forward to seeing their womenfolk again; happy, relaxed, not thinking of danger until unexpectedly, brutally, it had descended on them from out of the surrounding trees and they were battered to death before they could defend themselves. Had they known why? Had they recognized their attackers? Or had they simply thought – for the short interval of time that they could think – that they had been set upon by footpads? But nothing, according to tradition, had been stolen from them. They had been left to welter in their blood, their money undisturbed in their purses.

It would seem to have been the handiwork of a madman or madmen; in which case, where had the person or persons come from? The village they had just left perhaps? Or from Lower Brockhurst? And if the latter, were the murderers' descendants still living there, tainted with the same strain of insanity? I found, to my annoyance, that I was shivering, standing in the silent wood, listening now to nothing more sinister than the steady drip-drip of the trees. Hercules had returned to blowing down the rabbit hole, evidently satisfied that the interruption had been a false alarm and intent on digging his way down to visit Master Coney, if Master Coney didn't have the good manners to come up to visit him.

'All right!' I said disgustedly. 'I understand. You didn't really hear anything. You were just making a fool of me.'

My nervousness had had the inevitable effect on my bladder, so I was forced to struggle with my laces and relieve myself in the long grasses that now rioted all over what had once been Upper Brockhurst's main street (although a few patches of cobbles were still visible in places). Then I prised a furious Hercules away from his excavation, tucked his squirming body under my cloak and proceeded to follow the line of the old watercourse until I was back beside the Draco, maybe half a mile further on from where I had left it some fifteen minutes earlier.

I released Hercules and directed my footsteps downhill once more, walking beside the stream as it purled over its stony bed, cutting deeper and ever deeper into the new channel that the men of Lower Brockhurst had dug for it a hundred years ago. No doubt, while they were about it, those men had also knocked down and removed much of the masonry from the upper village, a free source of building material for the lower. (There was always gain to be made out of other people's misfortune, as I had reason to know only too well. I should not now be the owner of a house in Bristol's Small Street had it not been for the unlawful death of an innocent and lovely young woman.)

I passed again the spot where the Draco had originally curved out from Upper Brockhurst village, and which marked the end of the new watercourse. The stream plunged onwards now between a strip of scrub and some stunted trees, whose topmost branches made a pattern like the hands of skeletons arched against the gloomy afternoon sky. An easterly wind was rising that drained the landscape of what little colour it had, turning everything to a uniform greenish-grey, and the dank smell of decaying leaves and rotting wood hung in my nostrils. It was as if the year were dying around me instead of being almost within sight of spring.

I judged, from the sudden levelling out of the ground, that Hercules and I were now crossing the ridge that overlooked the valley. Abruptly abandoning the Draco, I turned to my right and went in search of the remains of Upper Brockhurst Hall. They were more difficult to find a second time amongst all that dense foliage, but eventually I repeated my fall of yesterday when I again stumbled over the lid of the well in what had once been the Hall's outer courtyard. Hercules came bounding through the undergrowth, a silly, doggy grin on his face that looked up into mine, where I knelt on the soft, damp grass, cursing my luck.

'It's all very well for you,' I complained bitterly. 'You have four feet, and that's what's needed to keep your balance on this sort of ground.' Hercules curled his lip, making it plain that he thought it a poor excuse for my clumsiness, and began to forge ahead through the overgrown grasses until I called him back. 'Not so fast,' I said. 'Now we're here, I'd like to take a look at the well.'

Hercules watched with interest, head cocked to one side, as I shed my cloak and cudgel and removed the heavy lid; but he was less enthusiastic when I began to climb down the iron ladder fixed to the wall.

'It's all right,' I assured him as he whimpered and began running around the rim of the well. 'It's quite safe.'

But a moment or two later, I was not so sure. After a hundred and thirty years, the iron was badly corroded. I could feel the jagged flakes of rust beneath my fingers, and some rungs were missing altogether, causing me almost to lose my footing the first time that I encountered such a gap. Afterwards, I proceeded more cautiously, groping around with one foot before lowering myself another step. In at least two places, three or four rungs had rotted away together, and it was only my long legs that enabled me to find the next one safely. And here and there, the ladder was coming loose from the brickwork that lined the shaft, making the whole thing shake.

I had no idea how far off the bottom I was, and I called to Hercules, whose face I could just make out, still peering over the rim of the well. His answering bark sounded anxious and a long way off. The daylight filtering through the canopy of trees above him was dim and diffused, and I wondered if I dared descend any further without risking life and limb. Then my left boot squelched into an inch or so of soft mud, and I knew I must have reached the bottom of the ladder. My eyes had by now grown accustomed to the gloom and I was able to look around me.

The walls of the shaft were running with damp, ferns and mosses sprouting in abundance between the bricks. The floor, as I have said, was thickly coated with mud, but Dame Jacquetta was right: there was no longer any water in it. I did notice a slight seepage where the base of the shaft had been roughly patched with stones and mortar; but the diversion of the Draco, a century or more ago, had doomed the well to dry up and become a hazard to the children of the district; until, that is, the Elders of Lower Brockhurst had had a lid made to cover it. I sighed. Eris Lilywhite was most certainly not buried here. Perhaps, after all, she wasn't yet buried anywhere. Perhaps she was still alive, although I didn't really believe so.

Ten minutes later, I emerged from the well-shaft, dirtier and decidedly smellier than before I went down. The fetid air at the bottom seemed to have permeated all my clothes. Even Hercules, not known for his particularity, backed away from me with a reproachful look. My hands were filthy and covered with flakes of rust.

'All right, boy,' I said, heaving the wooden lid once more into place. 'I know I stink. I'm hoping the breeze will blow some of it away. I've a clean shirt and hose in my pack, and if I have a good wash under Mistress Lilywhite's pump, I might just be fit company for the Fair Rosamund by this evening.'

'Ah!' exclaimed a voice behind me, nearly making me leap out of my skin. 'You must be the pedlar who's lodging with the Mistress Lilywhites, or so I hear. I think I saw you at our Patronal Mass this morning.'

I turned to see the priest, his arms full of kindling, standing a yard or so away from me, smiling benevolently. My heart was still beating unpleasantly fast; but at least his presence in the woods explained the cracking twig I had heard earlier.

'Sir Anselm,' I said, filled with an inexplicable relief. I really was becoming far too jumpy, but the whole atmosphere of death and decay – the ruined Hall and village, the dried-up well, the tale of violent murder – was beginning to make me nervous.

The priest smiled. 'You prefer the old-fashioned form of address, do you? My flock are more up-to-date.'

I returned his smile. 'I'll call you Father, if you prefer it. In Bristol, where I live, both modes of address seem to be acceptable nowadays.'

He nodded. 'Either will do, my son. I'm not choosy. Are you returning to the Lilywhites' now? If so, perhaps you'll be so kind as to give me your company. But I'm afraid I must hurry

81

you, otherwise I shall be late for Vespers, although my long-suffering flock are used to my tardiness. Tonight, however, there is to be an alefeast and a game of Nine Men's Morris to celebrate Saint Walburga's Day. They won't be happy if either is delayed.'

'I know. I'm a member of Mistress Rosamund's team,' I said. 'She enlisted my services yesterday evening.'

The priest regarded me with amusement. 'Did she? I can see why, of course. You're a very good-looking young man.'

'I'm married with three children,' I answered shortly before he could start adding two and two together and making five. I put on my cloak, picked up my cudgel and whistled to Hercules. 'Come on, boy! We're going home.' (Hercules wasn't fussy. Home to him was anywhere there was warmth and food. Before he had attached himself to me, he had run wild on the hills above Bristol.)

I followed Father Anselm, who, happily, appeared to know exactly where he was going, and within a very short space of time, we were clear of the woods and descending the pasture towards the Rawbone farm. I explained that I had to retrieve my pack from their cowshed, where I had left it, a fact my companion seemed to find in no way peculiar. Nor did he ask me what I had been doing down the well shaft, although he must have seen me climb out. At last, I mentioned it myself.

'Why was that well never filled in?' I demanded. 'It would have been more sensible, surely, than fitting it with a lid.' (My sore shins could testify to that.)

The priest wrinkled his nose. 'You sound like Ned Rawbone,' he complained. 'He was saying the same thing to me only a week or so ago. Of course, he has a particular reason to hate that well. He fell down it when he was a boy and wasn't discovered for several days. Broke quite a few of his bones, poor lad. He still walks with a bit of a limp.'

'Oh, it was Ned Rawbone, was it?' I said. 'Someone told me that story in the alehouse last night, but mentioned no name. Master Rawbone's been down the well shaft again recently, so I believe, looking for Eris Lilywhite.'

Nine Men Dancing

'A complete waste of time,' Father Anselm snorted. 'You only had to look down the shaft to see that there was nothing there except a foot or so of water.'

'You were present when he went down to search?' I asked.

The priest nodded. 'Me and most of the rest of the village. The alarm had been raised that Eris was missing, but I wasn't at all surprised at that, not after what I'd been told about events that had taken place in the alehouse the previous evening.' He sounded disapproving.

'You didn't like Eris Lilywhite,' I suggested.

'My son, it is not for a priest to like or dislike members of his flock.' He smiled wryly. 'Let us just say that he is fonder of some than of others.'

'That's a sophistry,' I complained.

He didn't deny it. We were now abreast of the Lilywhites' smallholding and it was with regret that I told him we should have to part company. I had barely begun to pick his brains.

'I need to wash and change my clothes. I stink of the mud at the bottom of that well.'

'I can't offer you a change of clothing,' he answered, 'but the priest house has its own pump. You'll undoubtedly find it easier to strip off without two women on the prowl, hoping to catch a glimpse of your manly equipment.'

I burst out laughing. 'I'm sure neither Maud nor Theresa Lilywhite has any such ambition,' I protested. 'But it so happens that my clean hose and shirt are in my pack, so I accept your offer. There are a number of things I'd like to ask you.' We continued walking downhill. 'You still haven't answered my first question. Why has that well never been filled in?'

Father Anselm turned a slightly shocked face towards me. 'Wells, once dug, are like springs, my son. They are sacred to the gods and nymphs and hamadryads of the woods. Rumour has it that there was once a spring in these parts, dedicated to one of the Roman gods.'

We were within a few paces of the conjunction of the Draco and the stream that bounded Lower Brockhurst. I caught at Father Anselm's arm, forcing him to a halt.

83

Kate Sedley

'*You're a priest of God!*' I expostulated. 'What do you care for
the spirits of the old religion? What do your congregation care?
This is a Christian community. Isn't it?'

'Of course! Of course!' He raised guarded eyes to mine.
'But . . .'

'But?' I prompted.

'But . . . have you never felt . . . yourself . . . that there may
be more ways in which to worship than one?'

I nodded. 'Often. But I'm not a priest. We're talking heresy,
Sir Anselm, and you know it as well as I do. Do many of your
flock still worship the spirits of the trees? The gods of their
Saxon forefathers?'

He shook off my hand and preceded me across the little
bridge. 'This is neither the time nor the place for such a
discussion,' he said petulantly, as he led the way through the
sheltering belt of trees.

We emerged almost directly opposite the church, flanked on
one side by the alehouse and on the other by the house of the
priest. Beyond this latter, right on the northern edge of the
village, was a sheep pound, which, Father Anselm informed me,
was for lost or stray beasts, or for those that were awaiting
transportation to Gloucester or Tetbury market.

'Some come down from the farms on the opposite side of the
valley.' And he waved a hand vaguely in the direction of the
rising hills to the west. 'Stupid animals, sheep!' We crossed the
street. 'Come into the church with me first. I must set a taper to
the Alms Light.'

This, as in most churches, was a simple taper in a bowl
standing before the High Cross, and was lit during service time
to commemorate the souls of the dead. (Some priests, indeed,
prefer to call it the Dead or All Souls Light, but Alms Light is
the more common name.) While Father Anselm was busy about
his chores, I examined the rest of the church, Hercules snuffling
at my heels. The statue of Saint Walburga had been restored to
its niche above the high altar, and the Virgin, unmistakable in
her blue robes – the colour of spiritual and marital fidelity –
graced one of the other two. But it was the figure on the second

84

side altar that interested me. Crudely carved and painted, it depicted the figure of Our Lord, naked, lacerated, bleeding, with a halo made up of carpenter's tools – hammer, mallet, axe, knife, wheel, horn and pincers – around its head. It was the Christ of the Trades that had first made its appearance some hundred years earlier, just before the great revolt of the common people during the reign of the second Richard.

'Right!' exclaimed the priest, bustling up. 'Follow me, and I'll show you where you can wash and change while I ring the bell for Vespers. There will be food in the alehouse afterwards, if you're hungry, before Mistress Rosamund and Lambert Miller begin their game.'

The priest's house was bigger than it looked from the outside, boasting, in addition to a parlour, hall and kitchen, a buttery, larder and a handsome staircase leading to no fewer than three bedchambers (so Sir Anselm told me proudly) on the upper floor. Out of doors there was a pigsty, a stable (unoccupied), a garden plot for herbs and vegetables, a small barn and a pump. The late afternoon had turned extremely cold, with a bitter wind blowing through the valley and a hint of yet more rain to come in the air. Nevertheless, to the sound of the Vespers bell, I stripped naked and, shivering violently, washed away the stink of my excursion down the well shaft, which clung so persistently to my skin. Then I ran back into the warmth of the kitchen, where the priest was waiting for me with an old linen sheet which I used to towel myself dry. I pulled on my clean hose and shirt, and although there was nothing I could do with my still smelly jerkin, I felt sufficiently restored to face the coming evening with equanimity.

My only preoccupation now was my empty stomach. I begged a bowl of scraps and some water for Hercules, but knew that I should have to wait for my own sustenance at least until after Vespers. I accompanied Father Anselm into the church, where the congregation was already assembling, hoping desperately that my rumbling gut would not disgrace me in the fragrant presence of the younger Mistress Bush.

Eight

When Vespers finished, I went back to the priest's house to collect Hercules, my cudgel and my pack (into which I stuffed my dirty clothes) before taking myself off to the Roman Sandal for the alefeast. But before bidding Father Anselm farewell, I returned to the church to ask if we might continue our conversation the following day.

'There are still so many questions to which I need answers,' I said.

'Concerning?' He raised a ragged eyebrow, in which black and grey hairs were inextricably mixed.

'The disappearance of Eris Lilywhite, amongst other things.'

He regarded me thoughtfully. 'Has Maud Lilywhite put you up to this?'

I decided to be honest with him, as I had not been with Jacquetta Rawbone.

'Not Maud. The older Mistress Lilywhite. She's naturally anxious to discover what's happened to her granddaughter. But it's partly to satisfy my own curiosity, as well.'

He nodded, turning to unlock a cupboard fixed to the wall beside the Virgin's altar.

'Maud wouldn't be so anxious to know the truth, of course. That's understandable.'

He picked up the heavy silver chalice, beautifully chased around the bowl, used at Vespers, and placed it on a shelf in the cupboard, beside its twin. On other shelves, I noted a pair of silver candlesticks, the silver-gilt pyx that contained the Eucharist and an elaborate ivory and gold crucifix. There were also one or two other pieces I didn't have time to see in any detail.

'You have quite a few treasures here, at Lower Brockhurst,' I commented, as Father Anselm closed and relocked the cupboard door.

'A few.' He chuckled richly. 'Although it wouldn't do to enquire too closely how all of them were acquired.'

'Why not?'

He gave another chuckle, looking up into my face with a mischievous grin (he only came up to my shoulder).

'I'm going to shock you again, chapman. One of my predecessors, Ambrose Lightfoot, was known as Light-fingered Lightfoot. At least, that's the tradition in the village. How and why he obtained his soubriquet I've never bothered to enquire too closely, and I'm not sure I'd get an honest answer if I did. But these sort of stories that are part of the folklore of a place very often have some foundation in fact, however distorted or exaggerated they may have become with the passing years.'

'Sir Anselm, I'm going,' I grinned, pulling my cloak together with one hand and picking up my pack and cudgel with the other, 'before you undermine my faith in the priesthood altogether. Tree-worship, intimations of theft . . . whatever next?' I nudged Hercules in the direction of the door with my foot. 'I'll call on you, then, sometime tomorrow. With your blessing, that is.'

He patted me on the back. 'If I'm not here when you arrive, just wait for me. I shan't have gone far. You can share my dinner, if you'd like. It's Friday, so it'll only be fish.' I thanked him heartily and accepted his invitation. 'Enjoy your game this evening,' he added. 'I hope Mistress Rosamund wins.'

The alehouse was so full of people and smoke from the fire that it was almost impossible to see across the room. Not that I wanted to. My eyes were inevitably drawn to the long table in the middle, groaning under the weight of food and drink. As most of the villagers were already seated, I hurriedly set down my encumbrances and freed myself from my cloak. Then I forced myself on to a bench, between two men I hadn't met before, and proceeded to fill my empty belly with everything within reach, until it would hold no more. And by that time, everyone – including Hercules, who had been wandering around with the other dogs, gobbling up every scrap that fell in his way – was so full that it was agony to rise from the table and start shifting it and the benches to the sides of the ale-room, so that the game of Nine Men's Morris could begin.

But it was done at last, and Lambert Miller, with two of his friends, scratched out the 'board' on the beaten earth floor, which had earlier been cleared of its covering of rushes. Three squares, one inside the other, were marked by wooden pegs at each corner and in the middle of each side, so that there were twenty-four markers in all. (On a normal board, these would be the holes into which the morrells were slotted.) Rosamund and Lambert then set about assembling their teams, each one comprising nine members. Long strips of coarse linen had been dyed either red or blue, and these were worn as sashes by the players; blue for Lambert's, red for Rosamund's. As I draped mine across my right shoulder and tied it on the opposite hip, I found it being more tastefully arranged by the lady herself.

'You remembered,' she whispered coyly.

'How could I possibly forget?' was my gallant response.

A vision of Adela's mocking face flashed through my mind, making me choke a little over the last word. Luckily, Rosamund noticed nothing amiss.

'I shall call your name first,' she murmured, as she moved away to stand beside Lambert.

She was as good as her word. 'Roger, outside square, top left corner.'

I took up my position.

It was the miller's turn. 'Rob, outside square, middle peg.'

Rosamund spoke to a girl in a brown petticoat and kirtle.

'Lucy, middle square, top left corner.' Now, if she could only get a player at the top left corner of the inner square, she would have a diagonal three-in-a-row, and therefore be able to confiscate one of her opponent's players.

But Lambert, at this early stage of the contest, was neither so unobservant nor so chivalrous as to ignore the obvious, and quickly ordered his next man to occupy the position.

And so the game continued, until all eighteen players were moving around the board as their captains endeavoured to line up three men in a straight line in any direction, each team encouraged by its own vociferous supporters. In the end, after just over an hour, it was Rosamund who won, having managed to capture seven of Lambert's nine players, thus leaving him with two, and unable to make a row of three. I had been removed from the 'board' sometime earlier, after a momentary carelessness on my captain's part, and had watched the finish of the game from the sidelines along with four of my other team-mates. And it was while standing there, contemplating the dance-like movements of the remaining 'pieces', that I was seized with the ridiculous notion that if I could only line up my own three 'morrells' in a straight line, they would lead me to Eris Lilywhite, alive or dead.

Everyone was smiling – none more broadly than Lambert – and congratulating Rosamund on a game well played.

'Another one! Another one!' the man called Rob Pomphrey was shouting. 'Give Lambert his chance of revenge!'

There was a general chorus of agreement, and eventually, after a pretty show of resistance, Rosamund consented, even going so far as to express the wish that the miller might this time be the victor. I didn't believe her for an instant: the Fair Rosamund was a girl who liked to win.

Lambert knew this as well as I did. He was careful not to make obvious mistakes, but as he strode around the 'board', peering between the players, I twice saw him deliberately turn a blind eye to an empty place in direct line with two of Rosamund's 'pieces'. I smiled to myself: the man was more astute that I would have given him credit for. He was also possibly more serious about the landlord's daughter than I had thought him.

I was again captured early on, and was standing near the fire, a cup of William Bush's best home-brewed in my hand, when, just as on the previous night, the ale-room door was flung open and Tom Rawbone appeared. He pushed his way across to Rosamund, seized her roughly in his arms and kissed her.

'I'm sorry!' he said. 'I'm sorry! I'm sorry! *I'm sorry!* Stop avoiding me, girl, and giving me the cold shoulder. I was never in love with Eris. I know that now. She bewitched me. I don't care what's happened to her! I don't care what's become of her, if she's living or dead! It's you I want, Rosamund. It's you I always really wanted.' He kissed her again.

Until that moment, no one had moved. We had all, including Rosamund herself, been turned to stone by the sheer effrontery and unexpectedness of the attack. (For it seemed more like an attack than a wooing; an assault rather than a gentle plea for forgiveness.) But suddenly the whole room erupted. Lambert Miller gave a roar like an enraged bull and launched himself at Tom Rawbone, seizing him round the neck and dragging him away from Rosamund. Winifred Bush, furiously shaking off her husband's restraining hand, tried to hit Tom over the head with a billet from the log basket, and only missed because someone else got in before her. The rest of those present joined in with an almost manic gusto, sitting astride the now prostrate young man's legs and chest, punching him on any part of his anatomy that became available.

I looked on for a minute or two from a distance, and was coming to the conclusion that it was time for someone to intervene, unless the village was to have another murder on its hands – and not just a suspected one, either – when I felt an urgent tug at my sleeve.

'For goodness' sake, stop them, Roger!' pleaded Rosamund's frantic voice. 'They'll kill him!'

I looked down at her. 'Would that worry you?'

'Of course it would!' she cried passionately. She swallowed hard and rallied a little. 'I don't want anyone here hanged on account of Tom Rawbone. He isn't worth it!'

I grabbed my cudgel from its resting place against the wall and laid about me, pulling, pushing, hitting out where necessary, using both stick and fists to haul the avengers off the bleeding, groaning figure lying on the floor. I met, inevitably, with a good deal of resistance, and earned myself a cut lip and a bloody nose before, finally, common sense prevailed. William Bush backed my efforts with a plea for calm and order, pointing out, once he could make himself heard, the dire consequences for all of them if Tom Rawbone were to die at their hands. One by one the would-be assassins slowly rose from their knees and drew back to stand in a menacing circle around their victim. The sudden silence, however, was as ominous as the preceding uproar had been.

To my great surprise, before I could offer him a helping hand, Tom staggered painfully to his feet and confronted his persecutors with as much of a sneer as his bruised and bleeding lips would permit.

'Fucking scum!' he spat. Or, at least, I think that's what he said. It wasn't that easy to tell.

There was a low growl and several of the men made a half-movement towards him.

'Go!' Rosamund told him sharply, laying a gentle hand on his arm. (I wondered if I were the only one, apart from Tom himself, to notice her anxiety not to hurt him further, and decided that I probably was.)

'Can you walk on your own?' I asked, prepared to offer him assistance.

His only answer was a contemptuous grunt as he shoved his way towards the door and, for the second evening running, left the Roman Sandal with the imprecations of the villagers ringing in his ears.

His departure was the signal for a babel of talk, a mixture of regret that he had not been taught a severer lesson, and relief that matters had not been carried further than they had. Lambert Miller rushed across to Rosamund to envelop her in a protective embrace, while vilifying her former betrothed in terms that were hardly fit for a young girl's delicate ears. Not that Rosamund seemed offended by them, merely unresponsive. But once again, I doubted if Lambert noticed her reaction: he was too busy being the knight in shining armour, *sans peur et sans reproche*.

It was obvious that the second game of Nine Men's Morris would now be abandoned, and the rest of the evening devoted to discussing Tom Rawbone's outrageous behaviour, renewing the debate as to whether or not he had murdered Eris Lilywhite. I decided, therefore, that it was time to leave. Maud and Theresa might be wondering where I had got to, as neither had come to the alefeast, although I doubted that they would be worried. I was, after all, a big lad able to take care of himself. I found Hercules, ruthlessly interrupting his amorous advances to a large, shaggy-haired bitch, and, along with my cudgel, pack and cloak, removed him and myself without anyone noticing our going (I was becoming quite adept at this). Hercules vented his spleen by trying to bite my ankles.

'Don't be a fool, boy!' I admonished him. 'She'd have eaten you for breakfast.'

The evening air was cold and clammy against my skin, refreshing after the overwhelming heat of the alehouse. The rain had ceased, and a ragged sliver of moon showed now and then between the storm-tossed clouds that shouldered their way across the valley. The village street clove a deep shadow between the darker shapes of the houses, behind which rose the infinitely ancient hills, home of the elf-people, waiting for the blast of the fairy horn that would wake them at last from their enchanted slumber . . .

I shivered and reined in my imagination. Opposite me was the mill, and between it and the neighbouring cottage, I glimpsed the silvery glint of the stream as the moon reappeared and drowned its reflection in the swiftly flowing water. Something moved. Someone was sitting there, on the bank, and guessing who it might be, I crossed the street towards him. Tom Rawbone was wiping his mouth on the back of his hand, having, by the smell of things, just been violently sick.

I laid a hand on his back and he bucked like a startled horse.

'Let me give you my arm as far as Dragonswick,' I offered.

He shook his head and muttered indistinctly, 'Not goin' home. No' . . . No' like this.'

'Where, then?' I asked. 'You can't stay out all night in this condition.'

He gestured in the direction of the far end of the street, where it curved away into blackness, and said something that sounded like 'Alice's'.

'Alice's?' I queried, unconvinced that I had heard aright.

Surely there wasn't yet another woman in his life! He couldn't be that foolhardy! Everyday existence was complicated enough, as he must be only too well aware, without clogging its wheels with a third emotional entanglement.

But when, with my arm about his waist to support his tottering footsteps, he had directed me along the village street to a cottage that stood by itself, some two or three hundred yards distant from its closest neighbour, the mystery was solved. Alice, a large, buxom woman somewhere, I guessed, between thirty-five and forty, with sleepy brown eyes, painted cheeks and a loose mop of coarse, carroty coloured hair, introduced herself as the village whore.

'Alice Tucker, that's me, dear. All the young lads come to me when they're in trouble. I give 'em a shoulder to cry on.' And judging by her ample bosom, more than just a shoulder. 'Who've we got here, then? Oh, it's you again, Tom! What have you been up to, this time?'

It was a tiny, one-roomed cottage with a large bed that took up most of the floor space.

'Tools of the trade, dear,' Alice said, as she helped me lower Tom on to it. 'So, what's the story?'

I told her, and she sighed, raising her eyes to the smoke-blackened ceiling.

'What's the matter with the young idiot? Doesn't he realize that you can't treat a girl the way he treated Rosamund Bush and then, when other things go wrong, just raise your finger and get her back again? I suppose not. He's a Rawbone, isn't he? Conceited, arrogant, lecherous. They're all the same. Although, perhaps it's fair to say that the old man's worse than his sons.'

As Tom had lapsed into semi-consciousness, I helped her

strip off his clothes, so that we could see the extent of his injuries. Alice ran practised hands over his ribs.

'Nothing seems to be broken,' she said. 'It's mostly bruising.'

She fetched a small pot from a shelf opposite the bed and began to rub its contents over the bluish welts beginning to mar Tom Rawbone's skin.

'Primrose salve,' she explained, noticing my curious stare. 'I'll put some on that cut lip of yours after I've finished with him.'

'It's nothing,' I protested, wiping away a thin trickle of blood with the back of my hand. I went on, 'You were talking about the Rawbone family. Conceited, arrogant, lecherous were your words. But the elder son, Ned, seems a quiet-mannered, harmless enough fellow from what I've seen of him.'

'Oh, Master Edward's settled down right enough since his marriage. He was never as wild as Tom or the old man, but he sowed his wild oats in his youth. That Petronelle, though, she keeps him under her thumb.' Alice sniffed disparagingly. 'Don't get me wrong. She ain't a dragon like Dame Jacquetta. She's the sort who whines and snivels and sulks and makes a man's life a misery if she doesn't get her own way. But that's just as bad . . . Hey! Get that dog off my bed, if he's yours. Or is he some stray that's come in with you?'

'No, I'm afraid he's mine,' I admitted, retrieving Hercules, who had been about to settle down for the night, curled up against Tom's legs. I set him on the floor, then leaned my back against the cottage wall. My legs were beginning to ache, no doubt as a result of my exploration of the well shaft that afternoon. I ventured, 'Don't you like the younger Mistress Rawbone?'

Alice wiped her hands on the patched and faded counterpane. Her patient stirred a little, then sank back into a torpor, either real or feigned. Either way, Alice had no inhibitions about discussing his brother and the rest of his family within his hearing.

'Petronelle's all right, I suppose,' she conceded grudgingly after a few moments' thought. 'It's not her fault that she loves a man who doesn't love her. Nathaniel forced Ned into the marriage because of her dowry. He wanted to marry Maud Haycombe.'

'Mistress Lilywhite?'

'That's right, dear. And I reckon he'd have defied his father, too, if she hadn't gone and fallen for that Gilbert Lilywhite who'd come here from Gloucester to dig somebody's well. Of course,' Alice added hastily, 'I don't remember events very clearly. I was only a slip of a thing at the time.' She saw the blatant disbelief on my face and grimaced. 'Oh, very well, then! I was twenty and already beginning to practise my trade. I had no choice, dear. My mother turned me out of the house when she married again, and what else was I to do?' She gave a sudden belly laugh. 'My stepfather was one of my first customers. Now, what d'you think of that? A joke, eh? I never told her, although it was on the tip of my tongue to do so, often and often.'

Fortunately, the flow of reminiscences was stemmed by Tom Rawbone opening his eyes and asking for water, which Alice fetched for him from a barrel just outside the door. Supporting him in one strong arm, she held the wooden cup to his lips.

'Do you want to stay here the night?' she asked him. 'I've got no visitors this evening. Unless, of course, your friend, here . . . ?' She turned to look up at me.

'No!' I declined the offer with more speed than courtesy. 'It's . . . It's just that I'm married,' I added in a belated effort to soften my terse refusal.

'They're all married,' she said reproachfully.

'Happily married,' I pleaded in extenuation.

Alice sighed. 'There's nothing I hate more than a happily married man.'

'I'm sorry.'

'Not your fault, dear, I suppose. Well, there you are then, Tom.' She smoothed his hair. 'You can sleep in my bed tonight and I'll rub your bruises again in the morning.' She rose from her seat on the side of the bed and moved towards the door. I realized I was being dismissed and once more gathered up my belongings, nudging Hercules, who was snoring beside the corner hearth, with my toe. Furious, he again tried to bite my ankles. I should have to cure him of this painful habit.

Alice followed me outside. 'You don't perhaps want some powdered mandrake root?' she hissed. 'I always keep a pot for some of my gentlemen who have – well, you know – trouble.'

I laughed. 'I already have three children.' I didn't tell her that Nicholas wasn't really mine. 'I'm trying not to have any more. So . . . no, thank you.'

She shrugged. 'Suit yourself.'

She was turning to go back into the cottage, when I was struck by a sudden thought.

'Alice,' I said, 'last September, the night of the great storm, the night Eris Lilywhite disappeared, did Tom Rawbone spend the night here?'

She seemed mildly astonished that I should even need to ask the question.

'Of course! He always comes to me when he's in trouble. And that night, he was in a terrible state. Not surprising, really, when you think about it, I suppose. He'd thrown over Rosamund Bush because he thought Eris was going to marry him, only to find that she'd got herself betrothed to his father! I told you old man Rawbone was a worse lecher than his sons. An old ram – and that's being unfair to rams. He should have been castrated years ago. Mind you –' she giggled – 'I should have lost a deal of trade if he had been.'

'He comes here?'

Alice glowered at me. 'Why do you say it like that? There's nothing wrong with this place. I offer a necessary service, that's all.' Once more her sense of humour conquered her indignation. 'Mother confessor to the entire male population of the village, that's me. I bet I know more about the men of Lower Brockhurst than Father Anselm . . . Are you sure you don't want to stay, dear? I'm very reasonable.'

I countered her question with one of my own, desperate to give her thoughts another direction.

'That night, the night we were talking of, what time was it when Tom Rawbone arrived here?'

Alice stared at me with that mixture of suspicion and curiosity that I've noticed in a lot of people when I start probing for information.

'Nosy, aren't you? And I know what you're thinking. Would Tom have had time to do away with Eris before he came knocking on my door? Well, unfortunately, the answer's yes, he would. It must have been after midnight, because my last visitor didn't leave until late. He – Tom, that is – was soaked to the skin. Said he'd been walking for miles in the rain. Couldn't remember, he said, where he'd been, only that he'd been trying to overcome his fury, so that he wouldn't go back to Dragonswick to finish what he'd begun.'

'He meant, I suppose, his attempt to murder his father and Eris. Did you believe him?'

'I think so. Mind you, if I'm honest, when I'd heard the whole story I wasn't so sure.' Alice wrapped her arms about herself for warmth. 'Look, I'm freezing, standing here, chatting like this. I'm going in.' She made one last bid for my custom. 'You're positive you don't want to . . . to . . . ?'

'I'm very tired,' I pleaded. 'I've had a long day.' Which was true. 'I'll call tomorrow to see how Tom is.'

She nodded, accepting defeat, and turned back indoors.

I picked up Hercules, who was giving a good imitation of a dog who could go no further without falling over, and tucked him under my arm. Then, with my almost empty pack and cudgel clutched together in my right hand, I walked back along the village street to the footbridge opposite the church. There were still sounds of merrymaking issuing from the open alehouse door, but the priest's house was in darkness. Sir Anselm, for want of other occupation, had presumably gone to bed, ready to rise in the small hours to recite Matins and Lauds in the icy and deserted church. Rather him than me. It was the service I had hated and resented most during my years as a novice at Glastonbury Abbey.

I turned into the belt of trees, but before I could set foot on the bridge, an arm was clamped around my throat in a frantic effort to throttle me.

97

Nine

I dropped everything, including the dog, and raised my hands to claw at the arm encircling my throat. At the same time, I could hear Hercules barking like a fiend and trusted that he was attacking my assailant's ankles just as, earlier, he had tried to bite mine. I was finding it increasingly difficult to breathe and my senses were beginning to swim. My eyes felt as though they were bulging out of their sockets, which they probably were, and although I kicked backwards with my right foot, I was unable to find a target. Then, just as unconsciousness was looming and the situation growing desperate, I was released with a suddenness that sent me sprawling to the ground.

I lay there, gasping, for a moment, rubbing my throat and waiting for my vision to clear, then heaved myself unsteadily upright and turned to confront my attacker. Backed up against a tree, vainly trying to free his right arm from the vice-like grip of Hercules's teeth, was Lambert Miller. The dog, suspended several feet above the ground, was hanging on valiantly and refusing to be shaken off. (I had seen him perform this trick once before, the first time he had saved me from violent assault. I thanked God that I had brought him with me.)

'All right, boy,' I said, 'you can let go now.' I caught his little body round the middle, relieving the strain on his neck and stomach muscles, then helped him to unclamp his jaws. I made much of him before lowering him to the ground.

Lambert was swearing profusely and rubbing his afflicted limb. Fortunately, he was wearing a thick tunic made of that mixture of flax and wool we used to call byrrhus, and which had saved him from the worst effects of a mauling by Hercules's teeth. Not that he could expect any congratulations from me on this account.

'What was that for?' I demanded hoarsely, taking a threatening step towards him (perhaps tottering step would be a fairer description – I was still feeling extremely groggy).

The miller glowered at me, rolling up his right sleeve to inspect his wounds.

'I'm sorry,' he muttered. 'I thought you were Tom Rawbone. I'd come outside for a breath of air and saw you vanishing into the trees. I didn't notice the dog. I thought you and he were still in the alehouse. Look, chapman, you must believe me! I've no grudge against *you*. But I'll not tolerate that lecher making Rosamund's life a misery, now he's decided he wants her back. She's a wonderful girl. She deserves better than him.'

I wondered if young Mistress Bush would agree with her would-be swain, but I didn't say so. That was for Lambert to discover. I nodded, accepting his explanation, and dropped down to sit on the ground, propping my back against a neighbouring tree trunk and lowering my head between my knees. After a moment or two, when I began to feel a little better, I raised it again and looked at him.

'Just make sure, will you, that next time you have one of these murderous urges, you have the right man? And for heaven's sake, make certain that you don't actually kill anyone. Another minute and I'd have been dead meat, and you'd have been lucky to have escaped the gallows.'

It was his turn to nod as he sat down beside me.

'I just saw red,' he excused himself. 'A good job it was you. If it hadn't been for the dog . . .' He broke off, shuddering, suddenly aware that my narrow squeak had also been his.

The night lay dark and tranquil all about us. Somewhere, I could hear a small, nocturnal animal rummaging in the long grasses. Hercules laid his head on my thigh and I caressed his ears. Echoes of laughter and singing reached us from the Roman Sandal.

Lambert asked abruptly, 'Do you know where he is? Tom Rawbone, I mean.'

'No,' I lied. In the circumstances I felt it was justified; a small sin to prevent a possibly greater one. 'Do you often make this sort of vicious attack on people?'

'Of course not!' His indignant rebuttal rang a little hollow. 'But you saw what happened in the alehouse this evening.'

'I saw a man trying to rectify a mistake that he now knows has cost him the best chance of happiness in this life.'

The miller scrambled to his feet, giving vent to another explosion of anger.

'Rectify a mistake! What sort of mealy-mouthed nonsense is that? If that Jezebel hadn't thrown Tom Rawbone over in favour of his father, he'd have married her! He cast Rosamund off like . . . like some old shoe! He humiliated her in front of half the village. I know. I was there. I was a witness to everything. I saw the state she was in when he'd gone. That lovely, innocent creature! I tell you, chapman, if I could have laid hands on Eris Lilywhite or Tom Rawbone at that moment, there would have been murder done!'

I, too, struggled to my feet, suddenly realizing how cold I was, sitting on the damp February ground. I also realized, to my dismay, that I was shaking, a palsy that had nothing to do with the dank night air, but seemed to be a kind of delayed reaction to my recent fright (a phenomenon I had experienced once or twice before). I drew my cloak tightly around me.

'Murder was done,' I pointed out. 'Or, at least, there's a strong probability that it was.'

'Well, we all know the name of the killer, then, don't we?' my companion sneered. 'Eris Lilywhite's disappearance can only be laid at one person's door.' Lambert thought about this for a moment. 'One family's door,' he amended.

'You think another of the Rawbones could have murdered her?' I asked. My throat still hurt, making conversation difficult, but I might not find the miller in such a talkative mood again. Guilt was making him expansive.

'Well, apart from Nathaniel, I can't think of any member of that family, including the housekeeper, Elvina Merryman, who'd have wanted Eris lording it over them as the mistress of Dragonswick. I wouldn't even rule out the twins, for all they're only fourteen years of age. Strong as oxen, the pair of them.'

'But the body, if there is one, has never been found.' Now I was arguing against myself.

I could just make out that Lambert was wagging his head in agreement. It was getting very dark as the moon had vanished behind yet another bank of clouds.

'Not for want of looking, though,' he told me. 'The remains of the old village, the ruins of the Hall and its well were all searched, but to no avail. But you can't look everywhere, it stands to reason. A grave dug deep in the woods will never be found, except for some freak accident, maybe years in the future. And, of course, the girl *might* not be dead. She *might* just have run away, as the Rawbones keep insisting.'

'Do you believe that?'

The miller laughed. 'No one believes it. No one who knew Eris Lilywhite, at any rate. What? Forgo the chance to be mistress of Dragonswick? She couldn't do it, even if it meant being tied to a man old enough to be her father for the next ten years and more.' He shivered as violently as I was doing inside my cloak. 'Holy Mother! Why are we standing around here in this cold? Come into the alehouse, chapman, and I'll buy you a stoup of ale.'

I declined. 'I must get back to the Mistress Lilywhites',' I said. 'They'll be wondering where I am.' I scooped up Hercules, who had been sitting patiently and protectively at my feet. 'But, like I said, next time, miller, just make sure you have the right person before you try to throttle him to death.'

I slept soundly, after being fussed over by Maud and Theresa, and woke to a quieter, sunnier morning.

My long absence of the day before, which I was sure the younger woman had barely registered – except, perhaps, to hope that I had changed my plans and quit the district – was more than forgiven when I had been able to recount, at first hand, the evening's events at the alehouse. This, together with details of my visit to Dragonswick Farm and my conversation with Jacquetta Rawbone, had kept them entertained until it was time for bed. My torn lip and bloody nose were bathed with a sicklewort lotion; very good for cuts and bruises, so my mother had always told me; and my hoarse voice, the reason for which I didn't divulge, was treated with a linseed poultice. The result was that, by the next day, I was feeling much better than I could ever have anticipated.

The women and I followed the same procedure as on the previous morning, with the result that we were all three able to wash and dress in comparative privacy. While I shaved, I reflected that, come evening, there were only forty-eight hours left before it was March, and then just over a fortnight before the feast of Saint Patrick. By which time, I had faithfully promised Adela I would be home.

'You're very quiet, chapman,' Theresa commented while we were eating breakfast. 'Are you any nearer to finding out what has become of my granddaughter?'

I was forced to admit that I wasn't. 'But you must give me time,' I protested. 'There are other people I have to talk to. This morning I'm visiting Father Anselm, who has kindly invited me to share his dinner with him.'

Theresa was dismissive. 'You won't discover anything by talking to that old fool.' I suspected that the priest was younger than she was. 'He knows nothing of what goes on in this parish. Nothing of importance, anyway. Lives in a little world of his own. Sometimes I wonder if he's quite . . . well . . . you know!' She tapped her forehead.

Maud was up in arms immediately. 'You know nothing of Sir Anselm, Mother! He's been living here, in this village, for many more years than you have. He's a good friend to all his parishioners. A man who can be trusted.' I reflected that this was the first time I had seen Maud Lilywhite display anything akin to real emotion. Not even when discussing Eris's disappearance and the possibility of her murder had she been roused to such a pitch of animation. She went on, 'I should prefer it if you refrained from criticizing him in my hearing.'

Even Theresa seemed taken aback by her daughter-in-law's vehemence. She hummed and hawed and spluttered a bit, but evidently thought better of renewing the subject. Instead, she filled her mouth with another spoonful of gruel, looked across at me and said thickly, 'We shan't be having the pleasure of your company at dinner, then?' She added, 'I still say you're wasting your time. You won't find out anything from Father Anselm. You should be sniffing around the rest of the Rawbones.'

'I must do things in my own way and my own good time,' I remonstrated, finishing my fried herring and oatmeal. I hoped it didn't sound too much like a snub, but Theresa was beginning to irritate me.

She took it, however, in good part. 'Oh, I know I'm an interfering old woman,' she mocked. 'It's just . . . It's just that I want to know what's happened to Eris.'

There was a note of genuine pathos in her voice and I immediately felt ashamed of my spurt of annoyance. As I rose from my stool, I pressed a hand on her shoulder.

'I'll do my best,' I promised. 'But that's all I can do. You must reconcile yourself, Dame Lilywhite, to the fact that we may never know for certain what's become of your granddaughter.'

I left my pack at the Lilywhites' cottage and set out with Hercules, encumbered only by my cudgel. It still being not yet half-past seven, and barely daylight, I went in the opposite direction to the village, climbing the slope past Dragonswick Farm to the wooded heights above. I was beginning to know my way by now, and had no difficulty, this time, in locating the ruins of Upper Brockhurst Hall. The place drew me to it as if by some enchantment. The silence this morning was almost total, except for the trees dripping gently in the early morning mist, their leaves unstirring in the windless air. A squirrel appeared, woken early from its winter sleep, and stopped in front of me. Its wary gaze, more full of bright-eyed intelligence than seemed natural in so small a creature, encountered mine for a fleeting instant before it scrabbled through a pile of last year's leaves and vanished from sight. Hercules made no attempt to give chase. It had moved so swiftly and quietly, I doubted he had even noticed it, busy as he was about his own concerns.

For a while, I wandered around the ruins, trying to pace out the different rooms, attempting, without much success, to reconstruct the building in my imagination. But there was too little of it left, nature and the scavengers from Lower Brockhurst having done too thorough a job in either smothering or removing the ancient stones. The courtyard well was the only thing that remained intact; the well that had cost two men their lives and which had never had a chance to be of benefit to its owners before they were struck down and killed by the plague; the well that had dried up and lost its function when the bed of the Draco had been diverted; the well that had once nearly claimed the life of the young Ned Rawbone.

I sat down on the heavy wooden lid that had been fashioned by the village carpenter after that accident, carefully avoiding its handle, my legs sprawled out in front of me, and listened again to that silence which, in the countryside, is not truly a silence, but filled with a hundred tiny sounds, some of them barely audible to the human ear. The thin February sunshine slanted through the latticed branches of the surrounding trees, striking on a patch of dark ground-ivy in points of polished steel. I remembered what Lambert Miller had said to me the previous night; that Eris could be buried anywhere in these vast tracts of woodland, and it would be nigh on impossible to find her grave.

And yet . . . And yet . . . Why could I not believe that this was indeed the case? I felt in my bones that she was dead; murdered. The people who had known her in life were positive that she would not voluntarily have run away; that she would not simply have discarded everything that she had so obviously schemed for. Similarly, the idea of suicide was most improbable. Having accepted, therefore, that she had been killed unlawfully, why did I find it so difficult to believe that her body was buried anywhere other than here, in the ruins of Upper Brockhurst Hall?

There was no rhyme or reason for this feeling that amounted very nearly to a certainty. Any rational person would have laughed it to scorn. But it persisted and grew stronger the longer I sat there, refusing to be intimidated by any logical argument my brain put forward. In the end, angry with myself, I jumped to my feet, startling Hercules, and began a second detailed search of the ground, looking for some disturbance that might give the slightest hint of a recently dug grave. But of course, I found nothing. I returned and stared for a long time at the well, then lifted its lid and peered once more into its depths. Nothing. Nothing at all. It was as empty as when I had climbed down the ladder yesterday.

Hercules barked at me, plainly afraid that I was contemplating another descent. I thanked him for his concern and patted his head. 'Not this time, lad,' I reassured him.

Nevertheless, the feeling that Eris was somewhere close at hand persisted, refusing to be shaken off. It grew so strong that I began to sweat profusely, in spite of the morning chill, and I was suddenly aware of a mask-like face that stared at me from between two tree trunks. I froze with fear. It took a moment or two for me to realize that the face was indeed a mask, made from straw, the bulging eyes two black pebbles from the bed of the stream. When at last I could move, I approached it slowly and saw that it was hanging from the lower branch of an oak. There was other evidence, too, that someone had been here since my visit yesterday. There were fresh strips of cloth tied to neighbouring twigs and a corn dolly pinned to the trunk, the nail, as in the one I had seen on Wednesday afternoon, driven straight through the heart. Hercules was whimpering, lying flat on his belly.

'Come on, boy,' I said, 'let's go.'

He didn't need a second invitation.

It was still too early, when I reached the village, to present myself at the priest's house for dinner. Besides, I could hear that the morning service had not yet finished, so I decided to call on Alice Tucker to enquire after Tom Rawbone. If people saw me entering her cottage and drew the wrong conclusion, that was up to them. A clear conscience is all that matters in this life. (Do I really believe that? Perhaps. Then again, perhaps not. But it's nice to dream.)

'He's gone home, dear,' Alice said as soon as she saw me, guessing my mission. She beckoned me inside. 'First light this morning. Mind you, he still looks a mess. Brother Ned'll scold him, but I doubt the others will take much notice. They're all used to Tom being in trouble. Been the same ever since he was a little boy. Comes of being so much younger than Ned, I reckon. Must have been like having two fathers. Enough to make any red-blooded young fellow rebellious.'

'You're sure he's gone home?' I asked.

Alice shrugged. 'Can't think where else he'd be. He isn't going back to the alehouse, at least not yet awhile. Though I doubt he's given up on Rosamund. A beating won't deter Tom, not if he's really set his heart on winning her back.'

'He'd better watch out for Lambert Miller, then,' I said feelingly.

Alice raised her eyebrows and I found myself telling her about last night's encounter. When I'd finished, she pulled down the corners of her mouth. (By this time, we were sitting side by side on the bed, there being only one chair in the cottage.)

'I wouldn't be too sure it was a mistake, dear,' she said, patting my hand. 'Got a very nasty temper, has Lambert. How could he possibly think that you were Tom Rawbone? You're much too tall.'

'It was dark,' I pointed out, 'and Hercules was under my arm, beneath my cloak.' Hercules, lying at my feet, thumped his tail at mention of his name. 'The miller wouldn't have seen him.'

Alice pursed her lips, carmined with a mixture of raspberry juice and white lead, which, although early in the day, was already beginning to crack.

'I still say you're too tall to be mistaken for anyone else in this village,' she insisted, adding shrewdly, 'Was Rosamund flirting with you in the alehouse last night, when you were playing Nine Men's Morris?'

'She was very friendly,' I admitted, 'but nothing more.'

'It wouldn't need anything more if Lambert's now decided that Rosamund's his property,' Alice sniffed. 'And I've no doubt she's been encouraging him to think so, just to get her own back on Tom. She'd do anything to prevent people thinking she still cared. You and Lambert won't be the only two she's giving the eye to, but you'll be by far the best looking.'

'I'm married,' I repeated wearily. 'With three children.'

'And far from home.' Alice slewed round so that she could see me better. 'I'm not saying Rosamund has designs on you, dear, just that, since last September, she's been salving her wounded pride by setting her cap at any man who can still walk and has more than three teeth in his head.'

I laughed. 'You don't allow a man much self-delusion, do you?'

'Will you be serious?!' she exclaimed impatiently. 'All I'm saying is that I'd keep away from Rosamund if I were you. I told you, Lambert Miller has a nasty temper. He's attacked people before. I like you. I don't want to see you hurt.'

I thanked her, but abstractedly. My mind was only half on what she was saying.

After a moment, I asked, 'You say Lambert has a reputation for being aggressive?' Alice nodded. 'You also say he's set on people before?' She inclined her head again. 'So . . .' I clicked my teeth thoughtfully. 'In that case, I wonder where he was the evening that Eris Lilywhite disappeared.'

'Oh, now, wait a minute!' Alice looked alarmed. 'Lambert was in the alehouse, along with everyone else. I was there myself. I saw him.'

'I daresay. But he wasn't there all night. He might well have gone out later looking for Tom Rawbone and come across Eris, instead. From something he said to me, he holds her equally responsible for what happened. Which, in a way, she was. If he was in one of his rages, he could easily have attacked her, just as he attacked me yesterday evening. Maybe he didn't mean to kill her, but found she was dead all the same.' I rubbed my throat reminiscently. 'He's very strong. He almost did for me. A defenceless young girl would stand no chance.'

Alice shook her head. 'You're wrong, chapman. I told you I had a customer that night, who didn't leave until late, almost midnight – which was how I knew Tom couldn't have been here before. Well, that customer was Lambert Miller. He made the assignation before we left the Roman Sandal.'

'What time did he arrive?' I persisted.

Alice hunched her shoulders. 'I don't know. An hour, maybe an hour and a half earlier. Contrary to what you might think, Lambert isn't the in, out, thank you and I'm off sort. He likes to take his time. And that night, of course, there was a lot to talk about before we got down to business.'

'What kind of mood was he in?' I asked. 'Angry? Vindictive?'

Alice blew her nose on a corner of the counterpane, managing, at the same time, to wipe her mouth clean of most of its white lead and raspberry juice coating. The lips beneath were very pale, almost bloodless.

'As a matter of fact, no,' she answered. 'Of course, he called Tom and the rest of the Rawbones all the bad names he could lay his tongue to for Rosamund's sake. But I'd say that really he was delighted that Tom was going to marry Eris – because, of course, we didn't know *then* what had gone on up at Dragonswick Farm. Lambert just saw that at last the way was clear for him to start courting Rosamund on his own account. He'd always been fond of her. More than fond.'

Hercules roused himself, staggered to his feet and placed his front paws on my knees. He had had enough of all this idle chatter. He wanted to get on.

I stroked his head. 'In a minute, boy.' I turned back to Alice. 'When was it generally known that Eris had jilted Tom in favour of his father? When did news of her disappearance reach the village?'

Alice pursed her lips. A few remaining flakes of white lead dislodged themselves and crumbled.

'*I* knew about Eris and old Nathaniel when Tom arrived here just after midnight. He told me all about it. And a terrible state he was in, as I mentioned to you yesterday. But I don't suppose the rest of the village knew anything until the next morning, when Ned came down to enlist the men's help in looking for Eris. Then they learned the whole story. Of course, Tom and I knew nothing of that until we'd dressed and breakfasted. I went as far as the mill with him, when he left here, in order to get some bread. That was when Goody Miller, Lambert's mother, told us what was going on. Lambert wasn't there. He was off, with the rest, searching for Eris.'

'And Tom?'

'He went to help, naturally.'

'Did it strike you that he wasn't surprised by the news that Eris had vanished?'

Alice shook her head decidedly. 'No. I'd say he was stunned by the news. He turned so white I thought he was going to faint. Later on in the day, when they still hadn't found her, I went to help look, as well. I'd say that Ned was more composed than his brother.'

But then, I thought, Ned Rawbone had less reason to be discomposed than Tom. He hadn't liked Eris Lilywhite and, deep down, probably secretly hoped that they'd seen the last of her. I supposed he might have been afraid that Tom had murdered her in a fit of rage. But from the little I knew and had been told of the Rawbones, I guessed them to be quite capable of closing ranks, whatever their internal quarrels, and covering up even so dire a crime as murder.

I pulled myself up short. I was making an assumption that Tom was the killer. That, indeed, there *was* a killer.

I asked Alice, 'Do you think that Eris Lilywhite ran away?'

She shook her head vigorously, so that her carroty-coloured mop of hair flew in all directions.

'Why should she?'

'Conscience? Guilt at the mayhem she had caused?'

Alice screeched with laughter. Hercules hurriedly lay down again, hiding his head between his paws.

'No, dear! Not a chance! Eris's beauty of soul never matched her beauty of face. I doubt if she knew what a twinge of conscience was. Strange, really. Gilbert Lilywhite was a sweet-natured man, for all he was a foreigner from Gloucester.

And Maud, well, I've never known her play a dirty trick on anyone. Yet, between them, they produced a monster like Eris. No, you can take it from me, she didn't disappear of her own free will. But who killed her, and where the body's hidden, is a different matter. I wouldn't care to speculate.'

It was the same answer that I got from everyone. I rose to my feet. It was time I was on my way.

Ten

I walked back along the village street, encountering one or two curious glances, and several disapproving looks from people who either knew or guessed where I had been. Others, busy about their daily business, ignored me. A few hailed me in a friendly fashion, but with that element of reserve in their greeting that reminded me I was a stranger in their midst, and therefore to be treated with caution. I smiled at them all, but did not stop until I reached the priest's house, just beyond Saint Walburga's Church.

The main door stood hospitably open, and I entered without knocking. I found myself once again in the hall, with the staircase to my left and three doors to my right, the first two separated by a small stone hearth, empty except for a couple of logs, gathering dust.

I raised my voice and called, 'Sir Anselm!'

An answering shout invited me into the kitchen. This, if I remembered correctly, was the third door along. Hercules, however, had already preceded me, recalling where he had been fed and watered the previous afternoon and hoping for similar largesse today. I followed him.

The priest was standing by the table, in the centre of the rush-strewn floor, washing the silver chalice that had held the wine for the morning's service. Seated opposite him, keeping his balance on a rickety stool, was Ned Rawbone.

'Come in, chapman! Come in!' Father Anselm beckoned with a dripping hand, describing, as he did so, an arc of rainbow-hued droplets that hung momentarily in the air, and then were gone. 'Do you know Edward Rawbone? From Dragonswick Farm?'

111

I leaned on my cudgel and nodded towards my fellow visitor. 'I saw Master Rawbone in church yesterday morning, and again, later in the day, at the farmhouse, when I was there at the request of Dame Jacquetta. But so far, we haven't spoken.'

Ned looked startled. I guess he would have said he didn't know me: neither meeting had made any impression on him.

The priest continued, 'Ned is the Warden of our Lamp Fund, particularly the Alms Light. He ensures that we have sufficient money for lamp oil from the sale of fleeces from two of the Dragonswick sheep, especially earmarked for the purpose . . . Now, there's another stool around here, somewhere. Sit down and make yourself comfortable while I finish drying this bowl. Then I'll find us something to eat. It must be nearly ten o'clock and dinnertime.'

I found the stool, tucked away beside a pile of brushwood, and did as I was bidden, ignoring Hercules's reproachful stare. He had expected to be fed at once. I dropped my cudgel on the floor, rested my elbows on the table and smiled at Ned Rawbone.

There was no answering smile, only a suspicious glance from those extremely blue eyes, so like his father's. He had removed his hood, and now put up a hand to subdue his unruly thatch of hair. I noticed several streaks of grey amongst the brown. A handsome man, as I remarked earlier, in a weather-beaten way. (But what else should I have expected from a man who spent most of his life out of doors? I must be weather-beaten myself, when I stopped to think about it.)

'Are you the pedlar who's been asking questions about Eris Lilywhite?' he demanded bluntly, just as I had decided that I must break the silence, and had opened my mouth to speak.

'Er, yes,' I admitted.

'Why?'

'W-why?' My tongue stumbled a little, as I was caught off guard.

'Yes. Why? What's she to you?'

I took a deep breath and steadied my voice. I would not be browbeaten.

'Dame Theresa Lilywhite has requested me to find out, if I can, what has become of her granddaughter.'

Ned Rawbone muttered something under his breath that I was unable to catch, then asked, 'And has anyone talked to you on the subject?' He cocked a suspicious eye at the priest.

Sir Anselm suddenly looked very hot, but it could simply have been the exertion of giving the chalice a final, vigorous rub.

'Your aunt, Dame Jacquetta, was most voluble on the subject,' I answered, with a certain amount of malicious satisfaction.

'Oh, she would be!' Ned exclaimed, flushing angrily. 'I might have guessed it! She'd never be able to resist *you*.'

I ignored the jibe. 'Why don't you give me your account of what happened on the night of the storm?' I suggested.

For reply, he put a question of his own. 'What does Maud Lilywhite have to say on the subject of your interference?'

It would have been easy to resent the word 'interference', but it seemed as pointless as lying.

'I don't think she wants me to discover the truth,' I confessed. 'As long as she remains in ignorance of Eris's fate, she can imagine that her daughter is still alive.'

Ned Rawbone nodded. 'Exactly! Then why don't you respect her wishes? Maud's the person most closely concerned, after all.'

'I hate a mystery,' I told him frankly. 'And I hate even more the notion that there's a murderer walking around free somewhere. A man who's robbed a young girl of her life.'

'Why a man?' he wanted to know. He had absent-mindedly taken the silver chalice between his hands and was twisting it round and around. The priest had gone outside to empty the basin of water and to hang his washing-cloth on a bush to dry. 'Why not a woman?'

I glanced sharply at Ned, but his gaze was concentrated on the bowl, following the rotating pattern of leaves and figures. I watched it with him for a moment or two.

'You think a woman might have killed Eris Lilywhite?' I prompted at last.

He shrugged. '*If* Eris was murdered – and I emphasize that "if" – then why not? Rosamund Bush and her mother, Dame Winifred, are both known to have uncertain tempers.'

I put out a hand and gripped the rim of the chalice to prevent it revolving further: the movement was making me dizzy. Sir Anselm reappeared and, having put away his basin and polishing rags, carried off the cup to the church, presumably to lock it in the aumbry.

'Do you think it possible, or even likely,' I asked Ned Rawbone scathingly, 'that either Mistress Bush or her daughter would have been out of doors, running around the countryside on such a night? I understand there was a terrible storm.'

Ned got to his feet. 'How do I know? How can anyone know what happened, apart from Eris and her killer? If there was a killer.'

'You can't believe that she simply ran away!'

He turned on me, almost savagely.

'Why not? Anyone who was responsible for so much wickedness and deceit might well have been shamed into removing herself elsewhere.'

I asked levelly, 'Do you really believe that Eris Lilywhite ran away?'

'What I believe in is keeping my thoughts and opinions to myself,' he responded angrily, pushing past me and almost knocking me off my stool. The priest had again returned to the kitchen and was regarding us both anxiously, aware of raised voices and the heightened tension between us. The farmer clapped him on the shoulder. 'I'll call in sometime this evening, Father, and let you have the money for the lamp oil. You say Henry Carter is travelling to Gloucester tomorrow? He can purchase however much you need and bring it back with him.'

'You mustn't mind his brusqueness,' the priest consoled me when Ned had gone, banging the outer door behind him. (Not that I was in need of consolation. I was reconciled to rubbing people up the wrong way.) 'It's possible that he's secretly afraid that Tom's guilty and doesn't want you – or anybody else, for

114

that matter – turning up evidence that might seem to confirm it.'

He bustled about, setting a pot of fish stew over his meagre fire to heat, cutting up the heel of a coarse barley loaf and bringing out of a cupboard a piece of mouldy goat's milk cheese. Obviously, unlike many of his kind, he had never mastered the art of good living. (On reflection, I felt thankful that he had not invited me to stay to supper the previous evening.)

I said little until the meal, such as it was, had been set before us on the table. The priest put a third bowl of stew on the floor for Hercules, who seemed to have no difficulty with the fact that the broth was not only lukewarm and extremely greasy, but also full of lumps of dried cod that were as tough as leather. (A very dry cod indeed was my guess, and only partially soaked before it was cooked.) In fact, having wolfed down one lot, Hercules sat up and begged for more.

'I like a dog with a healthy appetite,' Sir Anselm observed, ladling a second helping into Hercules's bowl from the pot, which had now been removed from the fire. (The stew looked even more unappetizing than it had before.) I stirred my own portion and tried to appear as though I were enjoying it.

'So,' I said at last, 'what do *you* think is the answer to Eris Lilywhite's disappearance, Father?'

'My son, your guess is as good as mine, or as anyone else's in this village.' He rose from his stool and went to draw two cups of surprisingly tasty ale from a barrel in the corner, then returned to the table and resumed eating, all without once meeting my gaze.

'You must have some theory,' I persisted, but he only shook his head, still without looking at me. Finally, however, reluctantly, he did raise his eyes to mine.

'Chapman, my earnest advice to you is to leave matters well alone. The girl has gone and the village is a better place without her. That, you may think, is not a very charitable thing to say, but I can assure you it's the truth. From the time she first began to realize that she had the sort of beauty men run mad for, Eris was trouble, playing off one young fellow against the other. No one can say for certain that she's dead; that she's been murdered. If there was proof, it might be different. It *would* be different. The murderer would have to be brought to justice. But as things are, there's nothing anyone can do about it. A Sheriff's Officer came from Gloucester shortly after Eris was reported missing to make enquiries; but although he was naturally very suspicious of Tom Rawbone, without witnesses or a body, no arrest could be made.'

'If Eris has run away, where might she have gone?' I asked.

Sir Anselm scratched his head. 'There's her great-aunt, who lives in Gloucester. But as Theresa Lilywhite was staying with her sister when Eris vanished, it's reasonable to suppose that the girl didn't go there. Moreover, subsequent investigations at the great-aunt's house proved fruitless. There are also, I understand, some distant Haycombe cousins who live near Dursley, but they are almost total strangers even to Maud. She was adamant that the girl would never have thought of them. Although, once again, I believe someone did pay them a visit, just to check, but she hadn't been near them.' The priest picked a sliver of fish from between his teeth and regarded it thoughtfully for a moment or two before swallowing it. 'But it's perfectly possible,' he went on, 'that Eris just ran away, not *to* anyone in particular, but simply to seek her fortune. To make a new life for herself. Even as we speak, she could be working as a cook-maid in the kitchens of someone's hall or castle. Or as companion to some lonely old lady.' Sir Anselm paused, presumably to consider this charming picture. Then his eyes met mine once more, and he sighed heavily as though acknowledging my right to be sceptical.

With great difficulty, I managed to get down the last spoonful of broth and pushed my bowl aside. Then I cleansed my palate with a draft of good ale.

'Father,' I said, 'let's assume for the sake of argument that Eris *was* murdered. On her way home, somewhere between Dragonswick Farm and the Lilywhite smallholding, soaked to the skin, head down against the wind and rain, she ran into . . .

someone. Someone who, perhaps, did not at first intend to kill her, but who was so infuriated by the events of that evening that he – or she – was incapable of self-control when confronted by the cause of all the trouble. Who – again just for the sake of argument – do you think that someone could have been?'

Sir Anselm breathed deeply. 'My son, I cannot say.'

I was about to deride his caution and timidity, when I hesitated. There had been something about his reply, some slight inflection in his voice, the merest emphasis on the word 'cannot', that arrested and held my attention. As if sensing my sudden suspicion, he bent down and began to make much of Hercules, who immediately jumped on to his lap and started to lick his face. I said no more, but just sat there, thinking.

The priest knew something, I was convinced of it. But what? Was it possible that the murderer had confessed his or her crime, knowing the secret to be safe if made in the sanctuary of the confessional? Had all that Sir Anselm said so far been merely a blind in order to deceive me and everyone else into thinking him as ignorant as ourselves? 'I cannot say,' he had said. Yet that slight stress on the word 'cannot' was hardly a sound enough foundation on which to build a solid theory. 'Bricks without straw, my lad,' I told myself severely, but it had no effect. My conviction that the priest possessed the answer to the mystery had taken root and refused to be easily dislodged.

He was deliberately allowing himself to be distracted by Hercules, so I leaned over, lifted the dog off his lap and dropped the animal to the floor. Hercules, incensed, ran to the kitchen door, scratching at it and barking to be let out. I ordered him, pretty sharply, to desist; so, recognizing the tone of voice, he retired under the table to sulk.

I stretched out a hand and gripped the priest's wrist.

'Father,' I said gently, 'when you say that you cannot say, does that mean you know no more than I do? Or does it mean . . . something else?'

He disengaged his arm. 'It means just that, chapman. Don't read more into the remark than is intended. Let us hope that wherever Eris Lilywhite is now, she has repented of her sins and is happy.'

There was a protracted silence, then I nodded.

'Very well . . . But I beg you to be careful, especially if you are in possession of dangerous knowledge.'

'All knowledge is dangerous,' he answered tartly, 'as Adam and Eve discovered when they ate the apple in the Garden of Eden.'

'All right,' I laughed. 'Let's change the subject . . . What do you know about the murder of two men who sank the well in Upper Brockhurst Hall?'

Sir Anselm stared at me blankly while his mind adjusted to this totally unexpected twist in the conversation. At length, however, he said, frowning, 'I've heard the story, of course. I've been priest in this village for more then twenty years.' He indulged himself with a momentary reminiscence. 'It must be all of that, I daresay. I went through the usual progression, acolyte, subdeacon, deacon before being ordained a priest, but I eventually came to Lower Brockhurst in the same year that the Earl of Warwick, who was then Keeper of the Sea, defeated the Spanish fleet off Calais, on Trinity Sunday morning. That must be over a score of years ago, wouldn't you say?'

'Probably,' I agreed. 'But as I would only have been five or six at the time, I can't be certain. Anyway,' I continued, 'you're familiar with the story?'

'No one can live here for twenty years and not be familiar with it. It's one of the legends of the place, all the more enduring because the mystery of who did it has never been resolved.' He added curiously, 'Why do you ask? It can have nothing to do with what we've been talking about. Or are you hoping to solve a 130-year-old murder as well?'

I didn't reply directly. I leaned my elbows on the table and cupped my chin in my hands. 'Do you have any thoughts on the subject?' I asked him.

The priest laughed dismissively. 'My son, I have other things to occupy my attention than a murder committed all that time ago. What is the point? Even if there were the remotest chance of solving the mystery, it's far too late. No one can be brought to justice for the crime now.' He regarded me straitly. 'What makes you ask? You can't think that it has any connection with the disappearance of Eris Lilywhite, surely?'

I grimaced. 'I must admit I'm unable to see how the two events could be linked. It's just that I have this irrational feeling – a conviction, almost – that somehow or other they are. All nonsense, of course! A hundred and thirty years is a long time.'

'A very long time,' Sir Anselm agreed.

'Where were the bodies found?' I asked. 'Do you know?'

He puckered his forehead. 'In the woods not far from the Hall, I've always been led to believe. But whether or not that tradition is correct, I wouldn't like to say with any certainty.'

'But if you're right, the men hadn't got far before being set upon. Why do you think they were killed, Father?'

'What a question! How do I know? But judging by what I've been told, robbery would *not* seem to be the answer. Not unless, that is, the robbers were disturbed by someone or something before they could empty the men's purses.'

'I suppose that is a possibility.'

But there was no point in pursuing the subject. At this distance of time, the priest could have no more notion than I, or anyone else, of the truth of the matter. So I changed the subject yet again and invited him to tell me all he knew about the Lilywhites. 'Were you the priest here when Maud Haycombe and Gilbert Lilywhite were married?'

'Most certainly. I married them. In fact, I remember when Gilbert first arrived in Lower Brockhurst from Gloucester. He came to dig a new well for the village, and never went home again. Fell in love with Maud instead.'

'Someone –' I decided it might be better not to mention Alice Tucker – 'told me that Ned Rawbone wanted to marry Mistress Maud, but was forbidden to do so by his father. Is that true?'

The priest cut himself a piece of cheese with his knife and stuffed it in his mouth, thus rendering further conversation impossible for at least a minute. Finally, he admitted thickly, 'I think there may have been some tenderness between them. On his part, at least.'

'Not on hers?'

He cleaned around his teeth with his tongue. 'Well, if there was, it obviously didn't survive Gilbert's arrival. Gilbert and Maud were wed within two months of him appearing in the village. They wasted no time once the banns were called. Neither her father nor his mother were pleased about it, but it didn't deter them. Dame Theresa, who came from Gloucester for the wedding, made her objections plain from the start. She considered her son had married beneath him. She despised the country and country people. The fact that Maud was sole heir to her father's smallholding didn't impress Theresa. She looked on farming as "grubbing a living from dirt". That's what she said. She insisted that Gilbert could make better money as a weller.'

'He didn't continue in his calling, then?'

Sir Anselm shook his head. 'It was one of old Haycombe's conditions for consenting to the marriage that Gilbert should give up his trade and help out on the smallholding.'

'And he was willing to do that?'

'Of course. He and Maud were very much in love. It was no surprise to anyone when Eris was born just under nine months later.'

I thought about this. 'Are you suggesting that Maud might have been with child before they married?' Father Anselm nodded. 'Did they ever have any more children?'

'Two boys, both of whom died young. They were sickly from birth; fragile-looking, like Gilbert. Eris was the only one with health and strength, a fine child who grew into a beautiful woman. A beauty, alas, that was to prove destructive, not only to herself but also to other people.'

We were silent for a moment, contemplating that destruction, during which time Hercules emerged from under the table and went to scratch and whine again at the kitchen door. With a sigh, I got up and let him into the hall, where I was immediately conscious of a draught from the open front door, swinging wide on its creaking hinges.

'Master Rawbone must have left it open,' I said to the priest, who had joined me, tut-tutting under his breath.

'Not Ned's fault.' He hastened to close it. 'Sometimes the latch springs after it's been shut. The wood is old and has warped. There, that's got it. Does your dog want to go out? If so, take him into the yard at the back.'

But Hercules, perverse as ever, returned to the warmth of the kitchen, his urgent desire to relieve himself evidently having evaporated at the first whiff of cold air. Sir Anselm and I followed him, resuming our places at the table.

I asked, 'How old was Eris when her father died?'

My companion poured more ale.

'Well, let me see, Gilbert died the same year the Duke of Gloucester married the Lady Anne Neville. When would that have been?'

'Seven years ago next month,' I answered promptly. I had good reason to remember the date. I had been instrumental in helping Duke Richard to find his future wife after George of Clarence had hidden her in the city of London, disguised as a cook-maid.

If the priest was surprised by the accuracy of my reply, he didn't show it.

'Then Eris would have been about ten years old,' he said. 'A bad age for any child to be left without a father, but especially one left in the care of a mother and doting grandmother. Dame Theresa came for her son's funeral and, unfortunately perhaps, never returned home. I don't think her visit was intended to be permanent, not to begin with at least, and I'm sure Maud didn't want her to stay. The two women never really got on. Maud resented, not unnaturally, her mother-in-law's belief that Gilbert had married beneath him. But they rubbed along together without any overt hostility, and if the truth be told, they must both have been lonely. Maud's father had died several years before.'

'You said that Dame Theresa was a doting grandmother. What about Mistress Lilywhite? Was she a doting mother?'

The priest sucked his teeth, no doubt searching for more scraps of food. 'I think she did try to instil some sense of discipline into Eris, but the child was too self-willed, like Dame

121

Theresa. Maud herself is a biddable woman, shy and retiring; someone who dislikes confrontation. And now,' he added, swallowing his ale, 'I've talked enough about the Lilywhites. My advice to you, chapman, is to do as Maud wants. Leave well alone. Eris is . . . has gone. William Bush and his family and the Rawbones are just beginning to pick up the shattered pieces of their lives and put them back together again.'

I made no answer for a moment, then leaned forward and once more gripped the priest's wrist.

'Sir Anselm,' I urged, 'If you know anything, *anything at all*, concerning Eris, you would do better to share it with someone.'

'You, I suppose?' he asked mockingly.

'Not necessarily, although it might not be a bad idea. But if not me, then go to the Sheriff's Officer in Gloucester. Tell him what you know.' I shook his arm. 'You may be in some danger if you don't.'

He smiled and patted my hand. 'I'm in no danger, my son. Because,' he went on hastily, 'I don't know anything. Now, let us drop the subject. Is there something else you want to ask me? Provided, of course, that it doesn't touch on the subject of the Lilywhites.'

I removed my hand from his wrist.

'Very well.' There was nothing further I could say. After all, I might have been mistaken about the extent of his knowledge, my imagination running away with me as usual. So I accepted defeat on that score and changed the subject for a third time. 'Who is it,' I wanted to know, 'who hangs the corn dollies and clooties on the trees around Upper Brockhurst?'

'My son, I've no idea and I don't enquire. Oh, you probably think it very lax of me, but the old religion still flourishes in many places throughout the western counties. It does no harm that I can see. Not, I admit, a view that would find favour with my superiors. Indeed, it would probably be regarded as heresy and lead to my being hailed before a church court without delay. But I can, I'm sure, trust you to keep my secret. And I very much doubt if I'm the only priest who takes this stand. The early Church itself was built on the marriage of Christian rites with pagan. Easter, the greatest festival of all, is celebrated to coincide with the festival of Eostra, the Norse goddess of spring. Christmas was when our forefathers welcomed back the lengthening days. The Green Man, Robin Goodfellow, the gods of the trees, they all lead men to worship. God may not be one Person, chapman. He may not even be Three in One or One in Three. He may have many faces and forms.' Sir Anselm smiled. 'There, now! I've put my life in your hands. You see how I trust you!'

But not enough, I thought, to confide in me what you know concerning Eris Lilywhite's disappearance.

Eleven

I stayed another hour with the priest, both of us talking desultorily of this and that, but with our own secret thoughts running like undercurrents in the stream of idle chatter. I can't, of course, vouch for what was going through Sir Anselm's mind, but I recall that he seemed a little abstracted, asking questions at random and barely listening to the answers. For my part, I was concerned with how much he might know and how much danger such knowledge might put him in. On the other hand, I had no proof that he knew anything at all. I had convinced myself purely on instinct that he did.

'You and your instinct!' Adela would often mock me, at the same time entwining her arms lovingly around my neck in order to rob her words of their sting. 'It's just another name for drawing your bow at a venture.'

Perhaps she was right. In this case I was afraid that she might well be.

As I downed a further draft of ale, trying unsuccessfully to banish the after-taste of Sir Anselm's fish stew, I was forced to admit that, so far, I had no firm idea as to what had happened to Eris Lilywhite, except for an unshakeable belief that she had not run away. Yet there again, there was no evidence to support this conviction apart from the general agreement concerning her character, and an equally general belief that she would never have abandoned her plan to become mistress of Dragonswick Farm. Most of the people I had spoken to were persuaded, either openly or covertly, that she had been killed. And that Tom Rawbone was her murderer.

But there were others who had been out and about that night

who had had similarly compelling reasons for wanting Eris dead. It was high time, therefore, that I questioned members of the Rawbone family besides Dame Jacquetta.

I fancy the priest was relieved when I decided it was time to take my leave, even if Hercules was not. (He had made a warm and cosy bed in the rushes beneath the table and was indignant at being disturbed.) Sir Anselm cheerfully waved us off, before returning inside and closing his door.

It was nearly noon, judging by the position of the weak and watery sun high above the rooftops. A keen wind, that had arisen while I was in the priest's house, was blowing along the village street in a whirlpool of dust and scraps of food and household rubbish. Some shreds of rag wrapped themselves around my boots and had to be disentangled before I could proceed.

But proceed where? I could hardly call at Dragonswick Farm and demand to question its occupants, even presuming any of the men were at home. The women would be there, of course. Dame Jacquetta, Petronelle and Elvina Merryman were unlikely to be abroad in the cold of a February afternoon, but I had no excuse to return. Neither Ned's wife nor the housekeeper had evinced any interest in buying from my pack, and the oldest of the three had already done so. Moreover, Jacquetta had told me all she knew – or, rather, all that she intended to tell me. (And a night's reflection could well have convinced her that she had confided far too much in a stranger.)

A glance in the direction of the mill informed me that the water-wheel was turning, and even from where I was standing, I could hear the clatter of the millstones. Lambert Miller was evidently hard at work and therefore not pursuing his courtship of the Fair Rosamund. So I turned my feet towards the Roman Sandal.

There were very few villagers in the alehouse at that time of day, but neither was there any sign of my quarry, only her father, who was busy broaching a new cask of ale. All traces of the previous night's game of Nine Men's Morris had vanished, the floor being strewn with fresh rushes and the table and

benches back in their accustomed places in the centre of the
room.

I recognized one of the two men sitting at the end of the
trestle furthest from the fire as Ned Rawbone, deep in conversation with the second man, whose more fashionably cut
clothes suggested a city dweller. And indeed, as I passed them I
heard Ned say, 'Fourteen marks the sack, not a penny less.
That's the market price for best Cotswold wool. You won't get
it cheaper anywhere. That's two weys or three hundred and
sixty-four pounds to a sack. Standard weight.'

A buyer, I guessed, from either Gloucester or Bristol, check-
ing up on what he would have to pay for wool come June and
the sheep-shearing season. I didn't doubt that Ned Rawbone
would drive a hard bargain. I saw the man called Rob Pomphrey downing a lonely cup of ale in one corner, but there was
no one else among the scatter of early afternoon drinkers whom
I knew.

I approached William Bush, tapping him on the shoulder as
he stooped over the cask and making him jump.

'Oh, it's you, chapman.' He did not sound best pleased.
'What do you want?'

'I was hoping to have a word or two with Mistress Rosamund,' I said.

'She's gone out.' He bent once more to his task. 'Someone
came with a message for her while we were having our dinner.
And it's no good asking me where she's gone.' His tone grew
peevish. 'My womenfolk never tell me anything.'

I nodded sympathetically. I knew what he meant. I was
familiar with the sudden silence that descended whenever I
entered a room where my wife and former mother-in-law were
talking, heads conspiratorially together, either planning my
future for me or 'protecting' me from things they considered
it would be better for me not to know. And I could imagine only
too well what it would be like when my daughter was also of an
age to deceive me – entirely for my own good, of course! (Fears,
I may say, that over the years have proved depressingly well
founded.)

'You don't know where she's gone, then?' I asked unnecessarily.

The landlord straightened up again with a painful jerk and pressed a hand to the small of his back.

'I've just told you . . .' he was beginning fretfully, but was interrupted by his wife, who had come into the alehouse without either of us noticing.

'She's gone to meet Tom Rawbone,' Mistress Bush announced with a worried frown. 'I had my suspicions when she refused to say who'd sent the message, so after dinner I made it my business to seek out young Billy Tyrrell, who brought it. Fortunately, the message was by word of mouth, so he knew what it said, as well as the name of the sender.'

'And what did it say?' William Bush and I demanded almost in unison.

Mistress Bush's imposing bosom swelled to even ampler proportions.

'Tom Rawbone asked Rosamund to meet him in Upper Brockhurst woods, by the Brothers' Well as soon as she could. He would wait for her there until she came. He begged her not to fail him.'

'And are you telling me she went?' William Bush was incredulous. 'But why? She hates him.'

Mistress Bush looked witheringly at her husband, or as witheringly as her fear and distress allowed.

'Of course, she doesn't hate him! She's still madly in love with him, as anyone with two eyes can see. Well, any woman,' she amended scornfully. 'I sometimes think men can't see what's in front of their noses.'

'But . . . But after the way he treated her?' The landlord, poor, simple soul, was still struggling to make sense of it all. He shook his head sadly, uttering the time-worn cry, 'I'll never understand women!'

For the second time, my heart went out to him. Fellow feeling made me pat his shoulder.

'Never mind that!' Mistress Bush exclaimed impatiently. 'You must go after her, William! I don't know how long she's been gone, but if you hurry you may be able to find her before any harm befalls her.' She added furiously, as her husband stared stupidly at her, 'For goodness' sake, man! Tom Rawbone is most probably a murderer!'

There was the thump of feet as Ned got up and strode the length of the table, his handsome face suffused with blood. Nevertheless, when he spoke it was with restraint, something I guessed to be habitual with him.

'I should prefer it, hostess, if you wouldn't accuse my brother of a crime that we don't even know has been committed. Mistress Rosamund will come to no harm with Tom. Forgive me, but I couldn't avoid overhearing your conversation.'

Mistress Bush ignored him. 'William!' she cried, and there was now an edge of hysteria to her tone. 'Go after Rosamund! Now! At once! She mustn't be left alone with that man!'

'Let me go,' I offered. 'My legs are longer than Master Bush's. I don't doubt,' I added, turning placatingly towards Ned, 'that Mistress Rosamund is perfectly safe with your brother, but in the circumstances, it might be as well to make certain.'

'Yes, yes! You go ahead, chapman!' William Bush urged. 'I'll follow. But you'll go faster than I can.'

Ned Rawbone looked displeased. 'I think you're making a mistake. I suspect your daughter won't thank you for your interference.'

I had little doubt that Ned was right. If this meeting proved to be nothing more sinister than a lovers' tryst, the Fair Rosamund would react furiously to any interruption. But with the suspicion of murder still clinging like an invisible cloak about her former lover, I, for one, was not prepared to take any chances.

As I strode uphill with Hercules, now fully awake and ready for any adventure, trotting happily at my heels, I tried to calculate how long Rosamund had already been gone. William Bush had said that she received the message while they were at dinner. It was now past noon, so that would have been nearly two hours ago. However, the landlord had given no indication that his daughter had rushed away immediately, so I presumed Rosamund must have finished her meal first. Had she then given the message some thought before making up her mind to meet Tom, as he had requested? But even if that were so, she must still have been gone an hour at the very least. Probably longer. Why hadn't I thought to quiz Winifred Bush more closely? Sometimes I acted too impulsively, was too lax with my enquiries. It's a fault I've mentioned before, and one that's dogged me all my life (even now when I'm old).

Not that the length of time Rosamund had been absent was really important. Injury and death can strike a person down in seconds, with help almost at hand. I could only pray that if any danger did threaten her, I should not be too late to prevent it.

I followed the course of the Draco, to the woods cresting the Upper Brockhurst ridge. I saw both Theresa and Maud in the distance, as I passed the Lilywhite smallholding, and, further up the slope, I could just make out Billy Tyrrell, minding his flock. But there was no other sign of life at Dragonswick Farm. To my right, the stream glinted silver in the winter sunshine, then disappeared from sight as I plunged beneath the grey, over-hanging canopy of the trees. The desolate woodland had a certain fugitive loveliness all of its own, but I was too pre-occupied with Rosamund's fate to stop and appreciate it.

Just before turning towards the now familiar path leading to the remains of Upper Brockhurst Hall, I glanced back over my shoulder into the valley below. A frieze of goblin figures, heads down, bodies hunched against the driving wind, was immedi-ately recognizable. Just beginning to ascend the pasture from the village were three men, the first of whom, striding purpose-fully ahead of the others, was undoubtedly Lambert Miller. The two behind, in dogged pursuit, had to be Ned Rawbone and William Bush.

I cursed. What, in God's name, had possessed the landlord to enlist the help of the miller? He must be aware of Lambert's feelings for his daughter and of the latter's reaction to any attempt by Tom Rawbone to worm his way back into Rosa-mund's affection. And if this were, indeed, the purpose of this meeting, then Tom stood a fair chance of receiving yet another beating at the hands of his pugnacious rival.

I called loudly and insistently, 'Mistress Rosamund! Master Rawbone!'

There was no answering cry, only the echo of my voice among the trees and the dismal cawing of rooks.

They were not at the Brothers' Well, the meeting place named in Tom's message. But that meant nothing, I told myself. It was a cold day and they had probably decided to take a walk as a means of keeping warm. But in which direction had they gone? I stared around, while Hercules, sensing my uneasiness, ceased hunting for rabbits and came to sit at my feet, staring up at me with a puzzled look on his doggy features.

I shouted again. 'Tom Rawbone! Mistress Rosamund!' But still there was no reply.

Think, I ordered myself. They were hardly likely, in that weather, to have wandered into the long grasses and under-growth that shrouded the ruins of Upper Brockhurst Hall: not unless, whispered that inexorable voice of doom at the back of my mind, Tom's intentions had been malign. But I decided to ignore this suspicion: I must assume Tom's innocence until it was proven otherwise. Therefore, the only way they were likely to have gone was along the overgrown track leading to the old, ruined village, the track I had accidentally stumbled across when I had lost my way the day before yesterday (a time that already seemed remote, so much had happened between then and now).

I moved forward along the path, and almost immediately found myself, yet again, thinking of those two men, dead for a hundred and thirty years, homeward bound in happy anticipation of seeing wives and children after a prolonged absence, only to meet Death, with his empty eye sockets and leering grin, barring their way. They haunted me, that pair, and I didn't know why; except that, for some obscure reason, I felt them to have a connection with the disappearance of Eris Lilywhite. I accepted that the feeling was unfounded, but I was unable to shake it off. And in the eerie silence all around me, I was suddenly disorientated, seemingly transported back to another place and time, unsure of where or who I was . . .

'Chapman! Fancy meeting you here!'

I was back in the present, as if pulled by an invisible thread, and saw Rosamund, walking towards me, picking her dainty way along the muddy and overgrown path. Behind her was Tom Rawbone. I breathed a sigh of relief.

'Mistress!' I said, but making no attempt to move aside as she approached. 'Master Rawbone.'

Rosamund stopped in front of me. Her pretty face, framed by the hood of her grey woollen cloak, glowed from the bite of the wind and the coldness of the air – and possibly from some other reason, too. I couldn't be certain, and there was nothing to be gleaned from Tom Rawbone's expression; but to me, he didn't have the hangdog look of a man who had been repulsed too severely.

'Are you going to let us pass?' Rosamund asked sweetly, but with just a touch of acerbity in her tone.

'In a moment,' I answered. 'But you'd do well to listen to what I have to say, first.'

Her swain – if that's indeed what he was – took a step forward to stand beside her.

'Move aside, chapman. This is no concern of yours.'

I ignored him and addressed myself to Rosamund.

'Mistress, your father and Lambert Miller are not far behind me. Your brother, also, Master Rawbone.'

'How . . . How did they know where to find us?' Rosamund stammered. 'And who invited Lambert to poke his nose in?'

I explained the circumstances as briefly as possible (although without being able to account for the miller's presence), aware that it could not be much longer before the three men caught up with us. I finished by looking pointedly at Tom's bruised and battered face. 'If you don't want yet another beating, Master, you'll take my advice and make a run for it while you can. Do you know of any other way down from this ridge?'

Just for a second, I saw his eyes flicker shiftily from side to side. But, to his credit, Tom wasn't prepared to act the coward in front of his lady, in spite of Rosamund adding her entreaties to mine.

'For mercy's sake, go!' she exclaimed, giving him a little push. 'Go on! Before they get here! You've suffered enough in the last two days. You'll be nothing but a jelly if Lambert sets about you again.'

It was, of course, the worst argument she could have used. Perhaps she knew that. Perhaps she was testing him. You can never tell with women.

'I'm not afraid of Lambert Miller!' Tom said with, I suspected, more bravado than truth. Nevertheless, he was determined to stand his ground, declining to budge when Rosamund gave him another exasperated shove. 'If you'll let us pass, chapman, we'll be on our way.'

I could see it was useless to argue with him further and stepped aside into the long grass that bordered the track. Now it was Rosamund who refused to move, her body shielding Tom's, but he simply stepped around her, skilfully avoiding her detaining hands, and walked rapidly and determinedly ahead. Rosamund ran after him, almost tripping over the hem of her cloak in her agitation. I followed with Hercules nipping in and out of all our legs and threatening to bring at least one of us down.

We reached the clearing that had been the courtyard of Upper Brockhurst Hall, and there, beside the well, Tom slowed to a halt.

'I'll wait for them here,' he said.

'For pity's sake, get in amongst the trees,' I urged him. 'A man can't swing either a stick or his fists effectively when he's hampered by trunks and branches.' I offered him my own cudgel. 'Take this! I'm assuming you know how to use it.'

'Of course, I know to use it!' He was indignant. 'But I don't want it. I've done nothing wrong, as Rosamund will testify.' She gave him an odd look, grim and white-faced. Tom went on violently, 'I'm sick and tired of defending myself against accusations that aren't true. The only thing I've been guilty of is the crass stupidity of ever believing myself in love with Eris

132

Lilywhite. But that's nobody's concern except mine and Rosamund's. It has nothing to do with Lambert Miller!'

'What has nothing to do with me?' Lambert demanded, bursting into the clearing, panting heavily and red in the face from the exertion of running uphill. He paused for a moment to get his second wind, then lifted his stick and took a swipe at Tom Rawbone, which the latter dodged easily. It would be a minute or two before the miller recovered himself sufficiently to pose any real threat.

'Stop it, Lambert! Stop it at once!' Rosamund, hands clenched, stepped between her warring swains. 'I agreed to meet Tom to listen to what he had to say. This has nothing to do with you!'

I doubt if the miller even heard her. He simply reached out and pushed her to one side as easily as if she had been a feather, before raising his cudgel again. This time, his aim was truer, but not by much, and he caught his rival a glancing blow on his left arm. Enraged by this lack of success, Lambert seized the stick with both hands and swung it straight at Tom's head. Had I not moved almost instinctively to parry the stroke, it might well have cracked his opponent's skull wide open.

With a furious roar, the miller turned on me, playing dirty and lowering his stick to strike me a wicked blow across both legs; a blow which knocked me off my feet and left me rubbing my shins in agony. He now had Tom at his mercy, but that was the last thing he intended to show. He dealt him a buffet that felled Tom, then started belabouring him about the head and body just as, by God's good grace, Ned Rawbone and William Bush arrived on the scene. They took in the situation at a glance and threw themselves at the miller – the landlord, with a bravery and agility I wouldn't have expected of him, jumping on Lambert's back, while Ned stooped and grasped his brother's assailant around the knees, tripping him up. The fact that Lambert and William Bush then toppled, with a sickening thud, on top of Tom Rawbone, in no wise detracted from Ned's resourcefulness; not, at least, in my opinion. It was the lesser of two evils.

Tom, however, was disinclined to see it that way, and dragged himself to his feet, cursing his brother and the miller in equal measure. Lambert, too, was yelling and swearing as he tried vainly to free himself from the restraining clutches of William Bush. I had by now recovered sufficiently to assist by sitting firmly on the miller's chest while Ned straddled his feet. As for Rosamund, she was standing a little apart, looking down her nose and surveying us all as if we were a bad smell that had just come to her attention. Then, in scathing accents, she uttered the one word 'Men!' before stomping off through the trees, obviously washing her hands of the lot of us. A very sensible young woman.

With her departure, we picked ourselves up and sorted ourselves out. William Bush hurried after his daughter, anxiously calling her name. The two protagonists, with no one to impress, contented themselves with glaring and snarling at one another.

'Leave Mistress Rosamund alone in future,' Lambert warned Tom between clenched teeth. 'Or you'll get more of the same.'

Tom rubbed at various batches of new bruises – I could guess at them, even if I couldn't see them – and glared at his rival for a moment or two without responding. Then he said in a low tone, charged with menace, 'You'll be sorry for this, Miller. It's the second time in as many days that you've attacked me. I'll get my own back, just you see if I don't!'

Lambert sneered. 'Do you think I'm afraid of you and your threats? Just remember what I've told you. Leave Rosamund alone, if you value your hide. Next time, you might not have your bodyguard with you.'

He didn't wait for Tom's reply, but set off after Rosamund and her father, hoping, I supposed, to catch them up. But if he was expecting the lady's thanks for rescuing her, I felt sure he was doomed to disappointment.

I whistled for Hercules, who had been cowering in the long grass during the recent pleasantries, and now came crawling warily out from his hiding place, sizing up the situation before running to greet me, wagging his stump of a tail. I picked him up and looked into his eyes.

'Where were you when I needed you?' I reproached him. 'You could have sunk your teeth into the miller for me again.' But he wasn't a fool, that dog: he knew when the odds were stacked against him.

A sudden flurry of movement, seen out of the corner of one eye, made me turn, just in time to help Ned Rawbone catch his brother's sagging form. Three beatings in three days had finally proved too much for Tom and, for a few seconds, he had almost lost consciousness.

He recovered a little, but it was plain that he would need assistance to get home. He was leaning heavily on Ned, who had one arm around his brother's waist and the other supporting Tom's left elbow. They were strong men, these Rawbones, and it never really occurred to me that Ned couldn't manage on his own, even on the difficult downhill slope to Dragonswick Farm. But I saw an opportunity that I could not afford to miss. I put a steadying hand beneath Tom's other elbow.

'Let me help,' I offered. 'He may pass out again and he's no light weight.'

Somewhat to my surprise, for I had anticipated opposition, the elder Rawbone nodded.

'Very well,' Ned agreed. I judged him to be a naturally taciturn man, and so was surprised, after we had gone a hundred yards or so along the path, when he burst into a low-voiced tirade against his brother. 'The boy's a bloody fool! He's made an ass of himself once over Eris Lilywhite, now he's making a bigger fool of himself trying to win back Rosamund Bush. And threatening Lambert Miller like that! In front of witnesses, too!'

'Is he likely to do what he threatened?' I asked, taking my cue from the elder Rawbone; ignoring the semi-conscious figure between us and talking over Tom's head. 'I should have thought he'd had enough punishment these past three days.'

'Oh, he's quite capable!' Ned snorted disgustedly. 'He's been a hothead all his life. Father and I will just have to keep a close watch on him, that's all.'

He lapsed into silence, which lasted until we finally arrived at the farm. As I released my share of the burden, I was afraid that that might be the end of it; that I would be dismissed with a curt nod of thanks. But perhaps something in the way I stooped to rub my bruised shins, where Lambert had hit me, and also in the way I shivered and huddled into my cloak, convinced Ned that I was in need of refreshment.

'You'd better come inside,' he said grudgingly. 'You look as though you could do with a cup of ale or a mazer of wine.'

I didn't wait for a second invitation.

Twelve

Not for Ned Rawbone the servants' entrance and the kitchen quarters. Supporting Tom between us, we walked round to the front of the house and went in by the door to the great hall, where our appearance was met with a flurry of women's skirts and an outpouring of feminine concern.

'Tom! What's happened? Are you badly hurt?' That was Petronelle.

'Stupid boy! You haven't been in yet another fight, have you? Sweet heaven! What a fool!' But Dame Jacquetta's anxious looks belied the harshness of her words. 'Sit in my chair by the fire.'

The housekeeper said nothing, but tut-tutted loudly and hurried away to the sideboard to pour a mazer of wine.

Her presence in the hall was explained as soon as I saw that Nathaniel Rawbone was seated in the chair facing his sister's, on the opposite side of the hearth. He had removed his shoes and hose, and a bowl of water and a bottle of salve lay on a footstool alongside him. Elvina Merryman was evidently in the process of bathing and anointing his badly chilblained feet.

As Ned and I tenderly lowered Tom into Dame Jacquetta's abandoned armchair, Nathaniel took one look at his younger son and let out a roar.

'You quarrelsome young idiot! Who have you been laying into this time, eh? Answer me this minute, sir!'

'Leave him be, Father,' Ned advised quietly. 'He's taken enough punishment these last three days, without you yelling at him. And he wasn't laying into anybody, as Master Chapman here will confirm. Lambert Miller set about Tom.'

The housekeeper came back with a tray on which reposed three beakers of wine, handing one to each of the Rawbone brothers and one to me. I savoured mine slowly, hoping that no one would realize that it was far too fine a vintage to be wasted on an itinerant pedlar. But they were all too preoccupied to give it a moment's thought, the women fussing over Tom, and Nathaniel listening with a scowling countenance to Ned's account of the day's events as far as he knew them.

While Ned was speaking, the twins entered through the front door, their young faces healthily aglow from the cold and the wind, shedding their good frieze cloaks for their mother to pick up and tidy away, rubbing their hands and shouldering their way to the fire. They would have plunged immediately into an account of their afternoon's activities, but were hushed by the simple expedient of their grandfather striking them across the buttocks with the stick he kept propped against his chair.

'Silence!' he yelled. 'Your father's talking!'

Hercules crouched, shivering, between my feet. I wondered if Nathaniel ever spoke in a moderate tone of voice.

While Ned finished his story, I took stock of the eldest and the two youngest members of the Rawbone family. The latter, Jocelyn and Christopher, were pretty much what I imagined fourteen-year-old boys to be all over the world, in any age and time: self-centred, self-absorbed, loutish young puppies, constantly on the lookout – at least, if they followed my example – for the chance to bed a girl. Any girl, anywhere; but not as yet absolutely sure what to do about it if and when the opportunity offered. (But, of course, the girls would know. They always did.) They were big, handsome lads, more like their uncle in appearance and manner than their father. And there seemed to be nothing of the whey-faced Petronelle in either of them until I looked more closely, when I could see that they had her eyes; eyes of a very much paler blue than the intense colour of their grandfather's.

Nathaniel, himself, in spite of his fifty-nine years, was still of an upright, broad-shouldered physique, as I had noted in church the previous morning. I could see that Eris Lilywhite might well have been attracted to him, quite apart from the lure of his money and the status of being mistress of Dragonswick Farm. She could have found his high-handed, autocratic ways something of a thrill after Tom's slavering devotion. But what had been Nathaniel's feelings for Eris? Had he truly been fond of her or had he simply seen her as a way to demonstrate to his family that he was still the master? That he could make them all dance to his piping at any time he chose? More importantly, what had he felt when Eris disappeared?

'What are you staring at, chapman?' His voice cut across my wandering thoughts, making me jump.

I realized that Ned had finished speaking and that everyone was looking at me.

'I-I'm sorry,' I stammered. 'I wasn't meaning to be rude.'

Nathaniel snorted and turned back to Tom, first signalling impatiently to Elvina Merryman that she should continue bathing his feet.

'You randy young fool!' he exclaimed bitterly to his younger son. 'Leave Rosamund Bush alone. You won't do yourself any good. She'll string you along for a while, just for the pleasure of knowing she has the upper hand again, and to annoy that great hunk, Lambert Miller. But you won't win her back. Not now. Not ever. So don't you think it! Use your common sense, boy!'

I wasn't so sure that he was right, but felt obliged to hold my tongue. It was none of my affair. Besides, I was too busy wondering how I could have a private word with those two budding young bravos, the Rawbone twins. I suspected that they might have a productive line in indiscreet chatter if only I could get them on their own.

For once, fate played into my hands. Petronelle suggested to her husband that they take Tom, who still looked extremely green about the gills, upstairs to lie down. Ned agreed and she had to push past her sons in order to reach her brother-in-law's side. The contact obviously reminded her of something she wished to say.

139

'You two!' she ordered; and I could see that for all her timid appearance, there was a virago lurking somewhere underneath, just waiting to be let loose. 'Out to the saw-pit. We need more logs, and Jack Sawyer sent word by Billy Tyrrell that he and his son wouldn't be able to get as far as Dragonswick today. So off you go.'

The twins would probably have argued about it if their grandfather had not been present. They each sent him a side-long glance and grumbled under their breath; but they were palpably in awe of the old man and did not dare risk his displeasure.

'Let me help,' I offered, picking up my cloak which I had shed shortly after entering the house. 'Two to work the saw, one to stack the logs. It will be quicker.'

I saw Ned glance at me suspiciously, as he and his wife hoisted Tom to his feet. But apart from the twins, who greeted my offer with a surly gratitude, no one made any comment. Dame Jacquetta was too concerned with resuming her seat by the fire, while the housekeeper was engrossed in her task of treating Nathaniel's chilblains. And the elder Rawbone was having too much fun nagging Elvina, and grumbling about her clumsiness, to worry his head over any ulterior motive I might have.

I followed Christopher and Jocelyn across the yard, where the household animals were penned, to the saw-pit on the other side of a wattle fence. Here, a pile of fair-sized branches were stacked, waiting to be sawn into smaller pieces by the local sawyer and added to the dwindling mound of logs ready for use indoors.

We found the family saw, a blade of fearsome proportions, in a lean-to shack that also housed a long- and a short-handled pick, together with other implements. I took off my cloak and volunteered to work in the pit, holding the bottom end of the saw, while Jocelyn bestrode the planks above me, grasping its handle. That left Christopher the task of dragging the branches into position across the saw-pit, removing the cut pieces and shifting the branch forward as required.

140

As I had anticipated, a little of such back-breaking labour went a long way as far as the twins were concerned. After we had sawn up three branches, they suggested, as one man, that we repair to the kitchen for refreshment.

'No one'll be there except Ruth,' Jocelyn said. 'And she won't snitch on us. Mother will think we're still working out here. Coming, chapman?'

I certainly wasn't going to argue, and picking up Hercules, who had been patiently watching us from a safe distance, guarding my cloak and cudgel, I followed the twins back the way we had come, through the rear door and into the warmth of the kitchen.

Ruth was busy cutting up winter vegetables – leek and water parsnip and turnip – and throwing them into a pot of boiling water, bubbling over the fire. She took no more notice of us than the twins did of her. I nodded and smiled, but elicited no response.

Christopher disappeared, returning after a few minutes with a leather bottle and three wooden beakers, which he placed on the floor near the hearth. We seated ourselves on the rush-covered flagstones and held our hands to the flames, letting our numbed fingers thaw out before toasting each other on a job well done (as well as we intended to do it, anyhow). Hercules settled down beside me with a satisfied grunt and was soon asleep and snoring.

I decided there was no point in beating about the bush, or letting the twins seize the initiative in the choice of conversation. So I asked, straight out, 'Do you remember what happened the evening that Eris Lilywhite disappeared?'

The question took them by surprise and Jocelyn choked into his beaker. Christopher just stared at me as though I'd enquired about the Great Cham of Tartary.

'Listen,' I said patiently. 'Dame Theresa Lilywhite wants me to find out, if I can, what has happened to her granddaughter. That's natural enough, you must agree!' Even these unfeeling young brutes could surely understand that. 'Wouldn't you want to know what had become of someone you love?'

Christopher scratched his head. 'I s'pose,' he conceded eventually.

Jocelyn lowered his beaker, having recovered his breath, and eyed me narrowly. He had a less open expression than his twin. I felt that of the two, he would be better at concealing facts he thought I didn't need to know. But on the surface, he seemed willing enough to humour me.

'What do you want us to tell you?' he asked.

'Suppose you begin by describing what you both felt about Eris. After all, she was nearer to you two in age than to any other member of your family.'

'She was all right,' said Christopher. 'But she was more fun when she was younger. We used to play together when we were children. She'd come birds' nesting with us in Upper Brockhurst woods. She could climb a tree as well as we could. Better, in fact. And kick a ball or hit a shuttlecock. And she could whip a top with the best of us. She was bossy, mind you. I suppose because she was that bit older than we were.'

'You were close, then?' I suggested.

Christopher pursed his lips. 'Maybe. People who didn't know us very well – strangers to the village – used to think we were brothers and sister. But then she grew up, and men started noticing her and telling her how pretty she was, so she didn't have time for Josh and me any more. By the time she came to work at Dragonswick, a year ago, she was behaving like she was the Queen of Sheba.'

His twin said grudgingly, 'Be fair, Chris! She had cause. She was beautiful.'

'Oh, I know you thought so.' Christopher's tone was suddenly spiteful. 'I saw you trying to kiss her sometimes when you believed no one was looking. She wouldn't have anything to do with you, though, would she? Called you a silly little boy once. I heard her, so there's no point denying it.'

Jocelyn flushed painfully. 'The only reason she wouldn't have anything to do with me was because she was a mercenary little wretch who had set her sights on Uncle Tom. And then on Grandfather.'

Christopher laughed and his brother looked murderous. I hurriedly intervened before there was a major falling out between the pair of them.

'I know all this. What I want you to tell me, if you can remember, is about the night she disappeared. What happened after your Uncle Tom arrived home that evening and after your grandfather announced that he was going to marry Eris?'

'You mean after Uncle Tom tried to murder them both?' Christopher scratched his chin, ignoring a mumbled protest from his brother. 'Well, Uncle Tom rushed out of the house without his cloak or anything. It was a terrible night, pouring with rain. And then Mother started shouting at Eris to go home. She wouldn't stop. It was like she was hysterical. Father couldn't go to her because he was attending to Grandfather, but he kept telling her to be quiet. I think Great-Aunt Jacquetta managed to calm her down after a while.'

'But then Great-Aunt rounded on Eris.' Jocelyn had evidently overcome his scruples and decided to join in. 'She hated Eris because Eris had found out that her real name was Joan and not Jacquetta, and always insisted on calling her by it. And the way she used to say "Dame Joan" made it sound like an insult.' He shrugged. 'Silly, really! But women seem to set a lot of store by such things.'

I concealed a smile at his weary-man-of-the-world air, and asked, 'What happened next?'

They thought about this. 'I believe Father went out to look for Uncle Tom,' Jocelyn decided, looking at his brother for confirmation. His twin nodded.

'That's right.' Christopher rubbed his chin again, where his former scratching had made a pimple bleed. 'But he couldn't find him, and it was too stormy to stay out for long. Then Mother attacked Eris. Physically, I mean. Mistress Merryman and Great-Aunt Jacquetta pretended to hold her back, but I don't think either of them could have been trying very hard because Mother managed to claw Eris's cheek open with her nails. That's when Eris said she was going home and left . . . We

143

never saw her again,' he added, regarding me with his direct, ingenuous, boyish gaze.

It was impossible to tell if he were speaking the truth or not. I turned to Jocelyn.

'Your grandfather was all for going after her, so I've been told. But your father wouldn't let him and went instead.'

Jocelyn nodded. 'Yes. Father was gone about an hour that time . . .'

'Longer,' his brother put in.

'Possibly. He'd called on Maud Lilywhite to tell her what had happened, and waited to see if Eris came back. But she hadn't returned when he left. Grandfather was beside himself. Said Father hadn't done enough to find Eris. But Father just grabbed hold of Mother and they went to bed. So then Grandfather said he was going out to search for her. Great-Aunt and Mistress Merryman pleaded with him not to go, but he wouldn't listen to them. Wouldn't listen to us, either. So we went with him. There was nothing else we could do.'

'Couldn't let him go alone,' Christopher confirmed. He shivered. 'Holy Virgin! It was a terrible night. Pitch black and blowing a gale. The rain doused the lanterns and we got separated in the dark.'

'What did you do?' I asked, turning my head enquiringly from one to the other.

There was a moment's hesitation on both their parts. At least, it seemed so to me.

Jocelyn was the first to answer. 'Oh, I stumbled around a bit, then decided it was a fool's errand and went home. I didn't feel so guilty when I discovered that Chris and Grandfather had returned before me.'

'Go on,' I urged, when neither of them seemed inclined to continue.

'That's all,' Jocelyn said.

His brother agreed. 'Then Josh and I went to bed. I think everyone did. There was nothing else that could be done that night. Nothing until morning.'

I jogged their memories. 'Maud Lilywhite told me that she

came up to the farm later, when Eris still hadn't come home, and roused the household. Dame Jacquetta confirmed her story. Didn't her knocking wake you?'

'Once we're asleep, even the Last Trump wouldn't wake us,' Jocelyn announced proudly. 'That's what Mother always says.'

'That's right.' Christopher finished the wine in his beaker and up-ended the bottle to drain the dregs. 'We didn't know anything about it until we got up next morning. Father came in just as we were sitting down to breakfast, soaking wet and absolutely filthy, plastered with mud and muck. He was exhausted. He'd been searching all night. Mother and Mistress Merryman heated water and filled the bathtub, here, in the kitchen, and scented it with herbs to ease his aches and pains. Afterwards, Mother wanted him to go to bed to get some rest; but he wouldn't. He went off out again, down to the village to tell people what had happened and raise a posse to search the district. They hunted for days. Weeks.' Christopher brought his headlong narrative to an abrupt halt, then shrugged. 'But they never found her.' He gave a callous laugh.

There was something shocking in his lack of concern, especially in one so young. But then, of course, the young are more honest, less hypocritical, than their elders. He knew very well that Eris's disappearance, and probable death, had been a blessing for himself, his brother and his parents (and possibly for others). He wasn't going to pretend to a grief he didn't feel.

I allowed the silence to stretch between us for as long as one might count to thirty. Then I enquired, 'What do you two think happened to Eris?'

They both stared at me as if I had asked them if they really believed the moon was made of green cheese; then they glanced fleetingly at one another. Finally, Christopher shrugged again and said, 'Dunno. Never thought about it.'

'Oh, come! You must have done,' I protested. 'It was a puzzle that was occupying everyone's waking thoughts for weeks.'

'Not mine,' Christopher replied with devastating simplicity. 'She'd gone. That was good enough for me.'

I decided he was telling the truth. Christopher Rawbone had

an uncomplicated philosophy of life. *His* needs, *his* desires were all that mattered. He was never going to waste time entering into the feelings of others.

I looked at his twin. There was nothing simple about this one, I decided.

'Do you think your Uncle Tom murdered Eris Lilywhite?' I asked without preamble.

Jocelyn was shocked by the directness of the question. They both were, as I had intended them to be. But I had defeated my own object: I had frightened them into circumspection. Mumbling some sort of half-hearted denial, Jocelyn scrambled to his feet, followed immediately by his brother.

'Thanks for your help with the sawing,' he said ungraciously. 'Come on, Chris! Everyone'll be wondering where we are.'

They slouched out of the kitchen, banging the door behind them. The empty bottle and beakers were left where they were, on the floor. With a sigh, Ruth came across and picked them up, carrying them over to the table.

I got up, stretching and yawning, and stood with my back to the fire, enjoying the warmth. Hercules raised his head from his paws enquiringly, but, deciding that I was not yet ready to move, lowered it again and once more closed his eyes. I could hear the vegetables simmering in the pot behind me, and realized that while I had been talking to the twins, Ruth had finished her chores and was now snatching five minutes well-deserved rest, seated on an old, three-legged stool. She gave me the slow, sad smile of someone who was overworked and tired to her very bones. I could almost feel the ache in her weary limbs.

I glanced around for my cloak and cudgel. 'I must be going,' I said.

'I heard what you and the twins were talking about,' she remarked abruptly. 'I couldn't help it.'

I paused. 'No, I don't suppose you could.' I regarded her thoughtfully. 'Ruth, where were you on the night of the great storm? The night Eris vanished.'

I wondered if she might resent being questioned, but she

seemed pleased, rather than otherwise, by my interest. She leaned forward, clasping her hands between her knees.

'In the early part of the evening, I was helping Eris to serve the Master's birthday feast. The family was late eating, because Master had waited for Master Tom to arrive, but he hadn't turned up. The old man was furious. Called Tom all the names he could lay his tongue to.'

'What was Eris like at this time?' I asked. 'Was she excited? Nervous? Upset?'

Ruth considered this, swinging her feet, which failed to touch the ground by some three inches.

'I don't remember that she was like anything. Just her normal self, handing the dishes around, filling wine cups, doing whatever Mistress Merryman told her to.' I had a sudden vision of this beautiful sixteen-year-old girl, composed, self-possessed, efficiently carrying out her orders, waiting for the moment when Nathaniel would make his earth-shattering announcement. Ruth went on, 'She was always like that when the family was all together.' Her voice grew more vindictive. 'But I'd seen her, kissing and cuddling in corners with Master Tom and young Jocelyn. Mind, I never caught her with the Master. I don't know when that went on.'

'No,' I agreed. 'Nor does anyone else. They were obviously very discreet.' She made no reply, so I continued, 'You must have been present when Master Tom returned. You witnessed the terrible row between him and his father.'

'I saw and heard it all, yes.' She giggled nervously. 'I thought someone was going to get killed. I thought Master Tom was going to murder one or the other of 'em. And Mistress Petronelle was screaming so loud I thought she'd have a fit. "Go home!" she kept yelling at Eris, and calling her a slut and a whore and anything else she could think of. It was awful! She frightened me as much as the men did. Then, later on, like the twins were telling you just now, she went for Eris and laid her cheek open with her nails. That's when I decided I was going to bed. I'd leave the dirty dishes and wash them in the morning.'

'Do you sleep in the kitchen?' I asked, knowing this to be the lot of the majority of kitchen maids.

To my surprise, she shook her head.

'No, in Dame Jacquetta's bedchamber. I've a truckle bed under the window. She doesn't like sleeping alone because sometimes she gets nightmares. Says she always has, since she was a girl. She likes someone to be there when she wakes up. She's never married. Never found anyone round here good enough for her, I reckon. Thinks a lot of herself, does Dame Jacquetta.'

Which, of course, was why she could never stomach the idea of being just plain Joan; why she adopted the name of a duchess. And it was also why she would never have been able to tolerate the idea of her brother or nephew marrying Eris Lilywhite.

'When you went to bed, did you go straight to sleep?' I asked.

Once again, she shook her head. 'No. I was too upset. And although I latched the bedchamber door, I could still hear them shouting and shrieking at one another downstairs. The noise was faint, mind you, but I could still hear 'em.' She swung her feet some more. 'I saw Eris leave the house,' she said at last.

'You saw her leave the house?' I asked, my pulses beginning to race. 'How . . . How did that happen?'

Ruth looked surprised. 'Dame Jacquetta's bedchamber window looks out over the front yard. I felt a bit queer, so I opened the shutters to get some air. Not much, mind you. It was blowing and raining too hard to open them very wide. Only a crack. But it was just then that I saw Eris run out. She was struggling to get her cloak on, but the wind almost tore it out of her hands.'

'You're sure it was Eris?'

'Of course I'm sure. I could see her in the light from the open doorway, before someone slammed it shut.'

'Was there any sign of anyone else?' I pressed her. 'Tom Rawbone, for example?'

Ruth shook her head. 'No. Not that I could tell. But it was raining too hard to see much beyond the front paling. Once Eris

was through the gate, I lost sight of her pretty quickly. The
storm swallowed her up once she started to run.'

'But in which direction was she running?' I gripped one of
Ruth's hands and squeezed it. 'You must have been able to get
some idea. Downhill or up?'

She considered this, wiping her nose absent-mindedly on the
back of her free hand.

'Well?' I urged. 'Which was it?'

I was afraid she was going to claim that she couldn't
remember, but after a moment, she announced triumphantly,
'She went downhill . . . Yes, I'm almost certain she did, because
I thought to myself at the time that she'd taken Dame Petronelle's advice, after all, and gone home.'

Thirteen

I was dreaming.

I knew that I was dreaming in the way that you do when you are very close to consciousness, but not yet quite fully awake. I was dancing with my two elder children as we had danced last August, through the streets of Bristol, at the end of the Lammas Feast. We were celebrating the safe bringing-in of the harvest, the cutting of the ripened corn. Adela was nearby with Adam, not as he was then, but the dark, determined seven-month-old that he had since become.

Abruptly, as things happen in dreams, the crowds and my family vanished and I was standing alone by the well in Upper Brockhurst woods, holding a silver cup, twisting it between my hands. The day was dark and overcast, but suddenly a weak gleam of sunshine pierced the canopy of trees to strike the rim, and I could see that the figures carved around the bowl were moving. Little boys with tails and horns and goats' legs twisted in and out of a maze of trailing vine leaves and olive branches, picking the silver fruit. From somewhere behind me, Adela's voice called, 'She went home . . . home . . . home . . . You promised to come home . . .'

The scene shifted yet again. I was back in the alehouse, moving with the other players around the Nine Men's Morris board. Someone – I couldn't see who – was saying, 'Line up the three morrells and then you'll know who killed Eris Lilywhite. Line up the three morrells . . .'

I woke, sweat pouring down my naked body, just as something heavy landed on my chest. For one brief moment I thought I was in my own bed, enduring one of the daily, early morning assaults of Nicholas and Elizabeth that were fast turning me into the most flat-chested man in Bristol. Then realization dawned that the weight belonged to Hercules, and that I was lying supine on a narrow pallet in Maud Lilywhite's cottage, as I had done for the past three nights. I had just decided that it must be almost daybreak, when I heard a cock crow, but there were as yet no sounds of stirring from behind the linen curtain. Theresa was snoring gently.

I freed an arm from beneath the blankets and stroked Hercules's head. He returned my greeting by enthusiastically licking my face and thumping his stubby tail, then settled down until such time as I should rouse myself. I continued to lie still, mulling over my dream and thinking about my promise to Adela that I would be home by the feast of Saint Patrick.

Tomorrow was the last day of February, and if I was to redeem my promise, I should be setting out almost at once. At this time of year, there was no reliance to be placed on the offer of some kind-hearted carter to give me a ride; at least, not for any great distance. It would be a few weeks yet before the improving weather lured people into making lengthier journeys. And if my legs were to carry me home, I should leave Lower Brockhurst today. This morning.

That, of course, would mean abandoning my search for the truth about Eris Lilywhite, and I hated being defeated: unsolved mysteries were anathema to me. But even more than that, I hated breaking my word to Adela. If she had been the sort of wife whose reproaches took the form of beating me over the head with a skillet, or refusing me my conjugal rights in bed, I could have dealt with the situation. I should have asserted my manly authority as head of the household, ranted and postured a bit and generally pranced around like a cock on his dunghill. But I knew very well that, whenever I turned up, Adela would greet me with her customary warmth, listen without comment to my excuses – and enjoy watching me squirm with guilt.

Just thinking about her, picturing that little half-smile that played around the corners of her mouth, remembering the occasional sardonic gleam in her beautiful brown eyes, recalling the feel of her soft body curled up against mine, was having the most embarrassingly physical effect upon me; embarrassing, that is, if either of the Mistress Lilywhites made any sudden appearance, wanting me to get up so that she could stow away my bed. Resolutely, I switched my thoughts back to Eris's disappearance and the dream from which I had awoken ten minutes earlier.

What had it been about? Something to do with a silver cup with satyrs dancing among vine leaves and olive branches . . . It made no sense at present, but perhaps it would later. I sighed and tried going back to sleep. I had, however, barely lost consciousness before I caught the low murmur of Theresa's voice, followed by Maud's. Immediately I was wide awake and, heaving Hercules off my chest, swung myself out of bed and reached for my hose and shirt, pulling both garments on with expert rapidity. By the time Theresa and Maud appeared from behind the curtain, I had tied my points and was fingering my unshaven chin.

An hour later, having washed and shaved, cleaned my teeth with willow bark and combed my hair, finished dressing and taken Hercules for a trot around the yard – keeping him well away from the geese, to whom he continued to take great exception – I sat down to breakfast. This morning, alas, it was oatmeal and dried herrings yet again (not a favourite meal with me, I'm afraid – I like something more substantial).

'Now!' Theresa said abruptly, putting down her spoon. 'Tell us again what you told us yesterday evening. You were too tired then to talk much sense. First, what did you learn from Sir Anselm?'

'Not a great deal,' I hedged, not wanting to confess that I suspected the priest of knowing more than he had admitted to. 'As I said, I learned more from the Rawbone twins and their little kitchen maid, Ruth.'

'Ah, yes.' Theresa resumed eating. 'So how did you come to be at Dragonswick Farm? Something to do with Rosamund Bush meeting Tom Rawbone, wasn't it? You'd better start again and explain what followed.'

Patiently, I went over the events of the previous day, aware that my fatigue had been so great last evening that I might possibly have been less than coherent. But I suspected the truth to be that Theresa enjoyed any story that redounded to the discredit of the Rawbone family and wanted to hear it for a second time.

'The twins seem to have been good friends with your daughter when they were young,' I remarked, finishing my account and turning to Maud.

'They liked one another well enough when they were children,' she conceded. 'But they grew apart in later years.'

'That was because you discouraged the friendship,' Theresa cut in disapprovingly. 'Some stupid notion of Eris not being good enough for the Rawbones. Laughable, considering what followed.'

'You know nothing about it, Mother-in-law,' Maud rebuked her sharply. 'You weren't here when Eris was small.'

'I've lived with you since Gilbert died,' Theresa retorted. 'That's almost seven years. Eris was ten, still young enough to be sneaking off with Chris and Josh Rawbone whenever she thought she could get away with it. That is, without you reprimanding her and confining her to the cottage.'

'She was getting too hoydenish,' Maud replied with heightened colour. 'It was time she learned a woman's skills and did her share around the house, especially with Gilbert gone.'

Theresa looked sceptical, but let the matter drop. She rapped my hand with the back of her spoon, to ensure my attention.

'You made some comment about the Rawbones' kitchen maid. That she'd seen Eris set off in this direction the night my granddaughter vanished. In the direction of home, was what you said.'

Maud snorted. 'On such a night, no one could have seen which way Eris went once she was outside the Dragonswick pale.'

'I think that's probably true,' I admitted. 'Indeed, when I pressed her, Ruth owned that she would be unable to swear on oath that your daughter had set off for home. Nevertheless, it was her impression that Eris was heading this way.'

'Well, she didn't arrive,' Maud said shortly, and began gathering the dirty bowls and spoons together. I thought I saw her blink back tears.

'So, what next?' asked Theresa, folding her arms on the table and peering at me intently. 'What do you propose to do now?'

Her attitude that I was entirely responsible for finding out what had become of Eris irritated me.

'It's high time that I returned to Bristol,' I answered. 'If I'm to keep my word to my wife to be home by the feast of Saint Patrick, I should leave here today.'

'You can't do that!' Theresa gasped. 'You promised!'

Before I could speak, Maud sprang to my defence.

'Master Chapman promised nothing, Mother, other than to do his best. Which he's done. Like the rest of us, he knows that nothing can ever be discovered now. Thank you for all you've tried to do, sir, but you must get back to your wife, I can see that. We shall, of course, be sorry to lose your company, but we understand.'

I guessed that Maud Lilywhite would welcome my going. She had never wanted me to investigate Eris's disappearance in the first place. She was happier in her ignorance. But my decision did not please Theresa.

'You promised,' she repeated.

'I promised to do what I could in the few days I felt I could allow myself. That was all. My word to my wife must come first.'

'Of course,' Maud nodded.

Someone banged loudly on the cottage door, and a female voice called, 'Maud! Maud Lilywhite! Are you in there? Theresa!'

Without waiting for a reply, the visitor lifted the latch and walked in – a round-faced woman with a coarse woollen cloak flung hastily and somewhat askew over her everyday homespun attire, whose plump features I vaguely recalled having seen in church on Thursday morning. She was pink-cheeked and panting.

'My good soul, whatever is it?' Theresa asked, guiding her to a stool and pouring her some ale from the jug on the table. 'Anne, my dear, calm yourself. What's the matter?'

The other woman gulped down the ale before gasping, 'Such terrible doings . . . Down in the village . . . Came to tell you.'

'Tell us what?' Maud demanded, exasperated by the delay. 'What doings in the village? What's happened?' She muttered for my benefit, 'Goody Venables. Wife of the blacksmith.'

Mistress Venables nodded in confirmation and made a determined effort to impart her news.

'Lambert Miller . . . Someone broke into the millhouse during the night and tried to kill him. Beat him half to death with an iron bar.'

'Who? Who was it? Who did it?' I asked, the Mistress Lilywhites being temporarily bereft of words.

The blacksmith's wife shook her head. 'Lambert couldn't see. It was dark.'

'But he would have some idea, surely . . . Is he incapable of speech?'

'Oh, no! Far from it. His mother says he's cursing and swearing fit to bring the roof down. He's blaming Tom Rawbone, although as far as I can gather he's no shred of proof. According to Goody Miller's story, the man who attacked him had his hood on back to front, covering his face, with slits torn for his eyes.'

Maud's hand crept up to her mouth.

'Tom did take a beating from Lambert Miller yesterday. Ask Master Chapman, here. He witnessed it. So did Landlord Bush and Ned. Perhaps Tom was getting his own back.'

This was obviously news to Goody Venables, who struggled gamely to her feet, in spite of her former state of collapse, and made for the door.

'I must get home,' she said, 'and see what's happening. I thought you'd want to know.'

She was gone to spread her newly acquired knowledge around the village. I glanced reproachfully at Maud, then admitted to myself that her lack of caution was no great matter.

William Bush and Lambert would be making everyone free of the information at some time or another.

Maud unhooked her cloak from its peg beside the door. 'I must go and warn Ned,' she said.

'Heaven knows why!' her mother-in-law exclaimed resentfully. 'We owe the Rawbones nothing. Nothing! That wastrel, Tom, most probably murdered your daughter. Now he's half-killed Lambert Miller. Don't be such a fool, Maud!'

'Ned has always been my friend,' the younger woman answered quietly. 'The rest of them can rot in Hades for all I care, but I won't have Ned suffer because of his family.'

As she left the cottage, Theresa beat her hands impotently against her sides.

'What can you do with her? The truth is,' she went on, quietening down a little, 'that Maud has always felt guilty because she fell in love with my Gilbert and refused to marry Ned Rawbone. He wanted to marry her, you know.'

'So I was told. But didn't his father object?'

'Probably. But it was of no consequence in the end. Maud knew a better bargain when she saw one.' Theresa put water to heat over the fire, giving me a shrewd glance as she did so. 'If you're leaving us, chapman, you'd better get started while the day's still young.'

I hesitated, then laughed and gave in. 'Perhaps I'll stay a little longer, after all. I'll go down to the village and have a word, if I can, with Lambert Miller.'

I was not the only one with this idea. There was a crowd of villagers gathered around the millhouse, all hoping to visit the invalid, and little knots of people the length of the village street, talking earnestly and gesticulating violently in a way that boded no good for the miller's attacker. Lambert was popular in his loud, rather bombastic fashion, and there was no intention of allowing his assailant to go unpunished. There was also an undercurrent of menace which made the hairs lift on the nape of my neck, and I heard the name of Tom Rawbone muttered more than once as I pushed my way through the mêlée. I banged loudly on the mill door, without much hope of being invited inside by Mistress Miller.

It was, however, not Lambert's mother, but Winifred Bush who answered my knock.

'Oh, it's you,' she said, taken aback, then gestured at me to enter. 'You'd better come and talk to the village elders. You were witness to the fight between Lambert and Tom Rawbone yesterday afternoon. They'll wish to hear what you have to say.'

My admission was not well received by the people left outside, all of whom had known the miller far longer than I had, and all of whom wanted to proffer their condolences and satisfy their burning curiosity at the same time. But Mistress Bush had no compunction in shutting the door firmly in their faces.

She led me upstairs to Lambert's bedchamber, a narrow, sparsely furnished room on the second floor. Judging by the unaccustomed silence in the working section of the mill, there was no one in Lower Brockhurst who could grind the corn until Lambert had recovered.

At first sight, the little room seemed inordinately full of people, but after a minute or two these sorted themselves out into Mistress Miller, an unsurprisingly large woman for an equally well-built son, Rosamund Bush and her parents and a couple of solemn grey-haired, grey-faced men who were introduced to me as the two senior members of the Village Council.

Lambert himself was propped up in bed looking decidedly the worse for wear. His face was a discoloured mass of bruising and one eye was so swollen that it was completely closed, while he could just about squint out of the other. His lips, too, were puffed up to twice their normal size, while his bare chest was covered in weals and welts where he had received a savage beating. What was on view below the decorously drawn up sheet, I could only guess at, but from what I could see, I immediately dismissed the iron bar theory of Goody Venables's overheated imagination. These injuries had been inflicted with nothing more lethal than a good, stout cudgel.

For now, Rosamund's sympathies seemed to have veered once more in Lambert's direction, and she was intent on demonstrating her womanly skills in the sick chamber, sponging her swain's fevered brow with a mixture of water and vinegar and fluttering her eyelashes at him in a way that must have been seriously inhibiting his crying need for rest.

William Bush was giving the village elders an account of the previous afternoon's quarrel between Tom Rawbone and the miller, the latter either nodding in agreement or making inarticulate grunts of disapproval if the landlord suggested that he, as well as Tom, might have been to blame. Rosamund was evidently refusing to endorse her father's half-hearted claim that the miller had been the aggressor. I had no such scruples.

'Nevertheless,' I admitted in conclusion, after I had said my piece, 'It's no excuse for breaking into a man's house and belabouring him while he's asleep and defenceless.'

'Did you see anything at all of the man's face?' one of the elders enquired of Lambert.

He shook his head and said something through his swollen lips that I could make neither head nor tail of. His mother, however, appeared to have no difficulty in understanding him.

'He says the bugger had his hood on back to front,' she interpreted. 'He'd cut slits for his eyes and . . . and what, dear?' She bent closer as her son again attempted to explain some detail. 'Yes.' She straightened up. 'Lambert knows it was back to front because the liripipe hung down like a long, thin nose.'

I could imagine the effect in the dark: grotesque and possibly frightening in those first uncertain minutes after being so rudely awakened.

The two elders were muttering to one another, their expressions serious. Once again, I heard the repetition of Tom Rawbone's name: it was obvious they were considering no other suspect.

'We must go up to Dragonswick Farm,' the taller and greyer of the pair decided. 'We shall confront Tom with his crime and see what he has to say. If he admits it, it will be up to the Council to decide his punishment. I see no need, at present, for this matter to go beyond the village boundaries. And Lambert!' He fixed the invalid with a gimlet eye. 'We bind you over to keep the peace until we have completed our enquiries. It would seem that you have not been entirely blameless in this quarrel.'

The miller let rip with an obscenity that shocked the men but which appeared to have no effect whatsoever on the ladies present. Indeed, Rosamund and his mother hushed and crooned to him in a manner that was guaranteed to turn the average stomach, and certainly caused mine to churn.

The second elder now spoke up. 'We should be obliged, Master Chapman, and you, too, Landlord Bush, if, in view of your evidence, you would both accompany us to Dragonswick Farm. Thomas Rawbone needs to know we are in possession of all the facts.'

I thought that if Tom had sunk to being Thomas, he was already adjudged guilty in the elders' eyes. But they looked like a couple of fair-minded men, and with Ned Rawbone's additional testimony of the provocation suffered by his brother the preceding day, Tom's punishment – in all probability a fine, which Nathaniel would no doubt pay – should be light. Perhaps it was as well, for his sake, that I had not acted on my intention of quitting the village after breakfast.

I glanced at Rosamund Bush with what I liked to think of as my quizzical look, but she pointedly ignored me, giving a little toss of her head and once more bending solicitously over her patient. I wondered how fairweather a friend to Tom Rawbone she might turn out to be; but simple justice reminded me that the initial wrong had been his. She owed him no debt of loyalty.

I stood aside to allow the two village elders and William Bush to precede me out of the room. (I was a well brought up young lad: first my mother, then the monks at Glastonbury had taught me good manners with fist and rod. I still bear the scars of some of their lessons.) Before they could take advantage of my politeness, however, we were all arrested by the sound of someone running up the stairs, an urgent clatter that boded ill news. A moment later, Lambert's bedchamber door was thrust open and the man called Rob Pomphrey burst into the room.

He addressed the two elders.

159

'Best come right away to the priest's house, Master Sewter, Master Hemnall! Miller, here, ain't the only one who's been set upon. Sir Anselm, he's in a bad way.'

This was more serious. This was an attack unmitigated by provocation. If the priest died, or was already dead, this would mean the full panoply of the law and a noose for the culprit at the end of it.

As I followed the elders and William Bush downstairs, and was myself followed by Rosamund and her mother – whose curiosity, I noted, outweighed their concern for Lambert Miller's health – I recalled uneasily my conviction that Sir Anselm knew more about Eris's disappearance than was good for him. For there seemed no other reason for an assault upon his person.

He was lying unconscious on the floor of his kitchen, half frozen to death, the door to the back yard having been left swinging on its hinges. The parishioner who had discovered him and then run screaming into the street had not thought to close it, nor had the gaping fools who had subsequently crowded into the house to see the priest for themselves. The senior of the two elders – Master Sewter, as I now knew him to be – immediately cleared the room of its uninvited occupants and requested Rosamund to run for the village wise woman.

'Tell her to bring all her pills and potions,' he instructed. 'And, my child, shut that door as you leave.'

Winifred Bush volunteered to find blankets, but Master Sewter decreed that Sir Anselm should be carried upstairs to bed.

'It will be too painful for him once he recovers his senses. Master Chapman, you're a big, strong lad. I feel sure you could do it single-handed and without any difficulty whatsoever.'

Sir Anselm may have appeared a featherweight, but, believe me, he was nowhere near as light as he looked. By the time I had negotiated the stairs to the second storey – with a confused Hercules circling round my feet and twice nearly tripping me up – and deposited the priest on his bed, I was beginning to have serious doubts about my future ability to father any more children. But once my task was successfully accomplished and the two village elders, Landlord and Mistress Bush together with myself were able to take a good look at him, it became very obvious that whoever had attacked Lambert Miller had also carried out the assault on the priest. The injuries were almost identical: a severe beating inflicted with a good, stout cudgel which, in Sir Anselm's case, had resulted in unconsciousness.

The village wise woman arrived carrying a large basket containing what must have been her entire store of salves and ointments, healing draughts and potions, tut-tutting in horror at the sight of her patient. Even Rosamund's description had not prepared her for Sir Anselm's condition. He was still breathing, but only just.

Master Sewter and Master Hemnall, having conferred together in whispers, decided that there was no likelihood of the priest regaining his senses yet awhile and that we were wasting our time at his bedside.

'We must go to Dragonswick Farm and apprehend Thomas Rawbone,' Master Hemnall said. 'William, you and the chapman will accompany us as planned.'

The wise woman – a much younger woman than I had expected, with a round, pleasant face and a pair of workmanlike hands – looked up from her ministrations.

'You'd better hurry,' she advised, 'if you want him in one piece. There was a mob setting out for the farm as I came along the street.'

The two elders exchanged glances and Master Hemnall pulled down one corner of his mouth.

'We shall need weapons, I think, Master Chapman, I see you have a cudgel, not to mention that pesky little dog, who seems willing to bite anyone and everyone, including yourself.' He turned to the landlord. 'William, you live next door. Can you find Colin and me a couple of clubs? Strong ones. We'll set out now. Catch us up as fast as you can.'

The landlord nodded and parted from us at the church. The village elders and myself crossed the bridge over the stream and began the ascent to Dragonswick Farm, but long before we got there, we could see the angry mob surrounding the house, baying mindlessly for Tom Rawbone's blood. By the time we had forced a path through the crowd to where Nathaniel, Ned and the twins stood, snarling defiance and brandishing bigger and stouter cudgels than William Bush had been able to provide, the general atmosphere had turned uglier than ever.

'Nathaniel!' Master Sewter had to shout to make himself heard. 'Where's Tom? It's no good trying to shelter him. Tell him to come out and face us like a man. Philip Hemnall and I will guarantee his safety until he's safely under lock and key.'

Nathaniel raised his voice in reply.

'Don't make me laugh! You two old women couldn't guarantee his safety from this pack of vultures however hard you tried. Anyway, it doesn't matter. Tom's gone! Left an hour and more ago. Took one of the horses. You won't catch up with him now.'

Fourteen

Nathaniel's voice carried clearly, even to those on the perimeter of the crowd. There was a momentary faltering, a decrease in sound that died away to almost nothing – only to rise again in frustrated fury as the farmer's words sank in.

Elder Hemnall lifted a hand, while his companion, Elder Sewter, took a warning step in the direction of the villagers, who showed every tendency to surge forward and storm the house.

''E's lying!' someone shouted. 'I'll wager Tom's in there somewhere. Friends, don't let yourselves be hoodwinked!'

There was an angry murmur like a swarm of bees, and a concerted, threatening movement towards the Rawbones, where they stood, cudgels at the ready. But Elder Sewter remained firmly in the path of the ringleaders – Rob Pomphrey and his fellow shepherds – forcing them to halt.

'Master Hemnall and I will search the farmhouse in an orderly fashion,' he decreed. 'The chapman and Landlord Bush, here, will accompany us and bear witness to our efforts. If it proves true that Tom Rawbone is not within, then, and only then, will a posse be formed to go after him.' He turned to me, lowering his voice and shrugging. 'Although how we're to know which direction he's ridden in, the Virgin alone can tell us. For the Rawbones most certainly won't.' He gave me a quirky, but friendly smile.

I warmed to Colin Sewter. On closer acquaintance, he was less austere than he appeared at first sight. He beckoned to William Bush, who was still in some distress after struggling uphill with three stout cudgels, two of which he had handed to the elders. The third he had kept for himself, but he looked uncomfortable and was plainly reluctant to use it. I decided that the landlord was essentially a man of peace, dedicated to rubbing along with all his neighbours. And I was suddenly seized by the conviction that he was not Eris Lilywhite's killer, however upset he might have been on behalf of his daughter. I felt sure that I could safely eliminate him from my roll of suspects.

The Rawbone women were in the great hall, bunched together in an an angry and frightened little group. They greeted Nathaniel's reappearance with cries of, 'What's happening?' 'What's going on?'

Jacquetta was the first to notice Master Bush, the two elders and myself. 'What are they doing here?' she demanded.

'They're looking for Tom,' Ned informed her wearily. 'We've explained that he's gone, but Elder Hemnall and Elder Sewter insist on searching for themselves. The landlord and the chapman have been brought along to see fair play.'

'Fair play, my arse!' Nathaniel roared, causing his daughter-in-law to wince. 'Tom had nothing to do with this attack on Lambert Miller. He gave me his word.'

'Then why,' asked Elder Hemnall reasonably, 'has he run away?'

'And how did he know about it?' Elder Sewter added.

At this last question, I saw Ned glance warningly at his father. He obviously wished to keep Maud Lilywhite's name out of the matter if he could.

'Know of it? Know of it? How does anyone know of anything in this benighted place?' Nathaniel blustered. 'Gossip travels on the wind . . . Billy Tyrrell probably brought the news. As for why my son ran away, what do you expect, with the whole village taking the miller's part and baying for Tom's blood?'

'It wasn't so much Lambert Miller's beating that incensed them,' I cut in. 'It was the attack on the priest.'

'Sir Anselm?' Ned looked startled and hushed his father with a wave of his hand. 'Are you saying that Sir Anselm has also been attacked?'

'Beaten unconscious,' Elder Hemnall confirmed grimly. 'And for all we know at present, likely to die from his injuries.'

There was a horrified silence while the Rawbones, men and women, looked uneasily at one another. Petronelle drew a deep, shuddering breath and slipped a hand into one of her husband's. Dame Jacquetta sat down suddenly in her chair as though her legs would no longer support her. Elvina Merryman put her fingers to her mouth like a child. Only Nathaniel and the twins seemed unaffected by the information.

'It still has nothing to do with Tom!' the old man exclaimed defiantly. 'Creeping around in the middle of the night, breaking into people's homes, attacking defenceless men, that's not Tom's way of doing things, and you all know it. If he's a bone to pick with someone, he'll challenge 'em face to face and fight it out like a man, not behave like some chicken-livered coward.'

From the little I had seen of his younger son, I was inclined to agree with him, but felt it was hardly my place to say so. Nor, I guessed, would Nathaniel appreciate my championing him. I therefore maintained a diplomatic silence.

'Let the elders get on and search the house, Father,' Ned advised. 'The sooner they satisfy themselves that Tom's not here, the sooner they'll leave. And the quicker we'll be rid of that mob outside.'

I could see that it was on the tip of the old man's tongue to argue the point, but in the end, common sense prevailed.

'All right,' he conceded grudgingly, but shook a warning fist in our direction. 'Just don't go poking your noses into anything that ain't your business. Are you listening? You're looking for Tom, nothing and no one else. You won't find him, of course, 'cos he ain't here. However, if you want to waste your time, that's your affair and don't make any difference to me.'

William Bush and I – the former very reluctantly – followed the two elders from the hall and spent the next hour subjecting the farmhouse to a thorough scrutiny. We opened chests, peered into cupboards, searched under beds, went up and down stairs until our legs ached and, finally, provoked Ruth's fury when we descended in a body on the kitchen and interrupted her pastry-making. But we found no sign of Tom Rawbone. Speaking for myself, I had not expected to. Nor, I think, had the others.

As we left the kitchen, I suddenly realized that we had forgotten the existence of the cellar: the building's original undercroft that some previous Rawbone had had walled in. I hesitated, wondering if I should mention our oversight, then decided against it. I was tired of this fool's errand we were on, all to satisfy a parcel of village hotheads who were simply looking for an excuse to indulge their baser instincts and ransack the house. I was convinced Tom wasn't there.

We re-entered the great hall, a somewhat shamefaced little band, hot, dusty and dishevelled. Elder Hemnall, at his most urbane, admitted that we had failed to discover Tom or, indeed, anything at all to connect him to the crime.

'So, at the moment, it remains Lambert Miller's word against your son's, Nathaniel,' Elder Sewter added. 'Mind you, it will also depend on what Sir Anselm has to say when he recovers consciousness. If he does, that is.'

'Right!' Ned exclaimed, rubbing his hands, relief, if only temporary, making him expansive. 'You'll have a beaker of wine with us then, friends, before you leave? I'll fetch up another bottle from the cellar.'

He'd done it! He'd said the word! I cursed him silently, but the damage was done.

'Cellar! Colin, we forgot the cellar!' Elder Hemnall clapped one hand to his forehead while, with the other, he seized Elder Sewter's arm. 'Come along! You, too, William. And you Master Chapman. Let's get this over with before we have that wine.'

Ned's expression told me that he wished he'd bitten out his tongue before uttering that unfortunate remark. If only he'd realized that we had forgotten about the cellar . . . ! Nevertheless, he did not appear unduly worried, just angry with himself that he'd given us the opportunity to poke about still further among the family belongings. He knew we wouldn't find his brother.

'I'll come with you,' he said, 'and fetch up the wine at the same time. The trapdoor is difficult to lift.'

Ned moved ahead of us, out of the hall and along the corridor, before either of the elders could object to his presence. He lifted the flagstone with practised ease, descended a few steps, paused to strike flint on tinder and lit a candle. Holding its flame high, he directed us where best to place our feet on the worn treads, expressing his concern lest one of the three older men should slip and fall. He evidently considered that I was able to take care of myself.

I could see by the flickering candlelight that my companions were somewhat daunted by the cellar's clutter, but it was unlikely that anyone was hiding there: there was insufficient cover. The piles of logs, the abandoned household goods and furniture were not stacked high enough, and were too scattered, to conceal a much smaller person than Tom Rawbone.

'Well, sirs, my brother's not here, as you can see for your-selves,' Ned said after a few minutes' half-hearted poking around on our part. As he selected a bottle of wine from the line standing against the inner wall, he was quietly triumphant. 'Shall we go?'

But even as we turned to climb the steps again, Elder Hemnall made a sudden pounce on something that had become entangled on the toe of Ned's boot. When he straightened up, a hand pressed to the small of his back, he displayed his trophy.

It took us all a moment or two to recognize what he had found, but once we had done so, it was unmistakable. It was a grey woollen hood with shoulder-cape and liripipe; a perfectly ordinary hood – except that two slits had been cut in the back of it just about where a person's eyes would be if, for some perverse reason, it was worn back to front.

Nathaniel resolutely refused to accept the discovery as a token of Tom's guilt.

'You brought that hood with you,' he accused the two elders, 'and dropped it on Ned's foot when you were in the cellar.'

Elder Hemnall was affronted by this slur on his probity.

'Don't talk such bloody nonsense, Nat! If that were the case, we'd have "found" it an hour ago, when we first began searching the house, and saved ourselves a deal of trouble. Now! Be sensible and tell us where Tom's gone. Which direction has he ridden in?'

'He didn't tell us, and we didn't ask,' Ned answered shortly. 'If he's any sense, he'll have headed for the Welsh border. But that's not to say he's done so.'

I decided it was time for me to add my mite to the discussion.

'Finding the hood,' I pointed out, 'doesn't necessarily mean that Tom was the wearer. It could have been worn by any other member of this household.' I glanced at Nathaniel and the twins and then at Ned.

'It's Uncle Tom's hood,' Jocelyn Rawbone declared flatly. 'I've seen it on him many times. Only yesterday, in fact.'

'Hold your tongue, Josh!' Ned barked at him. 'And that goes for you, too, chapman, if you know what's good for you. I agree with my father. The hood proves nothing. It could be anyone's.'

Petronelle rounded angrily on her husband and father-in-law.

'Stop trying to protect Tom, both of you. He's not worth it. He's brought this trouble on himself. That's his hood and you know it. There's the rip in the cape where he caught it on some brambles when he was rescuing one of the sheep last month.' Nathaniel would have interrupted her, but she shouted at him, 'I won't have Ned or the twins made scapegoats for Tom. I don't know why you bother. You and he have never liked one another.'

'That may be so,' Nathaniel hissed, 'but we Rawbones stand together in times like these, so be quiet, woman! If you were my wife, I'd give you a damn good thrashing!'

'You old lecher!' Petronelle screamed at him, making claws of her hands and looking as though she might gouge out his eyes at any moment. 'This is all your fault! You're worse than Tom! Lusting after a girl young enough to be your granddaughter!'

She collapsed on to a stool, sobbing. The housekeeper hurried over, throwing her arms around Petronelle and rocking her gently.

'Hush, my dear! Hush! No need to upset yourself.' She added viciously, 'That nasty little trollop has gone now and she won't be coming back.'

Elvina spoke with an assurance that made me glance sharply in her direction; but she was too busy glaring at Nathaniel to be aware of my interest. Ned noticed it, however, and lost his temper, bringing his fist down on the table top with a thump that made everybody start and which must have badly bruised his hand.

'Shut up, the lot of you,' he roared. 'Can't you see that you're making a spectacle of this family in front of strangers?'

His fury was plainly so uncharacteristic of him that they all, without exception, subsided into silence. Even Nathaniel seemed to think better of exerting his authority, although judging by the expression on his face it needed all his self-control not to do so.

Ned Rawbone drew himself up and addressed the two elders.

'Will you please leave now. We have nothing more to say to you. We have no idea where Tom might be. As I said before, he didn't think to tell us where he was heading. Nor did we ask him, naturally.'

'Naturally,' Elder Sewter agreed drily.

'We shall have to search the outbuildings,' Elder Hemnall said, preparing to retreat in good order.

Ned shrugged. 'I don't care what you do,' he answered wearily, 'as long as you persuade that mob out there to go away.'

Colin Sewter nodded. 'You have our word on that. Nor do we hold any of you responsible for Tom's actions. You will be free to come and go in the village as you please. You may encounter a little hostility, but no one will molest you.'

'They'd better not try,' Nathaniel snorted. 'Rawbone men know how to defend themselves.'

'Be sensible, Nathaniel,' his friend urged him. 'Don't go looking for trouble.'

169

Ned said quietly, his anger having apparently burned itself out, 'You'll let us know what Sir Anselm has to say when he recovers consciousness?'

'Of course.' Elder Sewter laid a warning hand on his arm. 'But you do realize that if the priest dies, it can no longer remain a village matter? We shall have to send to Gloucester, to the Sheriff.'

Sir Anselm did not die, however.

By the time that the elders had organized a search of the farm outbuildings by Rob Pomphrey and his friends, persuaded the rest of the villagers to disperse and we had all tramped back to Lower Brockhurst together, a visit to the priest's house established that he was able to sit up and take some nourishment.

Propped up in bed, looking frail and badly shaken, the livid bruises staining his parchment-white skin like blackberry juice on linen, he was being fed bread and milk by Winifred Bush while the village wise woman packed her medicaments back into her basket.

The latter nodded to the two elders and William Bush, but treated me to a suspicious stare as though she thought I might be up to no good, especially after I had treated her to my most winning smile.

'I've put a honey, rue and borage poultice on his swollen knee,' she informed the room at large, 'and powder of puff balls, mixed with spiders' webs to staunch the blood of a nasty cut to his upper arm. And there are some lettuce juice pellets to help him sleep when he's finished eating. Father Anselm,' she continued, turning to her patient, 'I leave you in Mistress Bush's most capable hands.' She gave another nod, nearly tripped over Hercules, who had been skulking around after me all morning, and went on her way with the parting admonition, 'Send for me if I'm needed.'

When the bedchamber door had closed behind the wise woman, Sir Anselm forestalled our questions by announcing querulously, 'It's no use asking me who did this. I didn't see anything.'

'You must have seen something, Father,' Elder Hemnall objected. 'The attack must have wakened you.'

'I tell you, I didn't.' The priest sounded as though he might burst into tears at any moment. 'It was the middle of the night. It was dark. I woke up to find someone was beating me black and blue. I remember crying out and putting up an arm to defend myself, but then I must have lost consciousness. I can't tell you anything more. It'll serve no purpose badgering me. Besides, I'm tired. I want to sleep.'

'Lambert Miller was attacked in just the same way,' Elder Hemnall told him. 'He insists that Tom Rawbone was his assailant, even though the fellow was wearing his hood back to front. Sir Anselm, do you think it was Tom Rawbone who assaulted you?'

'I keep telling you, I didn't see anything,' was the peevish (and frightened?) response. 'Can't you understand English?'

'Tom Rawbone has run away.' William Bush proffered the fact as though he hoped that it might reassure Sir Anselm. But the hope was doomed.

'I didn't see anything or anyone,' the priest repeated in a fading voice, leaning back against his pillows and closing his eyes. 'Now, will you please go, and allow me to rest?'

Mistress Bush took charge, shooing us from the bedchamber with sweeping motions of her hands.

'Off you go, and let the poor man get some sleep,' she scolded.

I was only too willing. My stomach was beginning to rumble, giving me notice that it was well past my dinnertime. I was debating whether or not to return to the Lilywhites' cottage when William Bush tapped me on the shoulder.

'I can hear you're hungry, Master Chapman. Come and eat with me. Eel pie and a draught of good ale, how does that sound? My wife bakes excellent eel pies. I can recommend them.'

He didn't have to ask me twice. We took our leave of the two elders, who had expressed their intention of paying another visit to Lambert Miller – I presumed that Rosamund had also returned to her suitor's sick-bed, and wondered what she would make of the news of Tom Rawbone's flight – while we proceeded to the alehouse. This was, for the present, still locked, so the landlord led me up the outside staircase to the living quarters above.

The first room we entered was the kitchen-parlour with, presumably, two bedchambers somewhere beyond. My host sat me down at the table and from a cupboard produced a couple of wooden platters on which reposed two of the largest eel pies I have ever seen. I was famished. I took my knife from my belt and fell to with a will. Master Bush did the same.

It was several minutes before we were able to speak, and then only in grunts to signify the offering and acceptance of ale. But after a while, when both hunger and thirst had been assuaged, the landlord cleared his mouth and asked, 'Well? What do you think, chapman? Is Sir Anselm telling the truth? Or is he bent on protecting Tom Rawbone?'

'Or somebody else,' I suggested.

William looked up, startled. 'You think someone other than Tom might have been responsible for the attacks, then?'

'Why not? Lambert didn't see the man's face, after all. And he assumes it was Tom because of their quarrel yesterday. He thinks, naturally enough, that Tom was getting his own back.'

'Of course! Who else could it have been? No one else that I know of bears the miller that sort of grudge. And it was Tom's hood we found.'

'Maybe. But why would Tom attack the priest? Come to that, why would anybody attack Sir Anselm?'

But I could make a guess at the answer to that question. Someone who either knew or suspected that the priest had information about the disappearance of Eris Lilywhite. I was not, however, prepared to share that thought at present. Besides, it failed to solve the problem of who, apart from Tom Rawbone, had a reason to attack Lambert Miller.

I took a gulp of ale, trying to work out the equation. Firstly, Tom had every reason to avenge himself on Lambert in retaliation for the beating he had received the previous afternoon. Secondly, if I was right in my assumption that Sir Anselm knew something about Eris's fate, then the person responsible might either want to kill him, or at least to administer a severe warning to him to hold his tongue. Therefore, if the two attacks were connected – and in the circumstances it seemed impossible that they were not – the same man stood indicted for both crimes . . .

It was the logical conclusion to make. And yet, somehow, I still wasn't convinced that the perpetrator was Tom Rawbone, in spite of William of Ockham's dictum that, in logic, assumptions should not be multiplied: the obvious answer is usually the right one. But in my experience, there were times when the solution to a problem was too obvious to be true.

I folded my arms on the table and asked, 'Why would Tom Rawbone want to harm Sir Anselm? Can you think of a reason?'

William Bush shook his head. 'I've been puzzling about that, myself. He and the priest always seemed to rub along together pretty well. He wasn't involved in the church, like Ned, but he always attended every feast day and holy day and didn't hold any of those heretical Lollard views that seem so fashionable nowadays. Leastways, not that I've ever heard of. Mind you, that's all the good I will speak of him, after what he did to my Rosamund.'

'Were you looking forward to having him as a son-in-law?'

The landlord shrugged. 'It was a good match for Rosie, I have to admit. And she was mad to have him, so I couldn't say no. I've never been able to deny her anything. But there was always something a bit wild about Tom that neither Mistress Bush nor I approved of. And it turned out, of course, that our fears were justified. Not that we saw it coming – his jilting Rosamund like that, I mean. And for Eris Lilywhite of all people!'

'You didn't like Eris?' I enquired, although I had already guessed the answer.

'No, I didn't.' The landlord emptied his beaker and set it down rather forcibly on the table. 'To be truthful, I've never liked her mother much, either. I always thought Maud Haycombe a bit wild in her youth. Not as good as she should have been, if you know what I mean.' He leaned across the table and said in a confidential whisper, 'If you want my opinion, Eris's arrival was much too prompt for her to have been conceived after Gilbert and Maud were married. It was barely nine months. More like eight, if my memory serves me rightly.' He added defiantly, 'And that's always been Winifred's opinion, too.'

I detected a touch of pique in Master Bush's tone, and wondered if he might once have fancied Maud himself, but met with no encouragement. All the same, I saw no reason to doubt his memory concerning the date of Eris's birth. If Maud had been as much in love with Gilbert Lilywhite as Theresa had implied, they might well have anticipated their marriage vows. They would most certainly not have been the first, nor the last, couple to do so.

'What do you think happened to Eris the night she vanished?' I asked. 'Was she killed or did she simply run away?'

William returned the same response that I had received so many times in answer to that question.

'Run away? That one? When she'd just got what she wanted, to be mistress of Dragonswick Farm? Of course, she didn't run away! No, she was murdered, if you want my opinion.'

'Then who was the murderer?' I wanted to know.

The landlord poured us both more ale. 'Tom Rawbone, I should guess. But it could have been Nathaniel or one of the twins. Or even one of the women. If Eris returned to the farmhouse for some reason – because of the weather or because she'd forgotten something – I wouldn't it past the capabilities of any one of those three – Petronelle, Dame Jacquetta, Dame Merryman – to take a knife to her back.'

'But no one's mentioned that she returned after she'd left for home that night.'

'Well, they wouldn't, would they?' William gave me a condescending smile. 'Not if one of them had killed her.'

'But would Nathaniel have covered up for them? He was supposed to be in love with the girl.'

'Of course he would! You're a stranger. You don't know the Rawbones.' The landlord's condescension became even more marked. 'Besides, I doubt if Nathaniel ever was in love with Eris. In lust, perhaps. And delighted at the prospect of serving Tom a backhanded turn. But he would never betray any member of his family into the clutches of the law. Whatever their internal strifes, the Rawbones always close ranks against outsiders.'

'Would the family include Dame Merryman?' I asked.

My companion nodded. 'Oh yes! Elvina's one of the family, all right. She was Nathaniel's mistress for years. Probably still is. The fact is never referred to openly, of course, but most people in the village accept it as a fact. There used to be rumours that she paid regular visits to the village wise woman – not the one you met today; her mother – for infusions of pennyroyal in order to abort unwanted children. But it was only gossip, you understand. You wouldn't repeat it?'

I hastened to reassure him, then decided it was time to take my leave. I wanted to look in on Sir Anselm again, in the unlikely hope of finding him awake and alone. After that, I needed to be by myself for a while. I needed to clear my mind; to separate fact from assumption; to set my thoughts and ideas in some sort of order.

Fifteen

Sir Anselm was sitting up in bed, looking very pale and obviously feeling extremely sorry for himself.

Mistress Bush, who let me in, was busy in the kitchen, making soup – chicken and lentil if my nose was any judge – and anxious to return to it before it stuck to the bottom of the pot.

'What do you want?' she asked, none too pleased at being disturbed.

'A word with Sir Anselm,' I said.

She pursed her mouth and eyed me up and down in that infuriating, considering way women have when the power of decision rests in their hands.

'Very well,' she conceded at last. 'As long as it is just a word. I won't have you tiring him out. He's still very weak. And don't bully him.'

'Who? Me?' I was the picture of injured innocence.

She sniffed. 'I've had experience of your hectoring ways.'

'You're thinking of somebody else,' I assured her, obtaining and gallantly kissing one of her hands. I inhaled the mouth-watering aroma of chicken soup. 'And your eel pies are sheer ambrosia, too,' I added, with apparent irrelevance.

She gave another sniff and snatched her hand away.

'That's quite enough of that, Master Chapman. I know your sort. I wasn't born yesterday. I'm just sorry for your poor wife, that's all.'

'I make her the happiest woman in Bristol,' I protested.

'Between the sheets, no doubt. But where does that lead? Only to more children. You said you have three, I believe. Any girls?'

'Just the one.'

'Then I'm sorry for you.' Dame Winifred sighed. 'Girls are the very devil to bring up. At least, modern girls are. It wasn't so in my day, of course. We were much better behaved.'

'As every generation of mothers has no doubt said from time immemorial,' I laughed, and headed for the staircase.

'What do you want?' Sir Anselm demanded as I entered his bedchamber.

I ignored the peremptory tone and sat down, uninvited, on the edge of his bed. I didn't beat around the bush.

'Who did this to you and the miller?' I asked. 'And don't tell me you don't know. Or can't guess.'

'Well, I don't know. I didn't see his face. Go away!'

I put a hand over one of his which was lying, hot and dry as an autumn leaf, on the patchwork coverlet.

'Father,' I urged, 'this man, whoever he may be, is dangerous. He's most probably the murderer of Eris Lilywhite. If you know anything – anything at all – you must tell me. Or tell someone. Was it Tom Rawbone who attacked you?'

'How many more times do I have to repeat myself?' His voice rose peevishly. 'I know nothing. I saw nothing. Now, will you please go away? Preferably,' he added waspishly, 'back where you came from.' He turned his face to the wall. 'I've no more to say.'

His protests carried no weight with me. Indeed, their very repetition made me more suspicious.

'Father, you're being extremely foolish,' I chided him. 'I suspected, when I talked to you yesterday, that there was something you were concealing; some knowledge gleaned, most probably, from things told, or hinted at, in the confessional. Was this beating a warning to you to keep your mouth shut?'

'And if it were, I'd be a fool to ignore it, wouldn't I?' was the sharp retort. His head jerked round again to look at me face to face.

'So you do know something,' I said, seizing on his question as an admission of the truth.

He removed his hand from under mine. 'I didn't say that—'

'In so many words,' I interrupted.

'—but if you wish to interpret it in that way,' he continued as though I hadn't spoken, 'I can't prevent you. But you're forgetting Lambert Miller. Does such an argument apply to him?'

'No, not as far as I know. But I think there might have been a different motive there.'

'Might have been?' He eyed me shrewdly. 'I understood from Dame Winifred that the miller and Tom Rawbone had quarrelled over Rosamund. Lambert had attacked and beaten Tom severely.'

I nodded. 'True! I was present when it happened. And Tom has fled the village. But suppose that someone wanted to throw blame on to Tom, hoping that amid the general condemnation, he'd panic and flee, then breaking into the mill and assaulting Lambert would be the way to do it. The attack on you would be for a different reason; a warning, as I've said already. But no one would stop to consider that. The thinking would be that if Tom assaulted the miller, then he also assaulted the priest. The 'why' of it wouldn't be considered. Most people, in my experience, can reason from one to two, but very few continue reasoning from two to three. Don't you agree?'

Sir Anselm regarded me sullenly.

'You're making my head ache,' he complained, 'with all your arguments. Go away. Please.'

I sighed and got to my feet. 'You're a stubborn old man,' I told him. 'And a foolish one.'

'Chapman!' Mistress Bush bustled into the room, carrying a tray on which reposed a bowl of chicken and lentil broth and a heel of bread, torn from a newly baked loaf. 'I warned you not to bully my patient. Do as Father Anselm asks, and leave.'

I shrugged. I could see that I was getting nowhere, and now that his temporary housekeeper and nurse had arrived to join forces with the priest, I might as well accept defeat gracefully and go. I wished Sir Anselm a speedy recovery and made for the door, followed by Hercules. (Having shared my eel pie, the dog

178

was still fairly somnolent and had been lying quietly at my feet, patiently waiting for me to make a move.)

I was about to lift the latch when, to my surprise, Sir Anselm called me back. He fumbled under his pillow and produced a bunch of keys, which he handed to me.

'I'm not absolutely sure that I locked the aumbry yesterday evening before I came to bed. I woke up in the middle of the night, worrying about it, and intended going down to the church to make certain. But then, I must have dozed again. And, of course, the next thing I knew . . .' He broke off, trembling, but controlled it with an effort. 'Since when,' he continued gamely, determined not to give in to his weakness, 'I've forgotten all about it. When you leave here, would you step into the church and see whether or not the cupboard is fastened? If it isn't, would you do it for me? It's the small silver key on the end. You can leave it and the others on the kitchen table. Dame Winifred will return them to me later.'

I readily agreed, only too glad to be of service, and took the keys from him while Mistress Bush settled the tray on his lap. I wished her the time of day and left, clattering downstairs, Hercules racing ahead of me, delighted to be on his feet at last.

He was disgusted, however, when, instead of heading for the open country on the opposite side of the stream, I turned to my right and entered the church. He demonstrated his disapproval in the usual way, by trying to nip my ankles, but, fortunately, my boots were of tough and seasoned leather, doing more damage to his teeth than he could do to my legs. All the same, it was a habit of which I had to cure him, and soon.

I made my obeisance before the High Altar and then to the Virgin. But it was to the Christ of the Trades that my eyes were inevitably drawn; to that contorted, tortured figure that had proved the inspiration for the low-born and oppressed, giving them the courage to rebel against the injustice of the infamous Statute of Labourers that had been fashioned in order to keep them in subjection and deprive them of their rights. The peasants hadn't won, of course. How could they ever have expected to, when all the forces of law and order were ranged against them? They had been betrayed in the end – inevitably I felt – by a king who had posed as their friend until the trap was sprung and they were crushed between its iron jaws.

'And betrayed by You, too,' I whispered, staring up at the writhing Christ, His bleeding head encircled by His carpenter's tools. 'Sometimes, I wonder whose side You're really on. Are you truly the defender of the poor and the subjugated? Or, as Lord of Creation, are you the friend of the High and the Mighty? Is it like calling to like?'

He didn't reply. He knew, as I knew, that I should have to work out the answers to those questions for myself. He also knew that I was trouble, that I always had been, but I felt, nevertheless, a sudden rush of warmth along my veins. He was there somewhere in that cold, dank church. It was reassuring.

I tested the door of the aumbry, but Sir Anselm had been worrying himself unnecessarily. It was locked. I turned to leave the church, then hesitated, pricked by an unaccountable spur of curiosity that made me retrace my steps and unlock the cupboard to inspect the treasures within. There were the pair of silver candlesticks, the silver-gilt pyx, the ivory and gold crucifix. And there, also, were the two silver chalices, side by side, the fragile light gleaming on the elaborate chasing around their bowls. I was at once reminded of my dream; of the little satyrs dancing in and out of the trailing vine leaves and branches of olive, picking the silver fruit and gathering the grapes into baskets, no doubt to make wine for the great god, Bacchus . . .

Bacchus? What was he doing in this holy place? What was I thinking of? I must be seeing things . . . Mustn't I? Carefully, I lifted out one of the chalices, carried it to the open church door and examined it in the better light thus afforded me. But I had not been mistaken. I was looking at the little boys with their tails and horns and goats' legs, the vines and the olive trees. Without even realizing it, I must have made a mental note of its decoration when I had watched Ned Rawbone twisting it between his hands the previous morning, exactly as I was doing now.

Hercules barked impatiently. I hushed him. The metal felt very old and thin, and when I studied the base more closely, I could see that a double band of chasing depicted tiny, delicately wrought scenes of everyday life: a man ploughing, a shopkeeper (a seller of wine by the look of him), a smith in his forge. But this was not everyday life as I and my contemporaries knew it. These men wore tunics and sandals. They were . . . Yes, surely they were Romans!

I drew a sharp breath. This pair of cups had never been made for Holy Church. They were pagan relics of our Roman past, lost, or more likely buried, centuries before when the inhabitants of Cirencester – Corinium Dobunnorum – had spread out across the surrounding countryside to farm the rich and fertile soil. (Hadn't Rosamund Bush told me that the alehouse was named after an old Roman sandal dug up from beneath its cellar floor?) But the question was, of course, how on earth had they come to be among Saint Walburga's ceremonial plate?

I went back into the church and returned the chalice to the aumbry, placing it beside its fellow on the top shelf. A quick glance at the other pieces, before I relocked the cupboard, convinced me that there was nothing strange or odd about any of them. So, how had the Roman bowls been acquired by the village? I dredged around in my memory.

The answer suddenly hit me like a bolt of lightning.

'It was that priest you told me about, wasn't it? What did you call him? "Light-fingered" Lightfoot. Was that his name?'

Having slipped back into the priest's house, leaving Hercules tied up outside, and having satisfied myself that Mistress Bush had once more returned to the kitchen, I had run upstairs and, without compunction, roused Sir Anselm from his postprandial doze. I dropped the bunch of keys on the coverlet and told him bluntly of my discovery. I also explained my theory as to how the bowls had been acquired.

Sir Anselm, still sore and badly shaken, had used up his fragile store of energy on our previous encounter, and was in no fit state to prevaricate further. He admitted wearily that he had

always suspected that the chalices were Roman, but had consecrated them both to the glory of God, just in case any of his
predecessors had failed to do so. He, also, had guessed that
'Light-fingered' Lightfoot had probably 'donated' them to
Saint Walburga's, although how he might have come by them
in the first place, Sir Anselm had no idea.

'Perhaps he just dug them up somewhere,' the priest haz-
arded as an afterthought.

'Unlikely,' I answered. 'Not impossible, but unlikely. Articles
like the cups were usually buried pretty deeply to begin with, in
order to preserve them from some natural or man-made dis-
aster. Then you have to allow for accretion to the earth's
surface during the intervening centuries. A Roman sandal
was found in the cellar of the alehouse, I believe, and that's
something that would only have been lost or mislaid by its
owner . . . Has no one else ever noticed that the decoration on
the cups is pagan?'

'Not in my time.' Sir Anselm yawned involuntarily. 'At least,
no one has ever mentioned the fact. In any case –' he yawned
again, this time suggestively – 'I don't suppose it would have
worried anyone very much in this village. We live our own lives
here. Some members of my flock, as you know, pay homage to
the old gods of the trees and the stones, as well as to the living
Christ. There are more ways of worshipping God, as I told you
before, than that laid down by Holy Church.'

I was attending to him with only half an ear, busy pursuing
thoughts of my own.

'Do you know when this "Light-fingered" Lightfoot was
priest in Lower Brockhurst?' I asked. 'Was it much before your
time?'

My companion had to rouse himself with a conscious effort
to consider my question. He looked ill: I felt guilty.

'He wasn't my predecessor here,' he said at last, 'nor either of
the two incumbents prior to that. I think you might have to go
back quite a long time. The stories about him always struck me
as having a mythical quality to them. You know, tales that have
been repeated down through the generations until people aren't

quite certain whether they're true or not. Or whether Father Lightfoot's reported exploits were real or imagined.'

'Oh, I suspect they were true all right,' I said. 'I should think those two cups testify to that. But if we rule out the likelihood of him digging them up, where else could he have found them?'

A troubled moan, however, indicated that Sir Anselm had at last fallen into an uneasy slumber, his fingers plucking unconsciously at the bedclothes, his shifting body a sure sign of his discomfort even while he slept. I could also hear faint yelps from Hercules, tied up outside, and decided that it was time to leave before Mistress Bush went to investigate them. I tiptoed from the bedchamber and down the stairs, gaining the street undetected by the landlord's wife.

Hercules went half-mad with joy at the sight of me, and hurled himself towards me with such force that he pulled over the post to which his rope was attached. I stooped to untie him.

'I agree, you've been very patient and forbearing,' I said, patting his head. 'Now we'll go for that walk I promised you.'

We crossed the bridge over the stream, climbing the Draco's bank to the woods above and leaving Lower Brockhurst far behind us. I supposed I ought to return to the Lilywhites' smallholding to inform the women of the current state of the village's two invalids, but decided it would be folly to try Hercules's patience any further. Besides, I told myself, there were plenty of neighbours to keep Maud and Theresa informed of events, even if they had not, by now, paid a visit to Lower Brockhurst to find out for themselves. So the dog and I continued our ascent.

As we crested the final rise, I turned and looked at the view behind me. The surrounding hills lay grey and misty on both sides of the valley that clove a deep purple shadow between them. The encroaching forest mantled their tops and flanks, making them seem remote and magical in the thinning light that was already waning towards dusk, as the short February afternoon drew towards its close. A primaeval landscape that had stood here for aeons, long, long before the coming of Saint Augustine and Christianity, when men had worshipped the

Tree and the Stone and made blood sacrifice to their insatiable gods. I shivered. These hills and valleys, these forests held echoes of those ancient rites as a curved shell will hold the sound of the sea.

I was suddenly very cold, and turned to find the well-trodden path that led to the ruins of Upper Brockhurst Hall, a path that now seemed so familiar to me that I might have been walking it all my life instead of just for the past three days. The silence was intense. If I stood still, I could almost touch it. Only the dog's unconcerned snufflings amongst the undergrowth and gently waving grasses reassured me that I hadn't strayed into the middle of some enchanted woodland where I was the only living thing. Well, I'd wanted solitude, and here I had it in abundance.

Before I knew it, I found myself in the clearing where the old Hall and its courtyard had once stood. I wrapped my cloak tightly around me and sat down on the low rim of the well, first of all stretching out my legs and feet in front of me, then drawing my knees up to my chest and locking my arms around them.

It was not a comfortable position, but comfort was not conducive to serious thinking, which was what I had come here to do. It had been my intention to sort my thoughts and put in order such scraps of information concerning Eris Lily-white's disappearance as had come my way. Instead, I was unable to concentrate on anything but the discovery I had made that afternoon; the Roman bowls locked in Saint Walburga's aumbry. How had they got there, among the church plate? Who had put them there? Sir Anselm and I both thought that we knew the answer to what was really a single question. And perhaps that answer could also solve a 130-year-old mystery to my satisfaction.

But my theory hinged on one as yet unverified fact: the period when the priest known as 'Light-fingered' Lightfoot had been the incumbent of Saint Walburga's church. But who could I ask? Dame Jacquetta was old enough for her memory to reach back into the past, to recall something perhaps that she had been told by her grandmother, or even her great-grandmother, when she was a child. But it was not a good time to approach a member of the Rawbone family, with Tom a hunted fugitive, suspected of attacking the priest and Lambert Miller, and the rest of them tainted by association. They would have other worries on their minds and would be impatient, to say the least, with queries about a long-dead priest.

That Father Lightfoot was long-dead, I was very nearly certain; as nearly certain as I was that he had discovered the Roman chalices in the deserted Upper Brockhurst Hall after the great plague, when it was at last safe to enter and dispose of the bodies. Maybe his subsequent reputation and soubriquet had hinged solely on this one incident; the sudden appearance of the silver bowls among the rest of Saint Walburga's small store of treasure.

I thought it doubtful, however, that any of the then inhabitants of Lower Brockhurst would have commented on the fact. Those fortunate survivors of the worst pestilence ever experienced so far by man must surely have been too busy themselves, thanking God for their survival and picking over the contents of the Upper Brockhurst houses, to care much about what their priest was up to. And who could blame them? Pots and pans, chairs and stools, knives and blankets are of no use to the dead. And when finally, the goods and chattels of their deceased neighbours had been removed and shared amongst them, there were the empty houses themselves to provide extra building material for many years to come, and the Draco to be diverted in order to improve the lower village's water supply. And when all was said and done, the chalices benefited all of Lower Brockhurst, their beauty enhancing every service, their silver bowls a pleasure to drink from, their graceful lines a feast for beauty-starved eyes.

But if all these conjectures of mine were correct – and they were only conjectures I reminded myself severely – there still remained the question of how the Martin brothers had come by their treasure trove in the first place. Had they, or one of their forefathers, come across the bowls accidentally while digging somewhere? For truffles in the woods, maybe? Beneath their cellar floor, like the Roman sandal in the alehouse? Or – and here my imagination really did catch fire with the utter certainty of having hit upon the truth – had the two wellers from Tetbury dug them up while excavating the new well for the courtyard?

But if that were indeed the case, to whom had the right of ownership belonged? To the men who had found them? Or to the men on whose land they had been discovered? I could imagine only too well the dispute that might have arisen, the Martin brothers claiming the bowls as theirs, the wellers, seeing a potential fortune in silver slipping through their fingers, adducing the old law of 'finders keepers'.

So stalemate would have ensued. Perhaps one bowl each would have been the answer; but men confronted by the prospect of sudden wealth are not that reasonable. Probably the Martins would have won the day. They were on home ground, after all, always an advantage. But perhaps the wellers, having finished the job and been paid for their labours, had started for home, only to return by stealth, purloin the Roman bowls and set out once more for Tetbury, hoping against hope that the theft would go undetected until they had put enough distance between themselves and Upper Brockhurst Hall to make successful pursuit impossible.

But, unluckily for them, the Martin brothers had discovered their loss in plenty of time to go after their former employees, whom they ambushed and bludgeoned to death in the forest. They had then carried the silver bowls home again with a triumph that had proved shortlived. Within days, a week at the most, they had both died of the bubonic plague that had spread like wildfire throughout Upper Brockhurst, leaving not a single soul alive.

And many months later, scavenging with his pastoral flock through the possessions of their dead neighbours, the Lower Brockhurst priest, Father Lightfoot, had come across two magnificent silver chalices that would not only grace Saint Walburga's altar, but also greatly enhance and augment her insignificant store of plate. It would have been an opportunity too good to miss. The bowls would be used to the greater glory of God, and I doubted if the priest would even have thought of his actions as a sin.

Had 'Light-fingered' Lightfoot realized that the bowls were Roman? If so, would he have cared? As I had discovered on occasions in the past, in remote, isolated communities such as this, the people made their own rules, judged by their own standards and, while they were aware of the wider world beyond their boundaries, nevertheless considered themselves exempt from its laws. In times of trouble, they closed ranks against the outsider who would have imposed the King's justice upon them and theirs, and, when necessary, meted out their own punishments. Tom Rawbone had fled from the wrath of his fellow villagers, not from the threat of trial and imprisonment in Gloucester.

I stood up, stretching my cramped limbs, slowly looking around me. I felt sure, in my own mind, that I had solved the mystery of the wellers' murder, although I should never be able to prove it. Nor would my solution arouse much interest if I could. Most likely, it would only inspire incredulity and derision. The story was a part of the folklore of the district, and if there is one thing that people dislike more than another, it is having a good mystery ruined with a rational explanation. It is no longer any fun.

Instead, I reconsidered the totally groundless, but intuitive feeling that I had entertained since the very beginning of this case: that the disappearance of Eris Lilywhite was somehow linked to the 130-year-old murder of the wellers. So, now that I had, or thought I had, a solution to that particular problem, how were the two events connected? There was, of course, only one answer, provided that my instincts were correct, and that was the well. But I had climbed down the shaft and inspected it closely. There was nothing there. Nor, according to those who had helped in the search for Eris, had there ever been. This had to mean that the two were unconnected. My much-vaunted intuition had played me false . . .

Hercules came hurtling out of the undergrowth, whining and climbing up my leg in palpable distress. I picked him up.

'What's the matter, boy?' I asked.

But even as I spoke, I could smell burning on the air and saw smoke curling up amongst the distant trees. I made my way towards it, the dog gibbering and struggling in my arms. Then I saw the flames.

A small wicker cage had been hung from a branch and set alight. Inside, on the bottom, was a charred shape, black and still. What it was I could not tell. But one fact was certain. If it had once been a living creature, it had met a horrible death.

Sixteen

I set Hercules down and he scurried, whimpering, under the nearest bush, his eyes reproaching me for abandoning him so callously. Then, with my cudgel, I slashed out at the last fiery remnants of the wicker cage, hitting them to the ground. They fell in a shower of sparks and charred black specks that clung to my hands and sleeves, the wet grass effectively dousing the rest of the flames. Reluctantly, I approached the remains and stirred them with the end of my stick, prodding cautiously at the burned lump, half expecting to uncover what was left of some small animal or bird. To my relief, however, it disintegrated, and I could only guess that it had been another of the corn dollies that I had previously seen, along with the rag 'clooties', tied to the branches of the trees.

I knew what the wicker cage and the corn dolly were meant to represent. It was a re-enactment, in miniature, of the old Celtic practice of human sacrifice, burning the victims alive. Often, the wicker cages had been woven in the shape of a giant man – or, at least, so had said Julius Caesar in his condemnation of the ancient British Druids. (Which, when one considered the barbaric customs of the Romans was like the pot calling the skillet black.)

But that was beside the point; the point being that I was not alone here, on the Upper Brockhurst ridge, as I had fondly imagined. The hairs began to lift on the nape of my neck. Someone had been very close, and recently enough to set light to the little cage so that it was still burning when I found it. Its woven twigs would most probably, at that time of year, have been damp, but nonetheless, it would have burned quite quickly. Had that mysterious someone realized I was near? Was the 'sacrifice' a warning to me?

I took my cudgel in a firmer grip, hissed at Hercules to follow me – an injunction he resolutely ignored: did I really think he was that much of a fool? – and walked forward along the track that led out of the opposite side of the clearing. After advancing two or three yards, I paused to listen, but the only sounds were the sighing of the breeze through the leaves, the faint, barely audible rustling of grasses and the twittering of birds among the branches.

A sudden rush of wings made me start, as one of the birds flew low overhead. I called out, 'Hello! Is anybody there?' But it was a stupid question, and silence was the only answer. As I had realized once before, endless acres of woodland stretched all about me; and for anyone who was familiar with its secret paths and tracks, overgrown and invisible to the eye of a stranger, remaining concealed would pose no problem. I was wasting my time and possibly endangering my person, as well. It was time I returned to the Lilywhites' cottage. If I had signally failed in what I had come here to do – to sift through what I knew of Eris Lilywhite's disappearance – I had at least solved one mystery to my satisfaction, even if the solution was of no benefit to anyone living.

I retrieved Hercules from under his bush and tucked him beneath one arm. He remained unmoved by my accusation of cowardice, licking my face in slavering subservience as we started downhill, across the pasture, heading for the smallholding near the bottom of the slope. The winter day was fading, the darkening sky riven by a shaft of light as cold as steel. It was also beginning to rain, the drops slanting against my face like splinters of ice, yet another reminder that winter had not yet given up the ghost, even though tomorrow, Sunday, would be the last day of February. And the feast of Saint Patrick was only seventeen days away. I had to leave Lower Brockhurst soon or break my promise to Adela.

I tilted my head, looking up at the white sword of light drawn through the leaden clouds, and demanded irritably, 'Well,

Lord? What is it you want me to do? Am I performing Your work here? Or are You simply playing at cat and mouse? Is Eris Lilywhite safe and sound somewhere, while You're just laughing up Your sleeve to see me running around in circles? I mean, I'd like to keep my word to my wife, if it's all the same to You. So for pity's sake, give me a sign!'

But, of course, nothing dramatic happened. Why did I think it might? God doesn't work like that. Not ever. You have to wait, slowly and painstakingly piecing together the scraps of information that He condescends to give you until, finally, you can see the picture, whole and entire.

The bright day had settled into a stormy night of wind and driving rain. The Mistress Lilywhites and I huddled close to a fire where the logs crackled and sparked across the red-hot sods of peat, while the wind moaned and whistled through the hole in the blackened roof, blowing showers of wood-ash into our laps and faces, causing our eyes to water and smart.

The two women had received news of the invalids' condition when they had visited the village during the course of the afternoon, in order, so they said, to purchase flour from the mill. Their information was therefore more recent than mine, and they were able to reassure me that both Lambert and Sir Anselm were making good progress. Indeed, the priest insisted that he would able to conduct all services the following day and also to hear confessions first thing in the morning. Mistress Bush, who was still dancing attendance on him, had pursed her lips and shaken her head doubtfully, but her patient was adamant.

'And she won't dent the old man's determination, once he's made up his mind,' said Theresa. 'Sir Anselm's as obstinate as they come.' She added reproachfully, 'We expected you back by dinnertime, Roger. We didn't anticipate having to go chasing after the news ourselves.'

'Don't be silly, Mother-in-law,' Maud begged her tartly. 'The walk did us good. Besides, Master Chapman's our guest, not our errand boy.'

191

'No, no! Dame Theresa's right,' I apologized. 'I should have had the courtesy to call in and tell you what I'd learned. But is there any more news, do you know, of Tom Rawbone? Has he been found yet? Have the village elders organized a posse?'

The older woman shook her head. 'We've heard nothing on either count. Between ourselves, I think the Rawbone family – Ned and his father, to be more precise – have brought pressure to bear on members of the Village Council to let matters rest as they are. Or, at the very least, to delay sending anyone in pursuit until it's far too late to catch up with Tom. No one's dead, after all –' her voice faltered for a moment, thinking of her granddaughter no doubt, but she rallied and went on – 'and, so long as Tom doesn't return to Dragons-wick, there's no occasion to make an enemy of Nathaniel. Generally speaking, communities like Lower Brockhurst – isolated, dependent on one another's goodwill, especially in winter – prefer to keep on speaking terms with their neigh-bours. Tom's the one people have it in for. His treatment of Rosamund Bush disgusted them: she's well liked in the village. And in many ways, they secretly admire the old man for being able, at his time of life, to sneak Eris from under Tom's nose. They feel it served him right.'

I asked, 'Do you both believe it was Tom who attacked the miller and Sir Anselm?'

'Of course!' Maud exclaimed sharply. 'What other explana-tion can there possibly be? He's run away, hasn't he? And the mask he wore was discovered in the Rawbones' undercroft.'

'But why would he beat up the priest? Lambert I can under-stand, but Tom seems to have had no grudge against Sir Anselm. At least, none that anyone has mentioned to me.'

Maud shrugged her thin shoulders. 'To make people ask that very question, I should suppose. To throw dust in their eyes so that, like you, they begin to doubt that it was Tom who assaulted either man.'

Theresa gave a snort of derision.

'Tom Rawbone hasn't the brains or the subtlety to think up a plan like that.' She turned to me. 'So what are you implying,

chapman? That someone else wanted to make people believe
that Tom Rawbone was the culprit?'

'Something like that,' I admitted.

'But why choose the priest as his second victim, when there's
no known quarrel between Tom and Sir Anselm?' She laughed
again. 'It seems to me we're going round in circles.'

'Perhaps. Or perhaps the priest knows something he
shouldn't. The beating could have been in the nature of a
warning.'

'I've never heard such nonsense!' Maud's tone was abrasive.
She had never spoken to me in so disrespectful a manner before,
and it shook me. 'You're making a mystery where none exists,
Master Chapman! I've no idea why. But I'll tell you now, for
what it's worth! I hold Tom Rawbone responsible for my
daughter's death.'

'You do believe that Eris is dead, then?' I intervened quickly,
before Dame Theresa could ask the same question, as she was
obviously about to do.

The tears welled up in Maud's tired eyes, overflowed and
spilled slowly down her cheeks.

'Of course, I believe she's dead! What sort of a fool do you
take me for? Do you really think that she wouldn't have tried to
get in touch with me, during all these months, if she was still
alive?'

'And you say you hold Tom Rawbone responsible for her
death?'

Maud took a deep breath and closed her eyes. 'Who else?' she
asked in a stifled whisper.

'Well, that's an admission,' her mother-in-law remarked with
quiet satisfaction. 'But if that's what you believe, Maud – what
you've believed from the very beginning – why are you so set
against Master Chapman, here, making enquiries? Oh, don't
bother to deny it! It's been apparent to me, as it must have been
to him, that you'd have preferred it if he hadn't meddled.
You've encouraged him from the start to be on his way, to go
home to his wife. Why?'

Maud's eyes flew open again. Still tearful, she looked, in the firelight, like Niobe, the very personification of maternal grief. It was the first time I had seen her display any great emotion about her daughter's fate.

'Why?' she spat at Theresa. 'Why? Because I've come to terms with the idea that Eris is dead. Because I've learned to accept it. Because I don't want to hurt Ned by accusing his brother. Oh, yes! I hold Tom Rawbone responsible for killing my child! If he hadn't been faithless to Rosamund Bush, if he hadn't put ideas into Eris's head about marrying into the Rawbone family, she would never have encouraged Nathaniel. And the whole sorry mess would never have happened.'

'Wait a moment,' I expostulated. 'What exactly are you saying, Mistress? Just now, you spoke as though you believed Tom Rawbone to be your daughter's flesh-and-blood murderer. But now, it sounds as if you merely regard him as precipitating a situation that might have provoked someone else to kill her.'

'What does it matter?' Maud demanded angrily. 'Whichever way you look at it, Tom's to blame! Without him, nothing would have happened!' She burst into noisy sobbing.

Theresa got up from her stool and went to kneel beside her daughter-in-law, putting her arms around her.

'If you'd give us a moment, chapman,' she said quietly.

I left them alone, wrapping myself in my cloak and going outside, sheltering from the wind and rain as best I could by flattening myself against the cottage wall. But the front of the building was receiving the brunt of the storm, so I walked round to the back, immediately setting the dogs off barking and the geese cackling, while I mulled over the recent scene indoors. I was almost certain that Maud's earlier remarks had been intended as an outright condemnation of Tom Rawbone; a naming of him as her daughter's killer. But she had had second thoughts, modifying her accusation against him from a specific to a general one. I wondered why.

I stared across the cottage palings into the windy darkness beyond. It was difficult to see much, the driving rain blotting out most of the landscape. And yet . . . Was there something, or someone, moving higher up the slope, on the shoulder of the hill where the Rawbones had their farm? I crossed the muddy yard in a couple of strides to stand beside the fence, screwing up my eyes and peering into the distance until my head ached. But all to no avail: it was impossible to tell if I had seen anything or not.

A gust of wind tore at my cloak, almost whipping it from my shoulders. I made a grab at it, then looked again with even greater intensity than before. It was useless, however. The rain had suddenly increased, blotting out all but the immediate vicinity from view.

Had I seen anything? And if so, what? Nothing more, probably, than a sheep that had strayed and failed to be rounded up for the night making its errant way back to shelter, waiting for someone to hear its bleating and take it in. But the greatest likelihood was that it was nothing more than my imagination, and, on reflection, I decided to keep my fancies to myself. I had no desire to be thought a fool by either of the Mistress Lilywhites.

It seemed to me that I had allowed Maud sufficient time to pull herself together and master her belated outpourings of grief for Eris. If I sounded mean and unfeeling to myself, I could no longer ignore the fact that I was getting soaked to the skin. I returned to the front of the cottage, tapped on the door and, without waiting for a response, went inside.

Dame Theresa rose from her knees beside the younger woman's stool and nodded in my direction. As for Maud, she now appeared perfectly composed, and only the redness of her eyes indicated that she had recently been weeping.

'Dear life! Is it raining that hard?' Theresa, shocked by how wet I was, relieved me of my cloak and urged me closer to the fire. 'As soon as you're dry,' she went on, 'we'll go to bed. Maud and I are both extremely tired. There's a spare chamber-pot under the chopping bench, Master Chapman, if you need it during the night. It'll save you having to go outside in this dreadful weather.'

It was plain that there was going to be no more discussion of events for that evening. Maud had reverted to her usual taciturn self, and I guessed that Theresa's conscience was troubling her. She intended, for the moment, to leave her daughter-in-law in peace. I could have prolonged our parley by telling them of my day's adventures: of the two Roman bowls I had found among Saint Walburga's plate, and of the conclusions I had drawn from that discovery, the possible solving of an ancient mystery. But I decided, for the time being at any rate, to keep the knowledge to myself. I wasn't sure why, except that I, too, was tired and possessed by a sudden desire for my bed.

I was suddenly awake, lying on my right side, facing the hearth and the dying embers of the fire. I had no idea how long I'd been asleep, but I reckoned it must have been for some little time, because the wind had dropped and the rain had eased to a steady drumming against the window shutters, together with a faint pattering, like ghostly fingers, on the roof. The storm had blown away to the west, across the Severn into Wales.

I lay still, wondering what had roused me. Whatever it was had been sufficient to jerk me fully conscious without any of that slow and drowsy emergence from sleep that is a part of natural waking. So I continued to lie unmoving on my narrow pallet, my ears straining to distinguish the slightest sound . . .

Gradually, I realized that what I could hear was not the rain, but someone outside the cottage tapping on the shutters; a slow, cautious, intermittent rapping which, with luck, and trusting to the fact that the other occupants were heavy sleepers, would only awaken the person for whom it was intended.

Hercules, who was lying across my feet, raised his head and growled softly. Hastily I shushed him, at the same time wondering why the Lilywhites' own two guard dogs had given no warning of a stranger's approach. The only conclusion I could draw was that whoever it was was known to them.

On the other side of the linen curtain, someone was moving with such careful stealth that I found myself holding my breath. I could hear Theresa snoring in the loud and snuffling way she always did; which meant, as I had already surmised, that it was Maud who was creeping out of bed to answer the summons. I continued to lie as still as possible, unable to see her because I was facing the other way, but fully conscious of the quiet movements behind me that caused little more disturbance than a draught of air passing through the room. I felt Hercules shift restlessly, but to his credit, he made no sound, showing an unaccustomed willingness to obey instructions.

Maud paused momentarily alongside the mattress, probably aware of the dog's eyes glittering in the darkness. But then, seemingly satisfied that he had not roused me, she continued her delicate progress towards the door. I heard her draw the bolt and lift the latch, letting in a sudden stream of icy air before closing it again behind her. The tapping at the window ceased abruptly.

Carefully, I raised my head from the pillow, but could hear no sound. Who on earth, I wondered, would be paying Maud a visit in the middle of the night? Could this event be connected with my earlier experience outside the cottage, and my conviction that I had seen movement in the neighbourhood of the Rawbones' farm? Maybe that had not been my imagination, after all.

I eased myself upright from the pallet and tiptoed across to the door, pressing my ear against one of the cracks in the wood. Hercules joined me, sniffing eagerly along the gap at the bottom, where the planking had shrunk away from the threshold.

'Silence!' I hissed and, to his great annoyance, returned him to the mattress, where I dared him to follow me a second time. Disgruntled, he lay down, burying his nose between his paws, but watching me, nevertheless, with those big, liquid brown eyes of his.

I went, this time, to the window in the forlorn hope that some faint murmur of sound might penetrate the shutters, but all I could hear was the steady dripping of the rain from the overhanging slates. Short of walking into the yard and catching Maud and her nocturnal visitor red-handed, there was nothing more I could do to satisfy my burning curiosity. And if I did confront them, what excuse could I give? That I needed the privy? But Theresa had forestalled me there, pointing out the benefits of using the chamber-pot on a night of such inclement weather. Besides, I should have to dress first and I doubted I had time for that.

My misgivings were immediately confirmed. While I stood, undecided, I was aware of movement outside the door and a shadow flickering across the gap at the bottom. Maud was coming back. Almost before I knew it, I was stretched out on the pallet, the blanket drawn up anyhow to cover my nakedness.

This time, I was facing away from the hearth, as though I had turned over in my sleep. As Maud passed by, I opened my eyes a slit and could see that the hem of her nightshift was liberally spattered with mud. Her shoes, too, were filthy. She vanished behind the curtain, there was a rustle of movement, then silence. I presumed she had returned to bed without her mother-in-law being any the wiser. Certainly, Theresa's snoring had never once faltered.

I waited as long as I dared before again easing myself up from the pallet. I wrapped my cloak around me, slid my feet into my boots and padded softly to the door. There, as Maud had done some ten minutes earlier, I slid back the bolt, lifted the latch and, with a warning gesture at Hercules to stay where he was, stepped outside. (And unless you have been out of doors on a wet and windy night in nothing more than a cloak and a pair of boots, let me advise you now not to try it. The chill will cut you to the marrow.)

The yard in front of the cottage was, as I had expected, empty, so I edged my way cautiously around to the back. Both guard dogs, chained to the fence, raised their heads briefly, treating me to a cursory glance, but they were too busy gnawing the meat from a couple of enormous bones to evince any real interest in someone whose smell and shape they had come to recognize during the past four days. The geese might have been a different matter had they not been greedily pecking at the decent sized mound of grain which had been tipped into their pen. Our visitor had come well prepared to silence any warning of his approach.

But whoever he or she was – and why should it not have been a woman? – was long gone. I could see the back gate of the little compound swinging gently on its hinges, as though the last person to pass through had been in too much of a hurry to close it properly. And the gate had been shut, I would swear to it, when I had been in the yard the previous evening.

Just as I had done earlier, I went over to the paling and stared into the darkness, but this time, with the almost total cessation of the rain, I was able to see further. A figure was climbing the slope at a good, round pace in the direction of the Rawbones' farm; a figure draped in a hooded cloak that billowed around it in the wind, making it impossible for me to make out a specific shape. But there was something about the way in which the figure moved that told me my first assumption had been correct. The length of stride that carried the person uphill at such a rate could only be that of a man.

He had moved too rapidly, was already at too great a distance, for me to go after him, not allowing for the fact that I should first have to dress: and there was no way I could confront a possible adversary in nothing other than a cloak and a pair of boots. The indignity of such attire would have put me at an immediate disadvantage.

I returned indoors as quietly and as circumspectly as I had left, although I half-expected Maud to be waiting for me. Had she been, I would have pleaded that something had wakened me and, as the storm had abated, I preferred to use the outside privy to the chamber-pot. (I cursed myself that I hadn't thought up that excuse earlier on, but, in mitigation, I must point out that it was the middle of the night and my brain was not at its sparkling best. Nevertheless, I knew I had missed an opportunity to identify the visitor through my slow-wittedness.)

Maud, however, was nowhere to be seen. The linen curtain still hung demurely between the two women and myself as I took off my cloak and boots and once again rolled, teeth chattering, on to the lumpy ticking of the mattress. I invited Hercules to join me and the pallet's lively colony of fleas under the blanket, which he was nothing loth to do, and I was able to use his bodily warmth to augment my own, like a hot brick wrapped in sacking. In my absence, Theresa's snoring had grown louder, but I found it difficult to believe that Maud had yet fallen asleep. Surely she must have heard me leave the cottage, but she hadn't challenged my reason for doing so.

The remaining embers of the fire made a glowing patch of red in the smoky gloom. I turned to face the hearth again, Hercules snuggling with a contented sigh into the crook of my body. Had the night visitor been Tom Rawbone? I wondered. Had he come sneaking back to the farm under cover of darkness? Had that been what I had seen the previous evening while I was loitering in the yard?

But why would he want to visit Maud? She had made it clear to both Theresa and myself that she held him, either directly or indirectly, responsible for her daughter's disappearance. He must be aware of her hostility. So it was unlikely to be Tom. Ned, then? There seemed, from what different people had told me, to be an enduring friendship between him and Maud, in spite of the fact that she had once rejected him in favour of Gilbert Lilywhite. Ned Rawbone, then, was more likely. But why? What would he possibly have to tell her that could not wait until their next meeting? And that must be at Mass tomorrow morning. No, this morning, for it had to be well past midnight, judging by the progress of the storm . . .

It was at this point that I must have drifted across the borderline of sleep, for I found myself, still repeating the words 'well past midnight', standing beside a giant Nine Men's Morris board in the main room of the alehouse, now the size of Westminster Palace. On the board were the players, consisting of the Rawbone family – the twins, Nathaniel, Jacquetta, Tom, Ned, Petronelle and Elvina Merryman – Rosamund and her parents, Lambert Miller, Sir Anselm, even Billy Tyrrell and the village whore, Alice Tucker.

Someone I couldn't see, but who I presumed was the other

captain, was saying, 'It's your turn, Roger. Come along! You know what you have to do. Line up three of your "morrells" in a straight line, and those three will lead you to Eris. Get on with it, now! You've asked for my help, so do as I tell you. And when you've discovered the answer, you can go home to Adela. You might even be there by the Feast of Saint Patrick. Come along, Roger! Come along . . .'

Seventeen

I awoke next morning with a headache, and possessed of the feeling that I had only just dropped off to sleep.

At some time during the night, Hercules had left the shelter of my pallet and was now lying beside the hearth, on which a recently laid, and newly lit, fire was burning. Someone had been busy while I slept. That someone was now shaking my naked shoulder.

'Wake up, chapman!' Theresa's voice sounded close to my ear. 'What's the matter with you and Maud this morning? You're both as dozy as if you'd been up all night.' She gave a sudden guffaw. 'Not an illicit assignation, I trust!'

'Don't be vulgar, Mother-in-law!' Maud begged curtly from behind the linen curtain.

'God save you, girl, I didn't mean it!' Theresa gave another hearty laugh. 'Don't you know a joke when you hear one? What's up with you? Didn't you sleep well?' She turned back to me. 'I'll give you ten minutes, Master Chapman, to make yourself decent enough for the company of a couple of respectable women. After that, you must take your chance. And so must we!' She vanished behind the curtain, chuckling suggestively and leaving me to reflect how often it was, in my experience, that older women had a coarser sense of humour than their juniors.

I heaved myself off the pallet, struggled into shirt and breeches, tussled with recalcitrant laces whose points refused to thread through their corresponding eyes with any degree of accuracy, tugged on my boots and made for the yard.

While I doused my head under the pump, the dogs and geese

started their usual cacophony, forcibly putting me in mind of the previous night. Before going back into the cottage, therefore, I checked on the animals to make certain that my adventure had not just been another, earlier part of my dream. But the bones, now picked clean, were still there on the ground beside the dogs, and the geese, pausing in their cackling, pecked at the few remaining grains scattered across the earth inside their pen.

Indoors, breakfast was almost ready, the oatmeal bubbling in a pot of water suspended over the fire, while the dried, salted herrings sizzled in a skillet placed among the embers. I groaned inwardly. I longed for a collop of pork or bacon such as we had had on an earlier morning. Breakfast in the Lilywhite household was fast becoming monotonous.

I donned my jerkin and pulled a stool up to the table. Maud placed a bowl of porridge in front of me just as I sneezed violently. I wiped my nose on the back of my hand.

'You're rheumy this morning,' Theresa remarked. 'Here, drink this. It'll warm you.' And she passed me half a beaker of ale to which she had added hot water and a spoonful of cinnamon.

I thanked her politely, although I would rather have had a drink made up entirely of ale. Then I sneezed again.

'You got thoroughly chilled, I expect,' Maud said, 'clambering about on Upper Brockhurst ridge yesterday afternoon. The woods are always dank this time of year.'

I grunted, but fatigue was taking its toll. Her remark failed to register properly with me until Theresa asked, 'Is that why you didn't return until late, then, chapman? And what were you doing up on the ridge? I thought you'd already explored it.'

But I was staring at Maud, who, in a sudden flurry of activity, was busying herself with the skillet of dried herring, bent over the fire as though her life depended on seeing that the fish was hot enough to serve. How could she possibly have known that I'd been on the ridge yesterday afternoon when I hadn't mentioned the fact the previous evening? There was only one answer, of course. The person who had seen me, who had set light to the cage, had been the same person who had called on Maud during the night. Whatever the main reason for his visit, his sighting of me had also been mentioned. But why?

Theresa was pressing me for a reply to her question in the hope, I realized, that I might have discovered something new in connection with her granddaughter's disappearance. Sadly, I had to disillusion her. But at least I was able to regale her, as we ate our herrings, with the story of the Roman bowls and my interpretation of what had really happened, nearly a century and a half ago, to the two wellers from Tetbury.

Her amazement at my deductive powers was gratifying; although I have to admit she was more concerned with the fact that, since coming to live in Lower Brockhurst, she had been drinking the Blood of Christ from a pagan vessel, than she was with the probable solution to a 130-year-old mystery, which had never interested her much in the first place.

'Did you know about these bowls?' she demanded of her daughter-in-law in outraged tones.

Maud shook her head. 'But I know the stories about Light-fingered Lightfoot,' she said. 'As does everyone else in the village.'

'So what do you intend to do about it?' Theresa enquired. 'Don't you think the village elders should be informed?'

Maud shrugged. 'You can tell them if you wish, Mother-in-law. The chances are that they know about it already. But if Sir Anselm has consecrated the bowls to the Glory of God, as he apparently assured the chapman that he has, then no one will worry. However they were come by originally, they belong to Saint Walburga's and the village now. We're not a wealthy community. We can't replace a pair of silver bowls except at great cost to ourselves. I'll have a word with Ned next time I see him, if you like. But I doubt he'll deem it necessary to do anything about it.'

Theresa breathed deeply, registering her disapproval.

'This is a heathen place, chapman,' she confided, lowering her voice to a whisper, 'as you've no doubt discovered for yourself by now. The old magic is still practised hereabouts, in the forest and in isolated villages like this one. It's so close to the Welsh marches that the ancient customs have spilled across the border and taken root for some miles this side of the Severn. Heresy goes hand in hand here with orthodoxy. And the priests, who should be the guardian of men's souls, become tainted by it, themselves, in the end. The Papal Commissioners don't venture into the wilds very often, and when they do, sand is thrown in their eyes. Everyone bands together to protect the village and its secrets, and the Commissioners go away satisfied that all is well.' She shivered. 'You must have seen in the woods, as I have, the clooties and the dolls. Offerings to the old Celtic gods.'

'I . . . I have noticed them,' I admitted.

'Of course, you have. How could you not? And the children are every bit as bad as the adults. They grow up with it.'

'That's enough, Mother-in-law,' Maud said sharply. She rose from the table and began gathering together the dirty dishes, adding unkindly, 'If you wish to return to a more civilized life in Gloucester, I shan't prevent you. Now, we must hurry or we shall be late for Mass.'

Theresa flushed painfully at Maud's words and I felt a sudden rush of sympathy for her, even though I realized how much her domineering ways must irk the younger woman. I tried to distract her by begging some scraps for Hercules from the meal she was preparing for their own two dogs. But when she would have left the cottage, she was intercepted.

'I'll take the food out to the animals,' her daughter-in-law said abruptly, seizing the bowls and picking up a small sack of grain for the geese.

As the door closed behind Maud, Theresa grimaced. 'She's in a bad humour this morning. I'd steer clear of her, if I were you.' And she set about washing the dirty dishes.

But I had already guessed the reason for Maud's insistence on feeding the dogs herself. It gave her a chance to remove and throw away the bones brought by the midnight visitor. If Theresa had noticed them, she might well have insisted on knowing how they got there and where they came from.

We walked to church in an oppressive silence, Maud and I

each busy with our own thoughts, Theresa carefully trying to avoid upsetting the other woman any further.

The stormy night had given way to a brighter morning, which once again prompted thoughts of the coming spring. The hills, rising up on the other side of Lower Brockhurst, were clearly visible, while the clouds, rolling past in the upper air, caught the last red gleam of a sunrise that turned their underbellies to fire. Away to our left, the glimmering surface of the Draco reflected the early morning light, and the sudden tolling of Saint Walburga's bell shattered the country silence.

As we crossed the bridge over the stream and made our way through the belt of trees opposite the priest's house, it seemed as though the entire population of the village was determined to attend the service. Everyone I knew, plus many more that I did not, appeared to be converging upon the church. Even Lambert Miller was present, still wrapped in bandages and extremely pale, but hobbling along manfully, supported by his mother on one side and Rosamund Bush on the other and plainly enjoying every second of the attention he was attracting. Most people stopped to speak to him and to enquire after the state of his health, making him the centre of interest. I doubted if he had ever been so happy, in spite of his injuries.

Once inside Saint Walburga's, however, it was a different matter. Both attention and interest had to be shared with Sir Anselm, who, as good as his word, had forced himself out of bed to conduct the service of Tierce as usual. He, too, still sported bandages, his crumpled face not so much pale as parchment white. And he tended to sway a little on his feet, to the great consternation of his congregation. But he lifted a hand in order to restrain those who would have rushed forward to assist him, then knelt in prayer before the altar while awaiting the arrival of the Rawbones, who were later than ever this particular morning. Not altogether surprisingly, I thought. Even they, with all their pride and confidence, must be a little worried as to the nature of their reception. And one of them, I was convinced, had been up and about in the middle of the night. But which one that was, I was still uncertain.

They came at last, all of them except Tom, heads held high, not deigning to glance either to right or left, and stood in their customary place at the front of the assembled villagers. Sir Anselm, continuing to refuse all offers of help, even from Mistress Bush, tottered to his feet, lifted his hands in blessing and the service began.

As the priest rolled out the familiar Latin phrases in a much stronger voice than I think anyone present had expected of him, my attention began to wander as, I regret to say, it invariably does in church. I twisted my neck slightly, in order to get a further glimpse of Lambert Miller, then turned back to look once more at Sir Anselm. It dawned on me that neither man had suffered as severe a beating as had at first been thought. Whoever their attacker had been, he had avoided extreme punishment and the danger of mortal injury. He had been careful to inflict damage but not death; and a man so in control of his emotions was, in my estimation at least, neither vindictive nor out for revenge.

What was he, then? In Lambert's case, I guessed him to be someone whose sole purpose was to lay the blame for the attacks on Tom Rawbone in the hope – and, as it turned out, the justified hope – that Tom would flee the village for fear of retribution. As far as the priest was concerned, I still thought the assault might be a warning of some kind to Sir Anselm to keep his mouth shut; a warning not to talk to . . . ? Not to talk to whom? The answer came like a clap of thunder. To me, of course! To me!

I suddenly remembered the open door of the priest's house, when I had dined with Sir Anselm on Friday morning, and cursed myself that I had not seen its implications sooner. After the meal we had found the main door into the hallway standing ajar. Sir Anselm had explained it by telling me that the latch was faulty, and that Ned Rawbone must have failed to close it properly when he left. But suppose that were not the case. Suppose someone, learning of my presence, had crept into the house with the intention of eavesdropping on myself and the priest, just to make sure that the nosy stranger was not being made a party to secrets he had no business knowing.

207

I thought back, desperately trying to recollect what Sir Anselm and I had discussed. Eris's disappearance for one thing. Eris herself . . . What more? The marriage of Maud and Gilbert Lilywhite and the fact that Ned had hoped to marry her, but been thwarted by his father and her love for another man. But there was something else, nagging at the back of my mind. While my lips framed the correct responses by rote, my eyes wandered from the side altars – from the Christ of the Trades and the Virgin – to the high altar and Saint Walburga, then back again to the Virgin in her blue dress and golden crown. The eternal Mother . . . children . . . the begetting of children . . . Yes, that was it! Sir Anselm had voiced a suspicion, later echoed by William Bush, that Maud might already have been with child when she married Gilbert Lilywhite. Eris, the first of the three children she bore him, had been born in just under nine months.

Yet, why should that fact be of any significance? No one with whom I had spoken had ever stigmatized Eris as a bastard. She had been born within the bonds of wedlock as had her two feeble young brothers, who had died in infancy. No, there was nothing in that. I must look for some other reason why my conversation with Sir Anselm might have provoked an eaves-dropper to feel uneasy.

The Mass progressed, but my errant thoughts could come up with no other recollections of what had been said between the priest and myself on Friday morning. I moved and responded like a man in a trance, receiving the wafer, the Body of Christ, on my tongue with an indifference that, later, filled me with shame. It was only when I was offered the silver bowl contain-ing the wine that I returned to the present, conscious of Dame Theresa kneeling beside me, and of her hesitation when it was her turn to drink. She forced herself to overcome her reluc-tance, however, and the slight frown of puzzlement that was creasing Sir Anselm's brow was smoothed away.

As soon as the service came to an end, the Rawbones left the church in a solid phalanx, Nathaniel walking with his sister, closely followed by Ned and Petronelle with the twins hard on their heels. Once again, they seemed unaware of the muttering among their neighbours and of the inimical looks they were receiving. Elvina Merryman, bringing up the rear of the column, was the only one who appeared at all flurried, tripping over a broken flagstone, one of several such hazards in the church. Being the well brought up and gallant young lad that I was, and being close at hand, I went to her assistance, gripping one of her elbows in a steadying clasp. Had I not done so, I might have missed the sudden turn of Ned Rawbone's head as he glanced in Maud Lilywhite's direction. It was a glance so fleeting, apparently so insignificant that I doubt if anyone noticed it but myself. Once alerted, however, I also saw the almost imperceptible nod Maud gave in return. Some sort of signal had passed between them, and I was suddenly convinced that Ned had been the nocturnal visitor of the previous night.

No one else seemed in a hurry to leave the church precincts, and as soon as the Rawbones had vanished across the footbridge on their homeward climb to Dragonswick farm, a deafening babel of conversation broke out, everyone talking at once. Lambert was surrounded yet again by well-wishers, as was Sir Anselm; while Elder Sewter and Elder Hemnall, together with several other grave and grey-haired men, who I guessed to be fellow members of the Village Council, were besieged by demands to know what was being done to apprehend Tom Rawbone. I had no chance to hear their reply as, at that moment, I was claimed not only by the Mistress Lilywhites, anxious to get home to their dinner, but also accosted by Rosamund Bush, who left Lambert's side for mine, pushing through the intervening crowd with her usual determination.

'Roger!' She gave me both her hands and her most attractive smile. 'Lambert has challenged me to another game of Nine Men's Morris, tomorrow night, in the alehouse. I want you to be one of my players again. You will say yes, won't you?'

She lowered long lashes over those beautiful blue eyes, then flashed them open again with practised artifice. At the same time, an involuntary dimple peeped at the corner of her rosebud mouth, as though mocking her own contrivance. Part of her great charm was the mix of contradictions in her nature.

I hesitated, but before I had a chance even to put my thoughts in order, Maud Lilywhite said firmly, 'You're out of luck, I'm afraid, Rosamund. Master Chapman will have to be on his way tomorrow if he's to reach Bristol by the feast of Saint Patrick. He's promised his wife and children to be home by then and he won't want to disappoint them. I'm sure,' she went on acidly, 'that there are any number of other young men in the village who will be only too anxious to oblige you.'

'There are not that many young men in the village, Mistress,' Rosamund retorted sharply. 'And I think Roger is man enough to answer for himself.' She turned back to me, laying a slender hand on my sleeve. 'Roger?' she queried. 'What do you say?'

I glanced at Maud. Her lips were set in a thin, determined line, although Theresa was looking bewildered.

'When did you make up your mind to leave us, Master Chapman?' she reproached me. 'You said nothing about it at breakfast.'

'I . . . I've only just decided,' I stammered.

'Then how does Maud know of your intentions?' the older woman rapped back at me. She rounded on her daughter-in-law. 'You're forcing his hand, aren't you? You're throwing him out!'

Maud avoided my gaze.

'No such thing,' she protested uneasily. 'Master Chapman has been saying for days that he must go home to his wife and family.'

I could see by the expression on her face that she had suddenly determined to be rid of me. She had been a grudging hostess from the beginning, and now she had had enough. She was telling me as politely as she could that I was no longer welcome in her house. Had it not been Sunday, I suspected that she would have suggested I leave at once. As it was, she would expect me and Hercules to set off immediately after breakfast tomorrow. Theresa was right: I was being thrown out.

I knew that I had no choice but to comply with Maud's wishes. It was her cottage. I could not stay where I was no longer welcome. The laws of hospitality must not be breached.

Besides which, at the back of my mind was the nagging thought that tomorrow was probably the last day on which I could set out with any realistic hope of reaching Bristol by the middle of March. Perhaps God was giving me a sign that there was, after all, nothing further for me to do in Lower Brockhurst; that maybe there had been nothing for me to discover in the first place.

So I said gently to Rosamund, 'You'll have to hold me excused from your game tomorrow evening, Mistress. Dame Maud is right. I must go home. It's true; I'm bound by a promise I made to my wife.'

The glow of that flower-like face dimmed. The blue eyes lost much of their sparkle and became dull, like pebbles; the rosebud mouth grew petulant. Women such as Rosamund Bush do not expect to have their requests refused; it is a negation of their beauty and of that beauty's power to subdue and hold sway over men. I could see that her rejection and humiliation by Tom Rawbone must have led to a nightmare of the soul. She withdrew her hand abruptly from my sleeve, as though I had suddenly been struck by the plague.

'Oh, very well, then,' she said, with a toss of her head. 'If you must go home, you must. Never let me be accused of coming between husband and wife.'

She swung on her heel and returned to Lambert Miller, hanging affectionately on his arm and raising her eyes to his in worshipful adoration. The poor fool, already weak from his injuries, almost swooned at her feet. I suppressed a smile and saw that Theresa was doing likewise.

But not for long. Her good humour evaporated very quickly once we reached the smallholding and entered the cottage.

Maud, carefully looking at neither of us, went to kneel by the fire where a clay pot sat among the glowing sods of peat. Seizing a cloth, she lifted the lid an inch or two, letting the tantalizing aroma of roasting coney linger briefly on the air before closing it up again. She set a pan of water to boil and went across to the chopping board in order to prepare the leeks, onions and garlic that would accompany the rabbit.

Theresa maintained her silence on the subject of my departure until I returned from giving Hercules a run around the
yard. As I stooped to pat him, she demanded fiercely, 'You've
given up hope then, have you, of finding out what happened to
my granddaughter?'

I glanced at Maud's rigid back, as she gathered the chopped
vegetables into the skirt of her apron and carried them over to
the pan of boiling water, tossing them in.

'Mistress,' I said, 'I've been here the better part of five days
and know little more regarding Eris's true fate than when I
arrived. That she was murdered, most likely by one of the
Rawbones, I have small doubt, which seems to be the opinion
of most other people I've talked to. But I have no proof of it.
Nor any solid proof that Eris is dead. I very much doubt that all
the Rawbones know the truth of the matter, either. One or two
of them might. Perhaps even three,' I added, remembering my
illogical conviction that I needed three morrells in a row to
complete the game of Nine Men's Morris that I had been
playing in my dream.

Theresa regarded me straitly. 'But was it really your intention
to leave tomorrow had not my daughter-in-law made it plain
that you were no longer welcome here?'

Still Maud kept her back to us, fussing over the pot hanging
from the trivet and poking at the vegetables with a long-
handled spoon. The smell was delicious. My mouth began to
water.

I had no desire to be the cause of more animosity than
already existed between the two women, so I said, 'I have little
option, Mistress, but to set off for home very soon if—'

'If you are to keep your promise to your wife,' Theresa
interrupted mockingly. 'I know. Everyone knows. If that promise was ever made, of course.'

'Mother-in-law!' Maud was shocked into breaking her self-
imposed silence.

'And why should I lie about it?' I asked Theresa angrily.

'It's better than admitting failure, isn't it?' she sneered. 'The
first night you were here, you told us – no, boasted to us – of the

problems that you've solved for other people. So you made sure that if this one proved too difficult for you, you could sneak off on the excuse of a promise to your wife.'

'That's most unfair—' I was beginning hotly, but broke off, suddenly aware of Theresa's game.

She was trying to goad me into staying. Even if Maud had given me my marching orders, there must be other lodgings to be had somewhere in Lower Brockhurst, and Theresa would willingly help me find them. She was taunting me with failure; and the word 'boasted' had been unkindly and undeservedly used to flick me on the raw. Maud, too, realized what her mother-in-law was up to and swung round to face her, arms akimbo.

'The chapman leaves tomorrow, and that's the end of it. It's my wish. It's also his. Please don't insult our guest with the suggestion that he's been lying to us, Mother-in-law. We had no right to ask his help in the first place. Now, sit at the table, both of you. Dinner's almost ready.'

Theresa took her place, looking suddenly old and defeated. I drew up a stool beside her, feeling that I had let her down. But my excuse was genuine, and she knew it. She did not really think me a liar.

All the same, her accusations and my own failure continued to haunt me throughout a largely silent meal. The roast coney and vegetables might have been sawdust for all the notice I took of their taste, in spite of the fact that I ate two helpings (although, to be fair to myself, I shared the second one with Hercules). Finally, as I pushed my plate aside and took a swig of ale, I put one of my hands over Theresa's, where it lay, fidgeting restlessly with a knife, on the table. The brown blotched skin of advancing age was dry and rough to the touch.

'I must start for home in the morning, Mistress. Dame Maud is in the right of it. But there's still the rest of today. I'll take one last look along Upper Brockhurst ridge, particularly at the well. I've no good reason to offer you for doing so, except a deep-rooted and completely unjustified feeling that it could hold the key to Eris's disappearance.'

Eighteen

'Why do you want to visit the ridge again?' Maud snapped. 'A waste of time and effort, if you ask my opinion, Master Chapman. We all know there's nothing up there. Ned himself searched the whole area, including the well, the morning after Eris's disappearance. So wherever she is, it isn't in the ruins of Upper Brockhurst Hall, a fact to which half the village can testify.'

Theresa nodded. 'I wasn't here, myself, but it's what everyone will tell you. And that well's been empty for years. It really ought to be filled in,' she added, her thoughts momentarily diverted. 'It's a danger to all the children of the village. Not so much at this time of year, I grant you, but in the summer months when the more adventurous of them go up on the ridge to play. Oh, I know the canopy's been removed and it has a lid,' she went on hastily, forestalling her daughter-in-law's objection, 'but children are perfectly capable of opening it, even if it takes two or three of them to do it. The village elders are fortunate that there have been no further accidents since Ned Rawbone was a lad. That rusty ladder's most unsafe. It was partially eaten away the last time I saw it, and that's some while ago now.'

'It still is,' I agreed. 'I can vouch for that. I've climbed down it. It's just that . . .' I shrugged unhappily, finding it impossible to explain the conviction that gripped me every time I visited the Upper Brockhurst woods that Eris was somehow close at hand.

Maud said again, 'It's a waste of your time. You might as well spend the rest of the day here, with us, by the fire. Conserve your strength. You'll need to be up and about first thing tomorrow morning if you're to make the most of the daylight hours. They're still short this time of year. Go early enough and you might fall in with a cart travelling in the direction of Bristol.'

'Oh, let him visit the ridge if he wants to,' Theresa grunted. 'A great lad like him doesn't need to worry about saving his strength. It stands to reason he doesn't want to be sitting around here all day, chatting to a couple of women, and one of them old enough to be his mother. He won't find anything up there on the ridge – at least, he hasn't so far – but if it keeps him happy, where's the harm in it?'

Maud opened her mouth as if she would argue the point; then, seeming to change her mind, shut it again.

I glanced at Hercules's recumbent form. Having finished his dinner, he had retired once more to his place by the hearth and was now stretched full length, fast asleep.

'I'll leave the dog with you, if I may,' I said. 'His little legs will find themselves overtaxed, I'm afraid, in the next week or so. I'll let him rest while he can.'

'He's no trouble.' Maud pushed the ale jug towards me, inviting me to pour myself another drink, which I did, not needing a second bidding. The simple action nudged my memory and I turned to the older woman with a smile.

'You overcame your scruples during this morning's Mass, Dame Theresa. You drank from the Roman chalice, after all.'

She pursed her lips in disapproval, partly, I suspected, at her own lack of backbone.

'There are times, chapman,' she said, 'when you know that taking a stand will achieve you nothing. You might just as well grin and bear whatever it is. And as, according to you, Sir Anselm has consecrated the cups to the greater glory of God, I've decided that this is one of those occasions. That must be my excuse for not speaking out.'

'But you have the added consolation,' I comforted her, 'of knowing that many generations of men, women and children have drunk from those cups without, apparently, having incurred the wrath of the Almighty. Ever since, if I'm right in my supposition, the priest known as Light-fingered Lightfoot chanced upon them in Upper Brockhurst Hall after the great plague.'

'This is only guesswork on your part, Master Chapman,' was Maud's acid comment.

Theresa frowned her down. 'He's admitted that. So, tell us again what you think happened,' she encouraged me. 'How did the Roman bowls come into the Church's possession?'

I was nothing loath to give my theory another airing.

'I believe,' I said, 'that the wellers who were working for Humphrey and Tobias Martin found the two chalices whilst digging the well, but did the bowls belong to the finders or to the men on whose land they'd been discovered? The silver was valuable, worth a great deal of money. If the wellers had had any sense, they would have kept quiet concerning their find, but perhaps they were unable to. One or both of the brothers might have been present when the bowls were dug up.'

'Go on,' Theresa urged as I paused for another swig of ale. 'I realize that you've already told us all this once, but I wasn't attending properly the first time.'

'There's nothing much more to tell,' I shrugged. 'I think it probable that the wellers walked off with the bowls. When the brothers discovered what they'd done, they went after them and killed them. They carried their treasure back to Upper Brock-hurst Hall, assuming that the murders would be put down to the work of outlaws or footpads. Sometime, doubtless, they would have intended taking their booty to either Gloucester or Bristol, or even, maybe, to London, in order to sell it. But they died in the outbreak of plague that wiped out the whole village a few days later.'

'You don't know any of this for certain,' Maud reiterated scathingly as she whisked the ale jug out of my reach and began once again to clear the table. I had often seen Adela move in just such a fashion, like a sleepwalker, as she performed a task that she did several times a day, barely conscious of her actions, her mind elsewhere. I would have given much to know what, or of whom, Maud was thinking just then, with that glazed, faraway look in her eyes.

Her thoughts, whatever they were, were interrupted by a knock on the cottage door. She called out, 'Come in! It's not bolted,' and, to prove her point, stepped forward to unlatch it.

Rob Pomphrey stood on the threshold, rubbing first one foot and then the other against the back of the opposite leg, in a vain attempt to rid his shoes of their coating of mud. His nose, red and running from the cold, sniffed appreciatively at the smell of roast rabbit that lingered tantalizingly on the air.

Maud laughed. 'Come and sit down, Rob. Have some dinner. If you don't mind the burnt scrapings from around the dish, I can probably top a trencher for you.'

I have rarely seen a man move faster. He was seated at the table before Maud had finished reaching into the bread crock to find a hunk of stale loaf. From this, she hacked a thick slice which she placed in front of him; then, with knife and spoon, she scraped the earthenware pot clean of its remaining meat and vegetables.

Rob set to with a will, producing his own knife and hacking the trencher in half. He then proceeded to stuff his mouth so full that it was impossible for him to speak for several minutes. He could only nod or shake his head in response to the two women's enquiries about his family.

Eventually, however, when he had washed down his impromptu meal with what was left of the ale in the bottom of the jug, he solemnly announced, 'Been talking to Billy Tyrrell.'

'What were you doing up at Dragonswick Farm?' Theresa wanted to know, ignoring the obvious question, to Rob's palpable irritation. 'I thought you were shepherding for one of the farms on the opposite side of the valley these days.'

Rob wiped his mouth on his sleeve. 'True enough, Mistress. But my master wanted me to consult with Billy 'bout washing the sheep.' He sighed, realizing from Theresa's bemused expression that he would be forced to give details before he was allowed to proceed any further with his news. 'We usually wash our flock and the Rawbones' together. This year, Master's keen

to do it as early as possible. Some of them old ewes get real dirty
during the winter. Lot o' foul wool and excrement trapped
round their udders. Washing sheep means we got to dam up the
stream fer a day or two, so Master tells me, "Get that Billy
Tyrrell to find out whereabouts Ned Rawbone's goin' to make
the pool this year." Further upstream than last, he's hoping.
Village folk get funny if water supply's dammed up fer too
long.' Rob stuffed the last piece of trencher into his mouth and
licked his lips. 'That was good, missus,' he complimented Maud
as he finished his ale. 'But none o' this is what I come to tell
you.'

At this juncture, Theresa pointedly moved her stool another
foot or so away from Rob, wrinkling her nose in disgust at the
strong smell of sheep emanating from his clothing. It was plain
to me that she had never really grown accustomed to the scents
and sounds of the countryside. She would have been happier,
and so undoubtedly would Maud, if she had gone home to live
in the city with its stench of drains and rotting garbage and its
eternal ringing of the bells.

Maud and Rob Pomphrey ignored her, the former out of
habit, the latter because he was completely unaware of giving
offence. Other people's thoughts and opinions didn't interest
him.

'Wouldn't call here just t' talk about sheep, now would I?' he
went on.

Maud smiled as her mother-in-law sighed in frustration.
'Why have you come, Rob?' she asked gently.

'Well . . .' Rob leaned his elbows on the table and cupped his
chin in his hands. 'Thought p'raps as how I ought to warn you.
Billy thinks Tom Rawbone's come back and is hiding in the
house up there.'

I again recalled the figure I had seen moving on the hillside
the previous evening, and at Rob's words, it occurred to me
that it might have been Tom sneaking home for the night.

'Then the village elders should be informed at once,' Theresa
said sharply.

Maud asked, 'Is Billy sure of this, Rob?'

The shepherd shook his tousled head and answered cautiously, 'Not sure, no. Not absolutely. But he's got the idea fixed in his head fer some reason or other. Mind,' he added fairly, 'you know what a feather-brain Billy can be. Anyone who'd graze sheep in same pasture as your geese . . . Well, 'nough said! But just in case he's right, I thought you goodies ought to be on your guard.' He pushed his plate to one side and belched loudly. 'That were a good dinner, Mistress Lilywhite, and no mistake. Better'n I'd get at home.'

Maud smiled, 'That's a slur on your wife, Rob Pomphrey.'

'No, it ain't,' was the positive answer. 'You know full well my Doll can't cook. Never could, lord love 'er.'

'Never mind your Doll and her lack of culinary talent,' Theresa cut in angrily, while Rob looked bewildered. 'Are you going to report Billy Tyrrell's suspicions to the elders or not?'

'No, why should I, Missus? Billy's only guessin'.'

Rob looked even more discomfited, and it occurred to me that he had only used the shepherd boy's story as an excuse to call on Maud Lilywhite in the hope of a better Sunday dinner than the one waiting for him at home. And he hadn't been disappointed.

'Why should you?' Theresa demanded wrathfully. 'Because, my good man, Tom Rawbone is wanted for assaulting both Lambert Miller and Sir Anselm, two innocent men asleep in their beds. He's a wanted criminal.'

Rob shook his head stubbornly. 'I ain't raising the hue and cry against any man, whatever he's done. I only come here to warn you and Dame Maud to be on your guard because you're two women on your own, and dwell away from the village. It might scare you if you come across Tom sudden like, and you weren't expectin' to see 'im.' He turned in some distress to Maud. 'I ain't peaching to the elders.'

She patted his hand. 'Of course you're not, Rob. And Billy's probably wrong. I don't suppose for a minute that Tom would be so foolhardy as to return to Dragonswick. Not so soon, at any rate.'

219

There was something about Maud's calm reception of the news, her lack of questions, her soothing reassurance that Billy Tyrrell was most probably mistaken, that suddenly convinced me she already knew about Tom. It also suggested to me a lack of animosity towards him that made nonsense of her earlier assertion that she believed Tom Rawbone to be her daughter's murderer. Had he, I wondered, been her midnight visitor, however unlikely that might seem?

'Maud—!' Theresa was beginning heatedly, but her daughter-in-law rounded on her just as angrily.

'Be quiet, Mother-in-law! Stop interfering in matters that don't concern you. You've never understood country ways, and you never will!' She swallowed hard and smiled at the shepherd. 'Thank you for warning us, Rob. You've put us on our guard. But Billy's story isn't worth taking seriously, I feel certain.'

'You won't breathe a word to anyone else, Mistress, will you? Not 'bout what I've just told you. Let Billy take the blame if anything's to be said. I don't want to get in bad with the Rawbones.'

'Of course we shan't say anything,' Maud assured him, as he rose to take his leave. 'Take care, now, and give my love to Doll. I'll be seeing her around.'

'Ar, I will that.' Rob sighed reminiscently. 'That were good food, that were, Missus. Gilbert always used to say as how you was a good cook, I remember. "Whatever else she is or isn't, Maud's a good cook. I'll give her that." Those were his very words, and he weren't wrong. I'll testify to that on oath.'

The cottage door closed behind him. There was a short silence before Theresa asked, 'What are we going to do, Maud?' She looked at me. 'Chapman, would you walk down to the village and speak to one of the elders? Tell him—'

'You're to do nothing of the sort,' Maud told me firmly. 'The story's a bag of moonshine, Mother-in-law. Oh, I don't doubt Billy said something of the sort to Rob, but I feel sure that Rob himself would have dismissed it as nonsense if he hadn't smelled the rabbit as he was passing and fancied a free dinner. It's true his Doll's a deplorable cook. What Billy had just told him served as an excellent excuse to call in. That's all.'

Faced with the younger woman's calm assertion, Theresa subsided on to her stool, defeated. In spite of all her domineering ways, it was Maud who really ruled the roost in the cottage, a conclusion it had taken me a day or two to reach.

'Very well,' Theresa conceded. 'But when we're discovered dead in our beds – especially now that you've given Master Chapman his marching orders, leaving us totally unprotected – perhaps you'll finally admit that I was right in wishing to take Rob Pomphrey's story to the elders.'

Half an hour later, as I climbed the pasture towards Upper Brockhurst ridge, having left Hercules twitching deliriously and dreaming his canine dreams before the Lilywhites' fire, I mulled over the shepherd's visit; in particular, his repetition of Gilbert Lilywhite's remark, 'Whatever else she is or isn't, Maud's a good cook.' Odd words indeed from a doting husband. 'Whatever else she is . . .' What else could she have been but the woman he loved? And who had loved him enough in return to reject Ned Rawbone's proposal of marriage for his own?

But was that version of events the true one? Something that Dame Jacquetta had told me surfaced suddenly in my mind; that Ned had married Petronelle to please his father. 'She wouldn't have been Ned's choice, I'm sure, left to himself, but Nathaniel insisted and, as ever, my nephew did as he was bidden.' Those had been the dame's very words. So, what was the truth of the matter? Was it that Maud had fallen head over heels in love with the handsome young stranger to Lower Brockhurst, and determined to ensnare him at all costs? This was Theresa's story. Or had Maud married Gilbert Lilywhite as second best, because Ned had obeyed his father's injunction to marry Petronelle? And was the fact of any consequence? Did the answer affect what had happened to Eris Lilywhite one way or the other?

I was following, as always, the course of the Draco, climbing upwards as it lisped and rippled downhill to the village below.

The noonday sky was growing stormy, torn into rags of cloud by a rising wind. Glancing behind me, I saw bigger, greyer clouds shouldering their way across the hills on the opposite side of the valley; hills that stood surly and black, humping their backs against the approaching rain until, suddenly, they were completely blotted out. And here came the rain, marching across the valley, trailing and swishing its long, transparent skirts with the fury of a woman scorned. Then it was falling all around me, doing its best to soak me to the skin.

I was by this time on a level with Dragonswick Farm, some quarter-mile away to my left across the sheep-bitten pasture, and I made a dash for it, telling myself that it was only sensible to seek shelter. (In the far distance, I glimpsed Billy Tyrrell running for the little shepherd's hut, higher up the hill.) I made my sodden way to the back of the farmhouse, knocked on the kitchen door and let myself in without waiting for an invitation.

Ruth Hodges was alone, boiling water over the fire preparatory to washing the dirty dinner dishes stacked on the table. She glanced up enquiringly as I entered.

'Oh, it's you,' she said, shrugging her thin shoulders.

'Can I stay here until the storm's past?' I asked, shaking myself like a dog and stripping off my wet cloak, which I flung over a stool near the hearth.

'If you want,' she answered indifferently, making it plain that she was a girl on whom my famous charm and dazzling good looks had no effect whatsoever. (Sadly, there were far too many of those in the world.)

'Dinner's over, then.' I nodded towards the pile of wooden platters and a line of cups and mazers.

'It's midday,' she answered scornfully. 'Course dinner's over. Supper's not more'n four hours away.' For the first time since my arrival, she gave me her full attention. 'You're wet,' she discovered. 'Is it raining?'

'Lashing down,' I said, gallantly suppressing a ruder retort. 'But I don't think it'll last long. It's too heavy to be prolonged.'

She poured hot water into a bowl, added a jug of cold from the barrel in the corner, found a cloth and a bunch of twigs for scouring the dirtier pots and set about her task, if not with a will, then at least with resignation.

I waited a minute or two, warming myself by the fire, before saying abruptly, and making it a statement, not a question, 'I hear Master Tom's returned.'

She was caught off guard. 'How d'you know that?' she asked involuntarily, then broke off, staring at me in round-eyed dismay. 'It's s'posed to be a secret. Master Ned'll kill me if he thinks I've said 'nything.'

'Rob Pomphrey knows. He says he got the information from Billy Tyrrell.'

'Billy ain't got the sense he was born with.' Ruth was dismissive.

'But it is true?'

'I didn't say so. Not in so many words, anyway.'

'Lying low in the house, is he?'

'I'm not telling.' She up-ended two mazers on the table, using them as props for the bowls and platters that she set to drain.

'And what does Master Ned say about it?' I enquired.

'What do I say about what?' asked a voice, and there was Ned Rawbone framed in the kitchen doorway.

Ruth screamed and dropped a pot which rolled around the stone-paved floor with an almighty clatter. Even I jumped, not having heard the door open.

Ned came forward and put two more dirty beakers on the table.

'You forgot these,' he said to Ruth, before turning once again to me. 'Master Chapman, I thought you were on your way back to Bristol.'

Now, what had given him that idea? I wondered. Then I recalled the look I had seen pass between him and Maud Lilywhite in church that morning, and it struck me that perhaps she was acting on his instructions. He was the one who wanted me and my prying nose gone before I discovered that Tom had returned to Dragonswick. I now felt convinced that my original guess was the correct one; it was he, not Tom, who had been Maud's midnight visitor.

'I leave tomorrow,' I told him. 'My journey's not so urgent as to warrant travelling on a Sunday. I've taken shelter here from the storm. I hope you don't mind.'

'And where are you off to now?' He eyed me suspiciously, his body tense, as wary as an animal guarding its lair.

'Upper Brockhurst woods. I promised Theresa Lilywhite that I'd take another look at the well before I leave tomorrow.' It wasn't quite the truth, but no matter. I had no wish to hold myself up to ridicule by admitting my own inexplicable feelings about the place.

'You won't find anything!' He was scornful. 'When Eris disappeared, the first thought in everyone's mind was that she might have fallen down the well. She hadn't, as I'm sure you must know by now. It was empty.' He echoed Maud. 'You're wasting your time. By the way, you haven't answered my first question. What do I say about what?'

I thought quickly. I saw Ruth's beseeching glance. Moreover, I had no desire to get Billy Tyrrell into trouble.

'I'm afraid we were discussing the attacks on Sir Anselm and Lambert Miller,' I said with apparent frankness. 'I wondered what your thoughts were on the subject, that's all.'

How he might have answered me, I have no idea because, just at that moment, Tom Rawbone sauntered into the kitchen.

'I'm damned thirsty,' he said. 'Ruth, my child, get me another stoup of ale.'

Ned cursed fluently before unceremoniously bundling his brother out of the room. He returned almost immediately to demand my silence, a demand that had a quiet but unmistakable undertone of menace to it.

I gave him my word that no one would hear of Tom's return from me, although I again failed to mention that the news had already leaked out. I silently wondered for how long Rob Pomphrey would be able to keep what he knew to himself.

'All the same, you won't be able to hide your brother for ever,' I said, pointing out the obvious.

My remark, though kindly meant, was not well received.

'I know that,' Ned snarled. 'Do you think I'm an idiot? I just want time to persuade Tom to go away again.' He thumped the table viciously, making Ruth jump a second time and drop another pot with an even bigger clatter. 'What does he think he's doing, coming back here and putting all our good reputations in jeopardy?' Ned's eyes had glazed over and I could see that he was really talking to himself. For the moment, he had forgotten my existence. 'I got him away safely once. The stupid bastard might not be so lucky next time.'

'Why has he decided to risk it?' I asked.

Ned gave a nervous start. 'What . . . ? Oh . . . Swears he didn't attack anyone. Insists he wants to clear his name. Not that it's any of your business, chapman! Can't keep that great nose of yours out of anybody's business, can you? It'll get you into serious trouble one of these days.'

'Oh, it has, on more than one occasion,' I answered cheerfully. 'Unfortunately, I never seem able to learn my lesson.'

Ned crossed to the back door and opened it, peering outside.

'The rain's almost stopped,' he said pointedly. 'But I don't think its' going to hold off for much longer. So, if I were you, I'd get back to the Lilywhites' while you can and stay in the dry for the rest of the day. You'll have enough to put up with for the next few weeks.'

I laughed. 'A bit of rain doesn't bother me. I'm used to being out in all weathers. I'm a pedlar, remember? However,' I added, as though deciding to humour him, 'maybe you're right. It's a long walk to Bristol.' I held out my hand. 'I doubt, then, we'll be seeing one another again, Master Rawbone, so I'll wish you goodbye.'

Something like relief lit the blue eyes, but was swiftly repressed.

'God be with you, also,' he said, grasping my proffered hand. 'I'm afraid Dame Theresa will be disappointed that you haven't been able to help her with the matter of Eris's disappearance. But my own feeling is that the little vixen is still out there somewhere, laughing at us all, just as she always did.'

'Perhaps.' There was no point in arguing with him. I doubted very much that he believed what he had said himself.

I bade farewell to Ruth, let myself out and walked round to the front of the house, then began climbing again towards Upper Brockhurst ridge. After I had gone some distance, I paused, looking back over my shoulder. A man was standing by the farm palings, watching me. To begin with, I assumed that it was Ned, who had come outside to check on my movements; to see if I really had decided to return to the Lilywhites' cottage. But it wasn't. After a moment or two, I realized that it was Tom.

Nineteen

It had stopped raining altogether by the time I reached the Upper Brockhurst ridge. Trees were outlined in bold, bare shapes against a sky clearing slowly from the west, and a misty sunlight, soft as a blanket, was already cloaking the hills on the opposite side of the valley. As I turned and looked over my shoulder, they quivered, like a mirage that might disappear at any second.

Once I had entered the belt of trees, however, it was a different story. Water still dripped dismally from the interlacing branches overhead, and my boots squelched noisily among the matted bracken and long stretches of sodden, slippery grasses. Wine-dark shadows assumed the forms of hobgoblins and the sprites of the woods, lying in wait for the unwary traveller, while drifts of last year's leaves made blood-red pools among the roots of the scrub. I felt suddenly as if I were suffocating in a cloud of silence and obscurity . . .

I pulled myself up short, both literally and figuratively. Such imaginings were ridiculous in a man of twenty-six, lord and master of an adoring wife and three equally adoring small children, hero to a dog of rare intelligence. (Well, a man could dream, couldn't he? There was no law against it that I knew of.) I paused to look around me, sternly identifying things for what they really were, then drew myself up to my more than six feet in height, squared shoulders that have been described by my admirers as broad, and by my detractors as hefty, renewed my grip on my cudgel and moved forward again with a determined, no-nonsense stride.

But there was no denying that my solitude had become

oppressive by the time I reached the clearing where Upper Brockhurst Hall had once stood; and it was with an over-whelming sense of relief that I stepped into the open space of the courtyard, the trees giving place to knee-high grass, studded with thickets of whin and stunted alder. Unable to shake off the feeling that I had passed safely through some sort of extreme danger, I sank down heavily on the ivy-covered stump of an ancient oak.

After a moment or two, my mind reverted to Rob Pomphrey's words – or rather to the reported words of Gilbert Lilywhite – concerning Maud. 'Whatever else she is or isn't, Maud's a good cook.' So what wasn't she? Or, rather, what hadn't she been in those far-off days when she was Gilbert's wife? And hard on the heels of that recollection came another; a remark made by William Bush while we were eating our dinner the previous day. 'I always thought Maud Haycombe a bit wild in her youth. Not as good as she should have been, if you know what I mean.' And as I mulled this over, something else, said by Alice Tucker, also came back to me. Alice had been speaking, if I remembered correctly, about Ned Rawbone. 'Oh, Master Edward's settled down right enough since his marriage. He never was as wild as Tom or the old man, but he sowed his wild oats in his youth.'

Other snippets of information, that I had gleaned haphazardly over the past few days, began floating to the top of my mind, in the same way as all sorts of debris rises to the surface when you stir up mud at the bottom of a pond. For instance, Dame Jacquetta had told me that when Tom announced his betrothal to Eris in front of his horrified family, Petronelle had shouted, 'You can't do that, Thomas!' An odd remark, now I came to think about it. I would have expected a barrage of protests, cries of dismay, but not the stark reprimand, 'You can't do that.' Why couldn't he? And the twins, as well as their great-aunt, had reported the fact that Petronelle had screamed at Eris to go home, not just once, but many times. 'Go home and tell your mother!' had been one phrase quoted by Jacquetta. And Ruth, the Rawbones' little kitchen maid, had claimed that from the window of Dame Jacquetta's chamber, where she had her truckle bed, she had seen Eris leave the house, running downhill, in the direction of the Lilywhites' cottage. Doing as she had been advised. Going home.

There were other things, too. Now that, at last, I had done what I had been intending to do for the past twenty-four hours, namely marshalled my thoughts into some sort of order, memories came flooding back. I recalled Theresa saying that, when the children were young, Maud had discouraged the friendship between Eris and the Rawbone twins; a friendship so close that, as Christopher had told me, strangers to the village had thought them all to be siblings. And despite her inimical feelings towards Tom and his family in general, Maud had never let them influence her fondness for Ned.

An idea was taking shape at the back of my mind, which, to begin with, was nothing more than a glimmer of light at the end of a long and winding tunnel, but which grew brighter by the minute the more I considered it. I might have reached a final, firm conclusion then and there, perched on that tree stump, but I was suddenly jerked out of my reverie by the scurrying of some small animal in the undergrowth, nearby.

How long I had been sitting, lost in thought, I had no idea, but judging by the stiffness of my joints, it had been for some considerable length of time. I found that I was shivering in spite of being wrapped in my cloak, and realized that if I were to avoid being laid up with an unwelcome and unwanted rheum, action was called for. I stamped my feet and clapped my arms around my body until I began to feel warmer, then decided it was time to make my second exploration of the well.

What I hoped to achieve by this, I had no clear idea. I had been down the shaft once and knew that there was nothing to be seen but an inch or so of mud at the bottom. Nevertheless, I could not shake myself free either of the notion that I might have missed something on that first occasion, or of the persistent fancy that in the well I was very close to the missing girl. There was no good reason why I should feel that way, so I reached the conclusion that maybe God was prompting me.

'I just hope you're not having a joke at my expense, Lord,' I grumbled peevishly as I unwrapped myself from my cloak and flung it across the tree stump. I dropped my cudgel in the grass alongside and cursed roundly as I tripped over one of the many loose stones lying about.

By the time I had struggled to lift the heavy lid of the well clear of the rim, I had stopped shivering and was sweating profusely. The iron ladder nailed to the wall of the shaft looked even rustier than I had remembered it. Indeed, it appeared positively dangerous, but I had negotiated it safely once before and presumably could do so again. I was thankful that I had decided to leave Hercules behind, with the Lilywhites: his large anxious eyes and reproachful expression would only have worried me further.

I swung both legs over the top of the well and cautiously began to descend. Once again, jagged flakes of rust adhered to the palms of my hands, and, as on the earlier occasion, I had to grope around in order to find a footing. The missing rungs, the diminution of the light as I climbed further down the shaft and the perilous swaying of the ladder as it worked loose from the brickwork, all told me that what I was doing was extremely foolhardy. And what should I discover when I reached the bottom? Exactly what I had discovered before. Nothing. Or, at least, nothing that gave me any clue to Eris's whereabouts.

And so it proved. There were the same ferns and mosses sprouting between the bricks and the same inch or so of mud and water still seeping through the rough patch of stones and mortar that had been used to shore up the well close to its base. I might have saved myself the time, the trouble and the possible danger to life and limb for all the good this second exploration had done me. Eris wasn't there, and never had been there as far as I could tell. I swore. My instincts were wrong. My sense of her presence, my conviction that she was close at hand, was not God-given intuition, but a trick of my own imagination.

Deflated, angry with myself for being such a fool, angry with God for what I saw as His cat-and-mouse games, I leaned against the wall of the shaft and stared up at the distant circle of sky, overlaid with its tracery of interwoven branches. In a minute or two, when I had calmed down and got my second wind, I would ascend the ladder, make my way back to the Lilywhites' cottage and, tomorrow morning, begin my homeward journey to Bristol. Failure was a bitter pill to swallow, but I made myself face up to the unpalatable truth that I would probably never now discover what had happened to Eris . . .

Someone was looking down at me, head and shoulders outlined against the backdrop of sky and trees, elbows bent, hands resting on the rim of the well. Man or woman? It was impossible to say at that distance.

'Hello! I'm coming up!' I shouted, and waved my arms before grabbing at both sides of the ladder and beginning an ascent that was more precipitous than prudent. Unsure if my presence had been noted, I didn't want whoever was up there thinking that the well had been carelessly left open, and replacing the lid.

In some ways, it was easier climbing up than down because I could see where the gaps in the rungs were. Even so, it required all of my concentration, and I didn't look skywards again until I was about three-quarters of the way up the ladder. Pausing to catch my breath, safe in the knowledge that I was now easily visible to the person above me, I raised my head, ready with some self-deprecating jibe about fools who possessed more curiosity than sense. But the words died on my lips as I realized, with a sickening jolt to the pit of my stomach, that the face I was staring at was no face, only a hood worn back to front – blue this time instead of grey – two slits cut for the almost invisible eyes, the liripipe hanging down like some obscenely elongated nose.

Fear held me paralysed – only for a minute, but it was a minute too long. The masked figure disappeared. I heard the grunt and thud as of someone moving a heavy object and knew at once it was the lid of the well. I began to climb faster, spurred on by the panic that was now driving hard at my heels. My whole body was jarred as I failed to spot another missing rung and my foot slipped back to the one below. I was breathing heavily and my hands were slippery with sweat, but I was nearing the top. A few more feet and I was there . . .

Something hit me squarely in the chest. In the few desperate seconds while I struggled to save my balance, I recognized it as the end of a good, stout cudgel – my own cudgel, in fact, which I had left lying beside my cloak. I could feel myself tottering and grabbed wildly at the ladder just before everything went black as the lid of the well was finally hauled, with a muffled curse, into place.

I have never understood, not even to this day when I am old and grey-haired, how I stopped myself from pitching head first to the bottom of that well, as I was undoubtedly meant to do. Perhaps it was nothing but sheer good fortune or the Hand of God beneath my elbow. Or maybe it was the determination born of rage at having been attacked with my own weapon that saved me. Whatever the reason, somehow or another I managed to regain my balance just as I began to wobble backwards off the ladder. Luckily, the masked man had been in so much of a hurry to seal me into my tomb that he didn't wait to make sure that he had done the job properly. (I was now convinced that my assailant was a man. No woman, I felt sure, was strong enough to lift the lid of the well single-handedly. Furthermore, the arms wielding my cudgel had displayed the sort of strength not possessed, in my experience, by females.)

I don't know for how long I clung to the ladder, not daring to move, still not entirely certain that I wasn't really lying at the bottom of the well shaft, seriously injured. My face was pressed so hard against the rung above the one I was clutching, that the flaking iron scratched my cheek; and I was shaking so violently that the whole ladder vibrated with my fear. Slowly, however, I managed to get my emotions under control, although my legs felt like lead when I started once again on my upward climb.

By this time, my eyes had grown accustomed to the darkness, and I could see enough to make out the curve of the walls and the shape of the ladder. I also discovered an added bonus in the light that filtered between the planks of which the lid had been made. It was not a solid circle of wood as I had at first imagined, but several separate pieces nailed together.

My nerves began to steady a little. I was now a mere foot or so from the lid and was able to reach up and push at it with my hands. I strained as hard as I dared but it didn't budge. I don't know what I had expected. Common sense should have warned me that it would be almost impossible to lift from beneath. It was too heavy and fitted too snugly around the rim. And while I was pushing and heaving, I had to maintain a precarious foothold or I could yet fall backwards into the depths. I lowered my hands and hung on to the top rung of the ladder while I regained my breath and assessed my situation.

I was trapped. How long would it be before someone else visited the ridge? People did go up there, I knew, to gather firewood – Sir Anselm, for example – but it might be days; days without water, food or warmth. Then it occurred to me that when I didn't return to the cottage by nightfall, the Mistress Lilywhites would raise the alarm – they knew where I had been headed – and relief washed through me. How stupid not to have remembered that at once.

Presumably, my attacker (of whose identity I was now almost certain) assumed that I was lying lifeless at the bottom of the well; although he, of all people, should have known that it was possible to survive such a fall. But why had he decided to make this attempt on my life now, when I had announced my intention of leaving the following day? Panic was the only answer, for he must know that there was nothing in the well to indicate what had happened to Eris; and without being able to prove that she was dead, whatever suspicions I entertained were useless as far as any hope of justice was concerned. And I wasn't even sure that justice was appropriate in this case. The longer I thought about it, the more I felt convinced that Eris's death had most likely been an accident . . .

I swayed and nearly lost my grip on the ladder. The darkness was having a disorientating effect upon me, and the stench that I had noticed on my first visit to the well now rose up and threatened to overpower my senses. If I wasn't careful, I really

233

would slip off the ladder, and if I pitched head first to the bottom, my assailant's prayers could be answered. Somehow or other I must try not to lose consciousness before help arrived. But how long might that help be? It would be hours before Maud and her mother-in-law began to get worried.

I forced myself to go over what facts I possessed again and again in my head, fighting off increasing nausea and dizziness. Three morrells . . . Three morrells in a row, that was what I needed. Petronelle Rawbone was the first. Go home, she had kept screaming at Eris. Go home! Tell everything to your mother. Tell her that you're going to marry Nathaniel Rawbone. But why? What could Maud do to prevent her headstrong daughter from doing exactly as she pleased? I believed I had the answer, and lined up Maud as my second morrell. Which left the person who had just tried to murder me as the third. Ned Rawbone – who had adopted the same disguise for this attempt on my life as he had done when he attacked Sir Anselm and Lambert Miller.

Which posed another question: why was Ned busy trying to incriminate his brother? Tom's quarrel with the miller had obviously given him the idea of a night assault on Lambert; and it would have been he, no doubt, who persuaded the younger man to escape the villagers' wrath by running away. 'I believe in your innocence,' he would have said, 'but who else will? Save your skin while you can.'

But why did Ned want Tom out of the way? Because Tom's increasingly aggressive and erratic behaviour was drawing attention to the Rawbone family once again? Because Ned was afraid that that attention would one day lead to a discovery of the truth? And to make matters even worse, I was being encouraged by Theresa Lilywhite to ask questions concerning her granddaughter's disappearance; questions that were starting to rekindle interest in a mystery that had begun to fade from the public consciousness. Since my arrival in Lower Brockhurst last Wednesday, Ned must have seen me as nothing but trouble.

I now felt certain that it had been he, and no one else, who had overheard my conversation with Sir Anselm on Friday morning. He had never left the priest's house, but stayed listening outside the kitchen door. Sir Anselm had said nothing that could point the finger of suspicion at anyone, but, like so many people burdened with other people's secrets, he had been unable to prevent himself from arousing my curiosity. Ned must have realized this; so while he was attacking Lambert in order to throw suspicion on his brother, he had also administered a beating by way of a warning to the priest . . .

Three morrells all in a row: Petronelle, Maud and Ned . . . And suddenly there they were, all smiling at me out of the darkness. Maud was saying, 'Strangers could see the likeness. Brothers and sister . . . Brothers and sister . . . Gilbert's children died young. Weaklings like him. But Eris was strong . . . Strong, strong, strong . . .'

Petronelle started floating around me, shaking her disembodied head. 'Go home, I said. Go home and tell your mother . . . I knew the truth, you see. I'd always known . . .'

Ned said nothing, but reached out slowly, but deliberately, towards me, hands extended, fingers splayed . . .

I came to my senses just in time to save myself from falling off the ladder. Fear gripped me as I realized that I had almost lost consciousness and that I was gasping for air in the stultifying darkness. I had to keep awake somehow, but lack of air was playing havoc with my senses. It was slowly dawning on me that I should be lucky to get out of the well alive . . .

'It serves you right,' Adela was scolding me. 'You can never keep your nose out of anyone else's business. I've warned you, time and again, Roger! The feast of Saint Patrick, you said. You won't be here, though, will you . . . ?'

Another woman joined her scolding to Adela's. 'Oh, dear God, what have you done?' she was screaming at me. 'You fool! What have you done?'

What had I done? Who was this harpy? Then my mind cleared as if by magic, and I recognized Maud Lilywhite's voice. It was real, not a part of my dream. Summoning up my remaining strength, I raised one hand, balled it into a fist and hammered as hard as I could on the lid of the well.

'Let me out, for pity's sake!' I yelled.

I could hear more shouting, voices raised in altercation. A fierce argument seemed to be raging. I yelled and hammered again. A moment later, the lid of the well was lifted and heaved aside. Maud Lilywhite, sobbing with relief at finding me still alive, reached down to help me climb out, watched by a sullen Ned Rawbone.

I only had time to gasp my grateful thanks before collapsing in an ungainly heap on the grass.

An hour later, after a walk I remember very little about except that Maud supported me with her arm around my waist, I found myself sitting in the Lilywhites' cottage before a blazing fire, swaddled in a blanket and drinking a cup of mulled ale. Maud, ashen-faced, was attending to my every need, while her mother-in-law stared morosely at Ned Rawbone, who was seated on a stool, elbows on knees, head clasped between his hands.

'Perhaps,' Theresa suggested grimly, when the silence at last grew too oppressive, 'one of you would care to tell me just what has been going on. I gather from the little that's been said already, that Ned has tried to kill Master Chapman by throwing him down the well, or some such lunacy. What I want to know is why. What has the pedlar done to upset him?'

When neither of the others answered, I volunteered, 'Master Rawbone's afraid that I know – or think I know – what happened to your . . . To Eris.'

'And do you?' The older woman whipped round to face me. 'Have you found proof that Tom Rawbone murdered her?'

I glanced from Maud to Ned, who both avoided my eyes. But they made no attempt to stop me speaking.

'Have you?' Theresa repeated fiercely.

'I feel pretty sure that Tom didn't kill Eris,' I told her, 'although his brother might like you to think so. In fact, I don't believe she was murdered at all. Oh, I'm certain she's dead, but I suspect that her death was an accident.'

Maud stirred suddenly and reached for Ned's hand, gripping it tightly. 'Go on,' she said, when I hesitated.

'Very well.' I regarded her straitly. 'I think Eris did come home that night, after the quarrel at the farmhouse. She did what Petronelle Rawbone wanted her to do: she told you what had happened. She told you she was going to marry Nathaniel. She was going to be mistress of Dragonswick Farm.'

Maud nodded, ignoring her mother-in-law's gasp of astonishment.

'Yes, Eris came home. She was triumphant. She gave me all the details of how she had managed to seduce Tom into deserting Rosamund for her and into proposing marriage; of how she had then received a better offer from his father. I was appalled at her conduct and told her so. But, of course, it didn't make any difference. She was determined to marry Nathaniel, a man old enough to be her grandfather. My disapproval meant nothing to her. She had been headstrong and wayward since babyhood. Like,' Maud added bitterly, 'all the rest of her father's family.'

Theresa interrupted furiously, 'That's an evil lie. The Lily-whites were all quiet, gentle people, just like my Gilbert.'

Maud raised her head at that and stared at Theresa for several unblinking seconds. Then she lowered her eyes again, but she seemed disinclined to continue. I glanced at Ned, but he said nothing, either.

I turned to Theresa. 'Your son wasn't Eris's father, Mistress.' I looked back at Maud. 'You said just now that Nathaniel was old enough to be Eris's grandfather. But he *was* her grandfather, wasn't he? You were pregnant with Ned's child when you married your husband.'

Theresa gave a great cry, then demanded harshly, 'Is this true, Maud?'

Maud took a deep, trembling breath. 'Yes,' she admitted at last. Her clasp on Ned's hand tightened. 'We loved one another. We always have. But Nathaniel threatened to disinherit Ned unless he married Petronelle, and I didn't want that to happen to him. He didn't deserve it. He had worked too hard to make Dragonswick prosperous. But I was pretty sure by then that I was carrying his child, so when Gilbert arrived in the village

237

from Gloucester, to dig a well for the Hemnalls, I set out to win his affections. And I was successful. Oh, as Eris grew up, I could tell that he began to suspect she wasn't his, especially as his children were puny creatures who died young. But he never said anything. He never openly accused me, but his attitude towards me became more distant and cold.'

'What happened when you told Eris the truth?' I asked.

Maud grimaced. 'At first, of course, she refused to believe me. Said I was making it up to stop her marrying Nathaniel. But I convinced her in the end, and then she went mad. She seized a knife that I'd been slicing bread with and attacked me. She was like an avenging Fury. I was sure she was going to kill me. There was a pot of water boiling on the fire. I picked it up and threw it at her.' Maud began to sob and it seemed for a moment as though she would be unable to continue. But, eventually, she managed to control her emotion and went on, 'It missed Eris, but she slipped in the puddle of water. She fell awkwardly and hit her head on the hearth stones. I heard her skull crack.' Maud shivered. 'It was horrible. I prayed that she was only stunned, but she wasn't. She was dead.'

I looked at Ned. 'Then you arrived.'

He nodded, speaking for the first time since our return to the cottage. 'Maud was hysterical, in a terrible state. But at last I managed to calm her down and then we had to decide what to do. I told Maud to wait an hour or so, then come up to the farm and say that Eris had still not come home. I would dress and return here and then . . .' He broke off, reluctant to say what I had no compunction in saying for him.

'You spent the remainder of the night burying Eris's body.'

He didn't answer at once, then he released his hand from Maud's, rose slowly from his stool and stood, looking down on me for a few moments. Finally, he said, 'You can't prove anything. If asked, Maud and I will deny everything you've heard here this afternoon. There's no proof. You have no idea where Eris is buried.'

'You're forgetting Dame Theresa,' I pointed out.

Ned Rawbone laughed. 'Oh, I doubt she'll say anything.

After all, what good would it do? I repeat, there's no proof. But if there were, she won't want to see Maud arrested and tried for Eris's death, any more than she can want to reveal her son, her precious Gilbert, as a credulous cuckold. You just make sure that you're on your way tomorrow, chapman, otherwise, next time, you cross my path, you might not be so lucky.'

Twenty

M aud said quietly, 'No, Ned. We can't spend the rest of our lives running away from the truth. We've done that for far too long. If Eris had known about her parentage, none of this sorry mess would have happened. And the chances are that if we'd admitted that I was carrying your child in the beginning, if we'd had the courage to face up to your father and take the consequences, Nathaniel might have relented and let us marry.'

'You know my father better than that,' Ned interrupted her roughly. 'I'd have lost the farm.'

'Perhaps.' Maud left fussing over me and sat down on one of the stools, hugging her knees with her arms. 'But nothing could have been worse than all these years of concealment, of deceiving both Gilbert and Petronelle . . .'

'I feel certain Dame Petronelle knows.' It was my turn to interrupt. 'Otherwise, that night, why was she so insistent that Eris came home to tell you of her plans? Surely it must have been because she thought that she could rely on you to tell your daughter the truth.'

Maud raised her eyebrows at Ned. 'Well?' she asked. 'Does Petronelle know that you were Eris's father?'

He nodded, adding quickly, 'I didn't tell her. She guessed. As Eris grew up, she could see the likeness, not so much between her and the twins, as between her and Nathaniel. And there *was* a likeness, quite a striking one, if you looked for it. But no one did, of course, except a jealous woman. Maybe Petronelle had her suspicions when she married me. I don't know. And it doesn't matter now.'

Maud answered steadily, 'You're wrong, Ned. It does matter. As I told you a minute or two ago, I can't continue with this life of deceit any longer. I'm going to see the village elders first thing tomorrow morning and tell them the truth. What they do about it is up to them.'

'No!' Ned's roar made both Theresa and myself jump violently, but Maud didn't even flinch.

'Yes,' she insisted in the same level tone as before. 'For one thing, there's Tom to be considered. I won't have him on my conscience, as well as everything else. I don't like what's happening to you, Ned. I feel I've lost you. You're not the same kind and gentle man I've been in love with all these years. That man would never have beaten up two innocent people just to throw suspicion on his brother, nor would he have tried to murder anyone, as you tried to murder the chapman this afternoon.'

'I was just warning him to keep his nose out of my affairs, that's all,' Ned blustered angrily.

Maud shook her head. 'That's a lie. You meant to kill him, and would probably have succeeded if I hadn't arrived to prevent you. You'd have left him shut up in the well until he was dead. He would have lost consciousness and fallen off the ladder.'

'Oh,' I cut in vindictively, 'Master Rawbone had already tried to speed the process by attempting to push me off the ladder with the end of my own cudgel.' Hercules, who had hardly left my side since my return to the cottage, growled and bared his teeth at that, almost as though he understood what I was saying. I lowered a hand and fondled his ears before asking, 'But what lucky circumstance brought you up to the ridge, Mistress Lilywhite? Whatever the reason, it was most fortuitous.'

'It was neither lucky nor fortuitous.' Maud gave me a wintry smile. 'I'd gone out to see if the dogs were all right after that heavy rain. I saw you leaving Dragonswick Farm – you're so tall I couldn't mistake you, even at that distance – so I guessed you'd taken shelter there during the storm. Then, a little later, I went out again to shut up the geese, and that time I saw someone I thought was Ned also heading for the ridge.' She closed her eyes for a brief moment while she fought to control her voice. 'It occurred to me that you might have told him where you were going, and why, and I began to feel . . . uneasy. So I decided to follow you both.'

'Thank God you did,' I said fervently.

'You're a fool,' Ned grated. 'No one would have missed him. People would have thought that he'd gone home at last. We could easily have disposed of his pack and that mongrel cur.' Once again, Hercules showed his teeth, but Ned ignored him. He put a hand on Maud's shoulder. 'Promise me you're not serious about going to see the village elders in the morning?'

She glanced up and made a gesture as though she would cover his hand with one of hers. But for some reason she thought better of it, and her hand fluttered back to her lap, where it clasped its companion so hard that the knuckles of both showed bone-white.

'I was never more serious about anything. I refuse to let you condemn Tom to a life of exile for a crime committed by you. What in God's name,' she cried, her voice rising suddenly like an animal in pain, 'possessed you to do such a thing?'

Ned withdrew his hand abruptly.

'Holy Virgin!' he shouted. 'Can't you see that it was to protect *us*? People blamed Tom for Eris's death, but they couldn't prove anything. They couldn't even prove that she was dead. If he'd just stayed quiet, if he'd only behaved himself, the whole affair would have blown over. Eventually it would have been forgotten. Indeed, it *was* being forgotten until this great oaf –' he glared at me – 'with his long, twitchy nose came blundering into our lives. I tried to frighten him away. But I very much doubt if anyone would have taken much notice of him and his questions if Tom hadn't also started to whip up their curiosity and speculation again with his outrageous behaviour. He's been making a right fool of himself trying to win back Rosamund Bush, and brawling with Lambert Miller. The chapman wasn't going to stay here for more than a day or two.

In fact, he kept telling us he'd promised to get home to his wife by the Feast of Saint Patrick. But Tom, once he gets an idea in that stupid noodle of his doesn't give up easily. He was going to keep on drawing attention to us, to the family, and keep the fact of Eris's disappearance fresh in everyone's minds. I thought it was time to be rid of him, and his last fight with the miller gave me the opportunity that I'd been looking for.'

'But why attack the priest, as well?' I asked. 'Is it because Sir Anselm knows the truth about you and Mistress Lilywhite?'

Maud raised her eyes from the contemplation of her hands, still locked together in her lap.

'I confessed to him years ago,' she admitted, 'not long after Eris was born. But he would never have betrayed us.' She glanced reproachfully at Ned. 'He couldn't, even had he wanted to. A priest can't reveal what he's learned in the confessional.'

Ned said impatiently, confirming the conclusion that I had already reached. 'But the old idiot couldn't conceal the fact that he knew something – at least, not from a sharp-nosed, sharp-brained fellow like the pedlar here.' I inclined my head in ironic acknowledgement of the dubious compliment. Ned ignored me and continued, 'Sir Anselm was getting far too friendly with Master Chapman, and I thought a short, sharp warning not to pursue the acquaintance wouldn't come amiss. Particularly as brother Tom could be foisted with the blame for that, as well.'

A sudden thought struck me. 'You said just now that you tried to frighten me away. Were the corn dollies and the burning cage anything to do with that attempt?'

'Only the burning cage. The dollies are hung up by some of the villagers just before, and during, the Feast of Saint Walburga, in order to propitiate the witches and wizards and general spirits of the forest who ride the night sky around this time.' (I should, of course, have worked that out for myself, having noticed the first corn dolly before ever I set foot in Lower Brockhurst.) 'From what I could gather, they made you uneasy, so I hoped to play on that superstitious fear of yours.' Ned laughed shortly. 'I should have known better than to waste my time. Nose-twitchers like you aren't easily discouraged. In the end, I had to resort to telling Maud to throw you out.'

'You were her visitor last night.'

He laughed again, but there was no mirth in the sound.

'I might have guessed that that quivering snout of yours continues to alert you, even when you're asleep.'

I was growing tired of these constant, sneering references to my nose, which I have always considered to be one of my handsomest features. I turned to look at Maud.

'Mistress, if you wish it, I'll delay my departure tomorrow morning and go with you to the village elders.'

'You needn't trouble yourself, chapman,' Theresa rasped, speaking for the first time in some minutes. 'I'll accompany Maud to make sure she doesn't change her mind. Or have it changed for her.' She glared defiantly at Ned Rawbone. 'After that . . . After that, I shall return to Gloucester. I can't stay here any longer, not now that I know the truth. My sister will be glad enough to share her roof with me.'

Maud turned her head quickly to look at her mother-in-law. 'You won't stay with me?' she asked.

I recognized the note of fear in her voice, and guessed that after years of wishing to be free of Theresa's company, when at last the chance was offered, she was afraid of the loneliness; of the days and nights with only herself and her thoughts for company.

Theresa demanded harshly, 'What is there to keep me here? Eris wasn't even my granddaughter. She wasn't Gilbert's child. You've deceived me, made a fool of me. No, I won't stay. But I'll make sure that everyone in this benighted village knows the truth before I go.'

'What truth?' Ned sneered. 'The pair of you can go to the elders if you want, but I shall deny everything you say. It'll be my word against those of a couple of hysterical women.'

'And against mine,' I said. 'I'll go with Dame Theresa and Mistress Lilywhite. I'll back their story.'

'You're a stranger,' Ned retorted. 'You've been in the village less than a week. Why should they take your word over mine?

Now, if one of you knew where Eris is buried, if you could direct the villagers where to find her body, that might be different.'

Maud smiled faintly and swivelled round on her stool to look Ned fully in the eyes.

'I know where Eris is buried,' she said. 'I've always known. Or, at least, I've always had a very shrewd idea.'

There was a moment's complete silence, broken only by the crackling of the logs on the hearth. Even Hercules seemed to be holding his breath. Then Ned Rawbone laughed uncertainly.

'You're lying,' he challenged, but without any degree of certainty in his tone.

Maud replied evenly, 'You forget that Gilbert was a weller. Do you really think that, during all the years we were married, I learned nothing about his trade? And you, Ned! You knew what was at the bottom of the well because you'd seen it as a boy, when you fell in. In fact, Gilbert told me that you'd once mentioned it to him and asked what its purpose was. So it's no use trying to deny that you knew it was there.'

Ned's face suddenly wore a defeated look. He sat down abruptly on another of the stools and buried his face in his hands.

'What are you talking about, Mistress?' I asked excitedly, recalling my conviction that Eris was somewhere in that well. And, on a more practical level, I remembered the overpowering stench of decay. But there had been nothing down there that I could see.

Maud rubbed her forehead with her hand as though trying to ease a headache. She was still extremely pale and Theresa, moved, I suppose, by some residue of affection, got up and poured her a stoup of ale.

'Here! Drink this!' Her tone was abrasive, but she meant well. 'Then tell the chapman what he wants to know.'

'Don't *you* want to know?' I asked her.

Theresa resumed her seat, pausing only to tuck my blanket more securely around me.

'My daughter-in-law's right, chapman,' she said. 'You can't live with a man for years and remain totally ignorant of his trade.' She glanced at Maud. 'Are you saying that the Upper Brockhurst well has a "drive"?' The younger woman nodded, an action that was echoed by Theresa. 'Of course,' she mused, 'That's why the foot or so of water that remained in the well has dried up to nothing since last September when he –' she glared at Ned – 'must have put Eris's body inside and then blocked up the entrance.'

I recollected two things simultaneously: the first was the patching of the wall at the bottom of the well, and the second was that not only Theresa, but also Sir Anselm had mentioned the fact of Ned stumbling around in water the first time he went down to 'search' for Eris's body.

'Could you please explain exactly what you're talking about?' I begged Maud.

'Wells are dug,' she said, 'on the recommendation of a dowser, who tells the weller that water can be found at a certain depth. But if the weller doesn't immediately strike water at that depth, then he has to dig a "drive" – a horizontal shaft – until he reaches the source of the water and the well begins to fill up. This must have been the case at Upper Brockhurst Hall . . .'

'Of course,' I breathed. 'It comes back to me, now. You told me that your grandmother had been told by *her* grandmother that the Martin brothers had to have their well *deepened*; that whoever sunk it originally, hadn't dug down far enough – or, as now seems possible, not close enough to the underground source of water. The two wellers from Tetbury must have cut this horizontal shaft, and that must have been when they found the silver bowls, near the original sacred spring of the Romans. And you think that Master Rawbone, here . . . ?' I paused, unable to continue.

Maud took a deep breath. 'Yes. I think – I'm almost sure – that Ned must have carried Eris's body up to the ridge, thrown it down the well and then . . .' Her voice, too, became suspended.

All three of us stared questioningly at Ned until, at last, he raised his head.

'All right,' he said in the toneless voice of a man who concedes defeat; who has come to the bitter realization that he has lost control of the situation. 'You're right, Maud. I knew about the "drive" at the bottom of the well. I'd seen it as a boy and found out from Gilbert what it was. He explained that when the course of the Draco had been altered by the men of Lower Brockhurst, after the great plague, it had dried up, except for a very small trickle of water that occasionally found its way through the "drive". Hence the foot or so of water always present at the bottom of the well. So, when I was wondering how to . . . to dispose of Eris's body . . . I remembered it.'

'But why didn't you just bury her in the woods?' I asked.

He shrugged. 'I don't know! I was in a panic, I suppose. I wasn't thinking properly. It just seemed safer at the time to conceal her body in the shaft. Apart from myself and Gilbert, I didn't think anyone knew about it, and Gilbert was dead. Stupidly, it didn't occur to me that he might have shared his knowledge with Maud.'

'So what did you do, the night that Eris died?' I asked as Maud seemed unable, or unwilling, to do so.

Ned seemed equally reluctant to dwell upon that night's events.

'I – er –' He glanced sideways at Maud before continuing, 'I dropped Eris's body down the well, then returned to the farm for a lamp and some tools.' (I recalled the lean-to shack where the picks and other implements were stored.) 'After that . . . After that . . .' He stopped, folding his lips together, refusing to say any more.

I didn't press him. We all had enough imagination to picture subsequent events. Ned must have descended the ladder, pushed the girl's body – his daughter's body – into the 'drive', then climbed up again in order to search for stones with which to plug the mouth of the horizontal shaft. There were plenty of those lying about in the grass of the old Hall courtyard, and he had spent the rest of the night completing his grisly task. It was small wonder, then, that Christopher had described his father's appearance the following morning as 'soaking wet and absolutely filthy, plastered with mud and muck . . . exhausted.'

Maud said accusingly, 'You've been advocating lately that the well should be filled in. I suppose, now, we all know why.' She gave a laugh that turned into a sob.

Ned was beside her immediately, pulling her up from her stool and into his arms, rocking her to and fro and caressing her hair.

'Sweetheart, sweetheart, don't. I'm so sorry. It was all my fault. You wanted to admit the truth, but I wouldn't let you. I was the one who persuaded you that it would be better if Eris just "disappeared". I was afraid of the consequences if my father ever discovered what a fool he'd made of himself, wanting to marry his own granddaughter.'

Maud clung to him for a moment while she fought to hold her tears at bay, then she gently pushed him from her. He would have reached for her again, but she drew herself up, straight-backed and at her most dignified, fending him off with her outstretched hand.

'No, Ned. We agreed long ago, when you married Petronelle and I married Gilbert, that we would never again allow our feelings for each other to get the better of us. We would be friends, but no more: that was the bargain. And you mustn't shoulder all the blame. The initial fault was mine. I should never have let Eris go to work for you at the farm. I knew it was playing with fire . . . And now, I'd like you to go. I think it's time you told your family the truth. But I should be deeply grateful if you would come to see the elders with me in the morning.'

Ned nodded, his hands falling back to his sides. He gave me a slanting look, as though in half a mind to offer an apology, but then, wisely, thought better of it. There's nothing adequate you can say to a man you've just tried to kill. He bade Theresa a brief 'Goodnight!', opened the door of the cottage and was gone, the dusk of late afternoon soon shrouding him from view.

Maud looked for a moment as though she might faint, but she was a strong woman, in mind as well as body. She had had to be to keep her secret for so many years, and for the past five months to live with the knowledge that, however unwittingly, she had caused the death of her child.

Theresa would have spoken, but Maud said tersely, 'No more, Mother-in-law. We're all of us tired and our guest has a day's walk ahead of him tomorrow. Supper, I think. And then bed.'

It was only just daylight when, with Hercules, I crossed the bridge into Lower Brockhurst village the following morning and turned to walk the length of the street. This way, according to both Maud and Theresa, would lead me eventually to the main Gloucester-to-Bristol track.

My two hostesses and I had said our muted farewells in the presence of Ned, who had arrived before daybreak, bringing with him his father, Tom, Petronelle and Dame Jacquetta. All of them were pale and heavy-eyed, as though they had slept badly the preceding night, and while Petronelle looked sulky and Tom dazed, Nathaniel's expression was murderous. But no one uttered a word of reproach or blame, either to Ned or Maud. At least, not during the time that I was there. The Rawbones were showing their customary family solidarity against the outside world.

I was huddled into my cloak, my pack settled firmly on my back. Hercules trotted happily by my side, not even straining at the length of rope knotted to the other piece that encircled his neck. There was a sharp wind, but, to my relief, it wasn't raining, and a glimmer of sunlight showed above the hills. A cock crew somewhere in the distance, I heard the rattle of wooden patterns on the cobbles of a yard, somebody shouted. But, for the most part, the village was silent, not yet fully awake to the coming day.

I glanced at the priest's house as I passed, wishing that I could have said my goodbyes to Father Anselm, but he was still unwell and it would be cruel to disturb him. I transferred my gaze, instead, to the alehouse, shuttered and quiet, and found myself wondering what would happen to Rosamund Bush . . .

'Roger!' She was descending the outside stairs of the Roman Sandal, a blanket covering her nightshift, her fair hair streaming about her shoulders, a pair of scarlet leather shoes on her dainty feet. 'It's true, then. You're really going home?'

'For Heaven's sake!' I remonstrated. 'You'll catch your death of cold. Your teeth are chattering.'

She came and stood close to me. 'Put your arms around me,' she invited. 'Then I won't feel the cold.' I did as I was bidden and she smiled up into my face. 'There! That's better!' She rested her head against my shoulder. 'I didn't think you'd go until you'd discovered what's happened to Eris.'

In my vanity, I couldn't bear her to think me a failure, so I told her all that had happened. I couldn't see that I was betraying anyone's confidence. The whole village would be in possession of the facts in a couple of hours' time. (Maybe even sooner, knowing how gossip travels in any community.)

'So, you see,' I finished, 'Tom's name will be cleared. You'll be able to marry him, after all, if that's what you want.'

She made no comment on this for some minutes, being too busy exclaiming at what I had told her and getting me to repeat the salient facts several times over. But when, at last, she had accepted my story as the undoubted truth, and come to terms with it, she said quietly, 'I shan't marry Tom. I could never trust him again, and trust is important in a marriage, don't you think?' I kept silent. What else could I do, with her wrapped in my arms and conscious of every curve of her body pressed against mine? Fortunately, she didn't wait for my reply. 'I shall marry Lambert,' she decided. 'He's a good, dependable man with a little money put by. His mother's too doting, it's true, but I daresay I can handle her.' She spoke with the confidence of youth. My heart bled for her and the years of disillusionment that lay ahead.

'I must be on my way,' I said, gently releasing myself from her embrace.

She reached up and kissed my lips. 'You're sure you wouldn't like to stay?'

'I've told you—' I began.

She sighed. 'I know. You're a married man with three children and you love your wife.'

'I do,' I said. But I couldn't help reflecting that the heathens of this world arranged things better. They, so I had been told, could have more than one wife. But then common sense reasserted itself. More wives, more children. I imagined the combination of Elizabeth, Nicholas and Adam multiplied three or four times over. And shuddered.

Nevertheless, I bent my head and kissed Rosamund on her tender young mouth. It warmed me up. I felt ready to face my journey with all its hazards and fatigue. She clung to me for a moment, then gave what might have been a sob – or then again, knowing my luck, it could have been a giggle – and ran back up the stairs. At the top, she turned and waved before going indoors.

Adela was unrestrained in her joy at having me home.

'And early, too,' she marvelled, hugging me tightly. 'Still three days wanting to the Feast of Saint Patrick. Oh, Roger, it is good to see you again.'

Her welcome made up for the children's offhand greeting of, 'What have you brought us?' and their indifference to my return once they discovered that my pockets were empty.

'I was lucky,' I admitted, 'in meeting up with several carters, who were willing to give me a ride in their carts in return for my company.' I kissed her once more. 'I love you,' I said fiercely.

It was a mistake. I saw her expression grow wary and that mocking glint light the back of her eyes. But she said nothing, merely drew me to the table and plied me with food and drink. She asked no questions. She knew that I would tell her all there was to tell in my own good time. Meanwhile, I was home, in my own house. My house! A proper house with a number of different rooms; with an upstairs as well as a down. Even now, I found it difficult to believe.

Elizabeth came rushing in to show me her latest toy, a present from her grandmother. 'It's called morals,' she announced importantly.

'Morrells,' Adela corrected her, smiling. 'Apparently, you move these little balls around in the slots until you get three in a row. I don't really understand it.' She broke off, frowning. 'Although I seem to remember, when I was a girl, that there was a version you could play using real people. Have you ever heard of that, Roger?'

'Oh, yes, I've heard of it,' I said. 'I've even been in a game where I was one of the "counters".' And, for the last time, I thought of Rosamund Bush, then dismissed her from my mind once and for all. 'That version of the game,' I added, blowing my wife a kiss, 'is called Nine Men's Morris.'

9 Blue

R

9 Red